ASSASSINS
ANONYMOUS

ALSO BY ROB HART

The Paradox Hotel

The Warehouse

Take-Out: And Other Tales of Culinary Crime

THE ASH MCKENNA SERIES

Potter's Field (Book 5)

The Woman from Prague (Book 4)

South Village (Book 3)

City of Rose (Book 2)

New Yorked (Book 1)

ASSASSINS ANONYMOUS

ROB HART

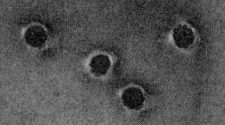

G. P. PUTNAM'S SONS
NEW YORK

PUTNAM
—EST. 1838—

G. P. Putnam's Sons
Publishers Since 1838
An imprint of Penguin Random House LLC
penguinrandomhouse.com

Copyright © 2024 by Rob Hart

Penguin Random House supports copyright. Copyright fuels creativity, encourages diverse voices, promotes free speech, and creates a vibrant culture. Thank you for buying an authorized edition of this book and for complying with copyright laws by not reproducing, scanning, or distributing any part of it in any form without permission. You are supporting writers and allowing Penguin Random House to continue to publish books for every reader.

Library of Congress Cataloging-in-Publication Data

Names: Hart, Rob, author.
Title: Assassins anonymous / Rob Hart.
Description: New York : G. P. Putnam's Sons, 2024.
Identifiers: LCCN 2024000706 (print) | LCCN 2024000707 (ebook) | ISBN 9780593717394 (hardcover) | ISBN 9780593717400 (ebook)
Subjects: LCSH: Assassins—Fiction. | Nonviolence—Fiction. | LCGFT: Thrillers (Fiction) | Novels.
Classification: LCC PS3608.A7868 A87 2024 (print) | LCC PS3608.A7868 (ebook) | DDC 813/.6—dc23/eng/20240112
LC record available at https://lccn.loc.gov/2024000706
LC ebook record available at https://lccn.loc.gov/2024000707
p.   cm.

International Edition ISBN: 9780593852057

Printed in the United States of America
1st Printing

BOOK DESIGN BY KATY RIEGEL

This is a work of fiction. Names, characters, places, and incidents either are the product of the author's imagination or are used fictitiously, and any resemblance to actual persons, living or dead, businesses, companies, events, or locales is entirely coincidental.

This one's for me.

"All of humanity's problems stem from man's inability to sit quietly in a room alone."

—Blaise Pascal

ASSASSINS ANONYMOUS

1

> Why is a caterpillar wrapped in silk while it changes into a butterfly? So the other caterpillar can't hear the screams. Change hurts.
> —Rory Miller, *Meditations on Violence*

Lower East Side, Manhattan
Now

Adrenaline is the ultimate painkiller. It doesn't last very long. But in those white-hot moments when your gut gets pierced by a bullet, or a knife cleaves your skin, you would be amazed at how little you feel it.

It screws with your perception of time, too. For most people, when pain is screaming for attention like a starving toddler, everything is a senseless jumble of limbs and grunts. The world moves at twice the speed, while you hover above your body watching the mayhem unfold.

But when you've been at this long enough—and I've been at this long enough—time turns into a thing you can hold in your hand. You can rotate it and examine the angles. You end up confronting things about yourself.

Like why you're sprawled on a cold linoleum floor, amid the shattered remains of a flimsy folding table, covered in cheap coffee and leftover donuts. You wonder which of your sins summoned the man who put his boot to your chest and sent you flying.

When I woke up this morning, I thought I didn't need a meeting. Those are the days when I need a meeting. So I dragged myself to the basement of St. Dymphna's on the Lower East Side. A tiny church, so forgotten it might as well be forsaken, tucked away in the wilds underneath the Williamsburg Bridge.

The details of the meeting aren't important.

What's important is stopping this guy from killing me.

He's that kind of tall where you wonder if he has to duck through doorways. He's right-handed. Not bulky, but the veins on his forearms are raised like ridges on a topography map. On his left forearm is a tattoo: a single black dot, surrounded by four more, like five on a die. His dark hair is buzzed to his skull, except for a narrow strip of black Mohawk. He's wearing cargo pants, black boots, and a navy thermal. I recognize the glassy deadness in his eyes because I see it in the mirror every morning. He might be Russian. He hasn't spoken yet, but the kick, his stance, and the smug confidence read as Systema.

I push myself to standing, careful not to slip on the spilled food. He's about ten feet from me. He should have tried to overwhelm me while I was down, but he hasn't done that. Instead he's sizing me up with a look of recognition and excitement.

I think he knows who I am.

Which means he's either insane or very confident.

"We can still talk this out," I tell him, glancing down at the floor. "I'd offer you a donut but we're past the five-second rule."

He smiles with the left corner of his mouth and mutters, "Kozyol."

Russian it is.

As soon as the insult leaves his lips, he comes at me, fast.

Too fast.

He's so excited about proving something, he's not paying attention to the floor. Three steps and he lands on a chocolate-frosted donut that causes him to slide forward. It interrupts his flow, which is all the opening I need.

In one movement I bend down, pick up the shattered coffeepot by the black plastic handle, and swing the jagged edge of glass at his leg. I'm hoping to hook it behind his knee and sever something important, incapacitate him, because I need to know who sent him. But also, it's not like I can kill him.

In this place, of all places.

He jerks back and I miss him by a hair. Same thing on the next three swings. I'm hunting for nonlethal cuts, but he's that kind of Bruce Lee fast where you see where he starts and finishes but not all those parts in the middle.

Already I'm feeling gassed. My muscles are covered in dust and cobwebs. It's been a while since I pushed myself. I go for the leg again but swing too wide and lose my balance. He uses his momentum to come back around and put his boot into the side of my head. I move with the blow and combat roll into a standing position.

The adrenaline is doing its job. The pain is outside, knocking at the door, but the disorientation is inside pouring a cup of tea.

I set my feet, ready for him to charge. The glass on the coffeepot is too fragile for it to be an effective weapon, but it's something. So of course, he reaches into his belt and pulls out a short black switchblade. It looks sharp enough to cut through the hull of a tank.

Another sign of his confidence. He could have knifed me at the start. I didn't hear him until he was right behind me, which is not the kind of thing most people could brag about.

He's here to test himself.

He holds the knife behind him, away from where I could effectively counter or knock it from his hand. He puts that veiny left forearm out like a shield. Knives are dangerous in the hands of idiots, but there's nothing worse than someone who knows how to use one.

He takes small steps toward me now, gauging the distance. Hopping forward a little before stepping back, daring me to swing. I'm matching his stance, forearm out, wrist facing me so he can't get at the tender part on the inside.

But I'm desperately outmatched.

What this guy doesn't know is that I will do anything within my power to avoid killing him, even as the most savage part of me roars with hunger to do just that.

While he puts on a show, I take a moment to breathe. Inhale for four seconds, hold for four, breathe out for four, hold my lungs empty for four. It calms my nervous system enough that I can focus.

The coffeepot is useless, so when he decides to strike I throw it at his face. He turns and staggers slightly to protect his eyes, which lets me come around low on his dead side and go for the knife. If I can control it, I might be able to walk away from this with a few cuts, maybe some light puncture wounds, without taking it handle-deep in my chest.

I get one hand over his wrist, and the other over his hand, then shove my shoulder into him, creating distance and pushing the blade away from me. From here it's chess at a hundred miles an hour. If I can throw my knee into the back of his, I can fold him to the ground and gain control. Get the knife arm down, use my leverage to keep it there.

But he's strong. He yanks back hard, creating an opening, and then the two of us are struggling for the weapon.

My fingers slip on something wet and it's harder to maintain a grip.

That's when my experience with adrenaline betrays me, and time gets fuzzy.

A jumble of limbs and grunts, an eternity in an instant.

He pulls away, a look of shock on his face.

His hands are empty. So are mine. I know the knife didn't land on the ground because I would have heard it. My heart is flooded with an acidic sense of regret.

Almost made it to a year.

I search him for the knife's handle, hoping it's a nonfatal wound. I can apply pressure, call an ambulance, tie off a tourniquet—whatever it takes to save this guy's life.

Except I don't see the knife anywhere.

And he's looking down at my stomach.

I follow his gaze to where the knife is sticking out of my left side.

"Oh, thank god," I say, gently touching the edges of the wound.

That's when the pain sets in, crashing into me like a wave, sending me to the ground. I roll onto my side, so as not to push the knife in deeper. Every nerve in my body flares to life and screams directly in my ears.

That's the thing about adrenaline—it's the ultimate painkiller, but it doesn't last very long.

He stalks toward me, and I think, *This is it*. I wonder what brought him here, how he found me, why he's doing this. It'd be nice if he would monologue a bit, but he doesn't seem the talkative type. I guess it doesn't matter. You could fill a stadium with the people who wish me dead.

And even though I didn't get to complete my steps, didn't get to make amends—maybe this is what I deserve. Dying painfully on the floor of a church.

He squats in front of me and pats me down. He pulls the small, battered notebook out of my breast pocket, flips through it, and nods. Seemingly satisfied that he got what he came for, he leans down to my ear, so close I can feel the heat of his breath, and says, "Disappointing, kotenok."

That just stings. *Kozyol* means "goat" but is pretty much Russian for "motherfucker." *Kotenok* means "kitten."

And also he stabbed me.

Just, overall this guy is a dick.

I start laughing, that my ego is my primary concern when I'm bleeding out, but I don't think he hears it. I'm pretty sure he's gone. I roll onto my back and stare at the fluorescent lights buzzing overhead. Through the pain, I am thankful.

Dying with my sobriety intact feels like *something*.

That said, maybe I still stand a chance. Blood is flowing around the knife but it's not oozing, and I don't smell shit, which means there's a decent chance it missed my intestines. All I have to do is keep the knife in, let it hold things together until I can find some kind of help.

The knife is the only thing keeping me alive, like a finger in a dam.

Footsteps behind me. The Russian reappears in my field of vision and gives a sheepish little wave, waggling his fingers at me. Then he reaches down and grasps the knife, pulling hard, yanking it out of me. That one overloads my system to the point I can't see straight.

"See you soon," he says.

I press my hand to my gut.

Hot blood gushes between my fingers.

This wasn't what I expected from the day.

2

> MATHILDA: Is life always this hard,
> or is it just when you're a kid?
> LÉON: Always like this.
> —*The Professional*

West Village, Manhattan
Earlier That Day

The timer goes off, the blare of it snapping me out of the trance induced by the rhythmic tapping of the jump rope. I stoop to pick up my phone from the surface of the roof and shove it into the pocket of my hoodie, gaze out over the rooftops of the West Village, and breathe in the brittle air.

It's a beautiful day.

Down the stairs and back in my apartment, I hang the jump rope from its hook next to the door. P. Kitty waddles over to his food dish in the kitchen and yowls, demanding tribute. I pull out a can of chopped chicken hearts and liver and dump it into his dish, give him a little scratch on the top of his big dumb orange head as he shoves his face into the bowl.

Part of me wants to stay home and watch movies and take a night off from processing deep emotions, but Kenji will be waiting for me at Lulu's and I don't want to stand him up.

That's enough to get me in gear. The temperature is somewhere in the twenties, but ten minutes of jumping rope is still enough for a sweat, so I hop in the shower, rinse, and get dressed. Then I make sure P. Kitty's water is filled. He ate half his food and retired to the couch, transformed into a shapeless ball of orange fur.

"No parties while I'm out," I tell him.

He doesn't stir.

I grab the trash and head for the door, then realize I forgot my notebook. It's on top of my tattered, beaten copy of the Big Book—the textbook for Alcoholics Anonymous—which is in its spot of reverence, next to the paper crane Kenji gave me in Prague all those years ago. I tuck the notebook into the pocket of my jacket and feel a bit safer.

The window is open a crack—the apartment holds heat like a pizza oven—but it looks too narrow for P. Kitty to wriggle through, and I'd rather not come home to a sauna, so I leave it.

I walk down a floor and knock on the door of the apartment directly below me. There's a shuffling sound from the other side, and the door cracks open, an eye peering out at chest level. It widens with recognition and Ms. Nguyen opens the door. She's wearing a heavy bathrobe and fuzzy slippers, her gray hair pushed flat against her scalp by a red headband.

"Trash service," I tell her.

Her face breaks into a smile as she holds up a small white plastic bag tied neatly at the top. "You're so sweet."

"Call it even for feeding my cat while I'm away. But you have to cool it on the treats. He's getting chubby."

"He's not chubby, he's big-boned," she says. "And if he's looking for food, it means he's hungry. You don't feed him enough."

"Agree to disagree."

"Do you need me to watch him over Christmas? Are you going anywhere?"

"I'll be the same place I am every year. Upstairs, drinking whiskey, watching *It's a Wonderful Life*."

"No family, no girlfriend?" she asks. "Or boyfriend?"

I shrug. "I don't do Christmas. I didn't get the BMX bike I asked for when I was a kid. It went downhill from there."

"Okay, Scrooge, I'll be making almond cookies for my son and his kids on Christmas Eve if you want to stop by." She raises an eyebrow. "I could use a strong set of hands."

"Doesn't matter how many times you hit on me, I'm not going to sleep with you."

She laughs and reaches up to smack me on the chest. "Like you would be so lucky. Thanks for taking the trash, Mark."

"See you tomorrow, darling," I tell her, heading for the stairs. "And stop sneaking food to my cat."

She calls after me: "Stop starving him."

I hit the street and drop the trash in the bins, then point myself toward the Lower East Side. Normally I would walk but at this point it's probably better to take the F, so I hustle over to West Fourth, then run down the stairs and manage to jump on a car as the doors are closing.

And of course, there's Smiley.

Smiley is a regular in this neighborhood. Not always the F, I've seen him on the A and the 1, too. He may live around here, or else it's just his hunting ground. As per usual he's swaying out of time with the rocking of the subway car, clutching a half-empty bottle of Hennessy, oozing with mid-twenties bravado. His unkempt hair is greasy, and then there are those ever-present scars on his face. One across each cheek, lending him the appearance of a grotesque smile.

My tack has always been to ignore him. Most people causing a stir on the subway are homeless or mentally ill, and I have sympathy for them; the city spends billions on the NYPD, which doesn't do much more than corral, harass, or beat them. And it gets that money by gutting the homeless and mental wellness agencies that could actually help them.

By and large, they're more a danger to themselves. If you ignore them, they leave you alone, and you can always get on the next car or wait for the next train.

But that's easy for me to say.

Right now he's talking at a pretty young brunette in expensive leather boots and a white bubble jacket. She is not picking up what he's putting down. Rather, her body is curled in on itself, like she's trying to make herself disappear. Fear permeates the car, people looking away, like maybe if they don't see it they don't have to feel guilty.

I sit in the empty seat next to her, but I look up at Smiley. "Hey, bud. What's your favorite ice cream flavor?"

The record in his head scratches. Then he says, "The hell are you talking about, bro?"

"Where's the best place to buy groceries around here? I go to Dags, but they're a little pricey."

"We're having a conversation," he says, taking a swig from

the Hennessy bottle, then staring at it in shock when he realizes it's empty.

"Didn't look like much of a conversation to me, but I saw how keen you were to chat, so I figured I would hop in. What's the last good movie you saw?"

The barrage of questions does exactly what it's meant to do—it confuses him and annoys him, but it's not aggressive enough to make him angry.

The doors open at Broadway-Lafayette and I give the woman a little nudge. She waits a second and dives off the train. As she's doing that, I get up, too, putting myself between Smiley and the door so he can't follow.

The doors close and he pushes me. Not hard, but I move with it to create a little distance between us, so I can watch his hands. Guy who gets his face slashed like that probably carries a blade of his own to assuage the memory. It's a safe assumption to make—I don't lose anything by being wrong, but I gain a lot if I'm right.

Such as: not being stabbed.

"You know who I am?" he asks.

"I don't," I tell him. "My name is Mark. What's your favorite color?"

"Red," he says. "As in, what I'm gonna see in a second if you don't back down."

"You're right, we don't want that," I tell him, struggling with all my might to hold at bay the shit-eating smirk that's begging to crawl across my lips.

He goes for another drag on the bottle—still empty—considering his options. The train slows as it pulls into Second

Avenue. I'm starting to wonder if this was a mistake. I don't regret drawing his attention to me, but I could have played a softer hand. As the doors slide open, he mutters, "Asshole," and stalks off.

Once the doors are safely closed, a few people clap. I give a little nod to the crowd, pleased at myself for keeping my cool, a little annoyed that no one stepped in before me. But most of all, wrestling into submission that toxically masculine urge that made me want to follow Smiley off and ask him: *You know who I am?*

Snowflakes whisper against the diner window. Not enough to stick, but enough to count as the first proper snowfall of the season. On the other side of Delancey, visible through a steady stream of traffic, is a small barren tree strung up with colorful twinkle lights. It looks sad, out there all alone like that, struggling to cast light in a dark and indifferent city, but that could just be a reflection.

Kenji brings my attention back to the countertop by tapping my notebook, which I helpfully took out and, unhelpfully, didn't bother to open. His long gray hair is pulled back into a topknot, and, as always, he has a bemused smile on his face, like someone told a moderately funny joke. Not enough for a laugh, but enough to earn his respect.

"How is your eighth step coming?" he asks.

I take a sip of my coffee-flavored water and shrug. "It's almost Christmas. Are we exchanging gifts? Because if you got me something, I don't want to be empty-handed and feel like a dumbass."

"Mark?"

"I'm a medium T-shirt. I have plenty of kitchen stuff. I don't need more kitchen stuff."

"Maaark?" Kenji says, drawing my name out in a low baritone, like he's lecturing a small child.

"It's coming," I tell him.

Kenji chuckles as he leans back on his stool, looking around to make sure no one is in earshot. Besides an old man sitting in a booth at the far end of the diner, disappearing into a moldy brown suit as he does the *New York Times* crossword, it's just us and the owner, Lulu. Her diner is a narrow little railroad-style joint, full of chrome, faux wood, and dust. The food is fine, but the privacy is top-shelf.

"What's wrong?" he asks. "You're distracted."

I tell him about Smiley. About how I should be proud that I de-escalated the situation, even though I wanted to pound on his skull until shards of bone sliced into my knuckles.

"If you're looking for affirmation, here it is." Kenji pats me on the shoulder. "I'm proud of you."

"Thanks, Dad."

"I know I keep saying it, but that's because it's easy to forget," Kenji says. "Choosing to change is not something you do once. It's something you have to wake up every day and choose to do again . . ."

Kenji stops when Lulu appears in front of us. Her red hair is going white, steely green eyes shining through crimson cat-eye glasses. She hefts a glass carafe of coffee and tops us both off without offering any kind of acknowledgment before shuffling back to the register, where she busies herself with paperwork.

"It's not easy," Kenji says, his voice a little lower now. With his right hand, he strokes the intricate, colorful tattoo that dominates his left forearm—the tail of a dragon, the body of which wraps around Kenji's torso. The dragon's head takes up the entirety of his back. He tends to touch the tattoo when he's remembering his previous life.

"The idea of actually sitting down with people . . ." I take a tentative sip of coffee, hoping the hot liquid will loosen up the thickening in my throat.

"Remember what I told you, all those years ago?" Kenji asks, spinning his mug on its plate.

"Willingness," I tell him.

"I did an amends two nights ago," he says. "I tracked down an old girlfriend who is living here, in Passaic." He puts down the mug and folds his hand. "She runs a restaurant. Japanese-Mexican fusion. Whatever that is."

"She didn't comp you a meal?"

"I went at closing," he says.

"And you just told her what you did?"

Kenji nods. "She seemed upset at first, a little scared, but she heard me out. When I was done, she said she didn't forgive me, but it had been so long she no longer held a grudge. She told me she set down that pain a long time ago, and it was now mine to carry. She asked me to leave and never come back."

"How did that feel?" I ask.

"In the moment, uncomfortable," he says. "But I felt lighter on the walk back to the train. It had to be done." He takes a long swig of coffee. "The more you do it, the easier it gets."

I laugh a little at that. The idea of any of this being easy sounds ridiculous.

The thing is, I'm lying to Kenji. My eighth step—the list of people I should make amends to—has been done for a while now.

But the ninth step is actually making those amends.

And moving on to that means admitting these things to be true.

"Here's the thing I don't get," I tell him. "The ninth step says we have to make direct amends wherever possible, unless to do so would cause further harm or injury. If that's the case, we can do a living amends. Just, you know, live a better life. One of service. Why isn't this whole program about living amends? How does it not cause further harm or injury to drop this kind of stuff in people's laps? We're just ripping off scabs. Putting them in a position of... What if they want payback?"

Kenji, with that smile again. "Spoken like every single person who doesn't want to start their ninth step."

My hands are flat on the counter, like I'm trying to hold myself down from floating away. These hands that have caused so much hurt, that have made my eighth-step list so goddamn long. Kenji seems to sense the shifting gravity and places his right hand over my left, to keep me grounded. My instinct is to pull away, but I appreciate the intimacy of it.

Especially because his hands have done the same kinds of things as mine.

"You're my fourth sponsee," he says. "Two gave up. One, his past caught up with him. You moved through the steps with real focus. You showed up for them. Then you got here and you hit a wall. I don't want to lose another one. Remember, this is a kindness. Not just for the people on your list, but for yourself. What you are doing is learning to forgive yourself."

"I know," I tell him. "I'm just being difficult."

"Very."

Four in, hold for four, out for four, empty lungs for four.

He's right. Moving into the ninth step means I can finish it, and then one day—well, I don't expect to truly forgive myself, or to find some kind of inner peace, but maybe I'll be able to sleep at night, or just hate myself a little less.

Maybe those things could be enough.

The door chimes behind us. A young couple comes in, holding up a phone at eye level, which they're both smiling into like lunatics. He's wearing a black skullcap and has a tattered scarf looped tastefully around his neck. She's got big thick glasses, a fuzzy pink coat, and a shaved head.

"On today's episode of *Undiscovered Eats*," the young man says, "we check out Lulu's Diner, which is so off the beaten path it doesn't even have a Yelp page, and—"

Lulu snaps her fingers, which stops him from talking, and without lifting her pen from paper, or her eyes from what she's doing, she points to the door and says, "Get out."

The two of them hover in the open doorway, the frigid December air chasing away the warmth. Neither of them knows what to say, and they look to us like we're going to help.

I offer them a half shrug. "I wouldn't mess with her."

Without another word, they leave.

And that's why we come to Lulu's.

I realize Kenji's hand is still on mine. We look down at where we're touching, then back up to each other, and we burst out laughing. It was the pressure release valve that both of us needed in that moment.

Kenji reaches for his wallet. But I'm ready, a fifty-dollar bill folded in my pocket and ready to go. I slap it on the countertop and he sighs.

"Please . . ." he says.

"It's all good, bud," I tell him.

Kenji is big on custom and tradition and doesn't like that I always pay. But I walked away from my old life with a sizable nest egg. He walked away with the clothes on his back.

"Thank you," Kenji says, offering a slight bow. "And yes, it would be nice to exchange presents this year. It's been a long time."

"Oh, that was just me being difficult. Again. After last Christmas . . ."

"Perhaps," he says, "we should take a bad memory and replace it with a good one?"

I'm struck by a couple of feelings at once: giddiness at the idea of doing something so normal as exchanging gifts, and then, of course, the noxious shame of what happened the last time I wrapped a Christmas gift.

But it feels like another small step on the path leading to the kind of life I want to build.

The kind where normal things happen.

"Spending limit is fifty bucks," I tell him. "Sound good?"

"Sounds good."

We get up and shrug into our coats. Lulu may notice, or she may not. I yell across the diner to her. "Hey, Lu, it's almost Christmas. You ought to put up some decorations."

"Hmm," she says, I think.

Kenji gestures toward the door. "We still have to get the donuts."

The church basement is sparse, but large enough to fit a few dozen people for a mixer or a fund-raiser. The coffeepot is gurgling next to an open box of donuts on the folding table in the corner. The walls are robin's-egg blue and the floor is a black-and-white-checkered pattern. It looks frozen in time, and that time is 1982.

Kenji leans forward, placing down a silver lipstick-sized device on the small table in front of him, which will prevent us from being heard or recorded outside this room. Next to that, his copy of the Big Book, even more tattered than mine. His is held together with a thick blue rubber band so the pages don't spill out.

"Welcome to Assassins Anonymous," he says. "My name is Kenji, and I am a killer."

Kenji looks around the room, regarding each one of us in turn. There are five of us in total, seated on brown metal folding chairs under the buzzing fluorescent lights.

Valencia is wearing a red flannel and jeans. Her jet-black hair is cut short and tousled like she just got out of bed. She has the same look she always has on her face: like she smells something terrible.

Booker is every inch the jarhead—bald, black tribal tattoos decorating his russet skin, combat boots, and fatigue pants. Eyes darting back and forth, waiting for something to happen so he has an excuse to explode.

Stuart is the youngest of the bunch by at least a decade, and dresses even younger than that—swimming in an oversize black sweatshirt and baggy cargo pants. He perches on his seat like an animal who steals food from larger predators.

"Assassins Anonymous," Kenji says, "is a fellowship of men and women who share their experience, strength, and hope with each other, that they may solve their common problem and help each other to recover. The only requirement for membership is a desire to stop. We are not allied with any sect, denomination, politics, organization, or institution; our primary purpose is to stop killing and to help others achieve the same.

"We do not bring weapons into Assassins Anonymous, nor prior political affiliations. If any of us were known by any particular handle or nickname, we do not use it here. We share our stories, but we obscure details as best we can. If any of us seek to bring in new fellows, we agree to have them properly vetted. This is to protect us, not just from prying ears, but from each other."

He's not kidding. The story goes, there was a meeting in Los Angeles a few years ago where two professional hitman revealed their stage names and inadvertently discovered they'd spent decades locked in a game of cat and mouse. By the time the meeting was over, four people were dead.

Anonymity is an important component of any recovery process, and it's especially important here.

"Valencia," Kenji says, "could you read the steps?"

Valencia shifts in her seat and closes her eyes, taking a moment to recall the words. In a regular AA meeting, there would be a handout you could read from; here, we prefer not to put things in writing.

"We really gotta do this every time?" Booker asks.

Kenji isn't chuffed. That's just Booker. "Remember," Kenji says, "we have steps to keep us from killing ourselves, and traditions to keep us from killing each other. Valencia?"

Booker exhales sharply, taking the wooden rosary beads from around his neck and wrapping them around his left hand, like he does at the start of every meeting. I want to point out the irony of that, but now is not the time. Valencia begins:

> "One, we admitted we were powerless—that our lives had become unmanageable.
> "Two, we came to believe that a power greater than ourselves could restore us to sanity.
> "Three, we made a decision to turn our will over to the care of a higher power, as we understood it.
> "Four, we made a searching and fearless moral inventory of ourselves.
> "Five, we admitted to our higher power, to ourselves, and to another human being the exact nature of our wrongs.
> "Six, we were ready to have our higher power remove all these defects of character.

"Seven, we humbly asked it to remove our shortcomings.

"Eight, we made a list of all persons we had harmed, and became willing to make amends to them all.

"Nine, we made direct amends to such people wherever possible, except when to do so would injure them or others.

"Ten, we continued to take personal inventory and when we were wrong promptly admitted it.

"Eleven, we sought through prayer and meditation to improve our conscious contact with our higher power as we understood it, praying only for knowledge of its will for us and the power to carry that out.

"Twelve, having had a spiritual awakening as the result of these steps, we tried to carry this message to others like us, and to practice these principles in all our affairs."

Hearing the steps has the same effect it always has on me: a desire and excitement to complete them, and an abject terror at the proposition.

Valencia continues: "No one among us has been able to maintain anything like perfect adherence to these principles. We are not saints . . ."

This line always draws a couple of chuckles.

"The point is that we are willing to grow along spiritual lines," she says.

Valencia looks up at Kenji, who nods.

"Thank you," Kenji says. "Now..."

Stuart's hand shoots up at teacher's-pet speed.

"Stuart," Kenji says, glancing at me, "we have some other business..."

"Nah," I tell him. "It's all good. We're not in a rush here."

Stuart twists his hands in his lap. "Yeah, so I..."

"This shit again," Booker mutters, looking at the rest of us like: *C'mon, right?*

Stuart immediately shuts his mouth, and his eyes drop to the floor.

"Booker, you know that's not how we do things," Kenji says, calmly but sternly. "Everyone is allowed space to share, without judgment. The only requirement is that you have the desire to stop."

"It's just," Booker says, waving a scarred hand in Stuart's direction, "he's a freak, right? We're all thinking it. I don't like that he's sitting here with us. What we did, we did to people in the game. I killed warlords and terrorists. Not innocent people." He looks at Stuart. "How the hell did you find out about this, anyway? It's called *Assassins* Anonymous. Not *Serial Killers* Anonymous."

Kenji looks at me, hoping I'll jump in. Another difference from a normal AA meeting, where people are given the runway to speak—our meetings often mutate into talk therapy sessions.

"Mark?" Kenji asks.

Booker's attention snaps to me.

Stuart gives a tentative glance in my direction.

"Couple of things here, B," I tell him. "You know as well as I do that he got vetted by Kenji, just like everyone else. Second, we take in hit men, and hit men ain't assassins. You're entitled to your feelings, but we've had this conversation more than once. What we did, we did for money, or the thrill, or because it's the only thing any of us is good at. Stuart over here"—I gesture toward the cowering figure—"he's got a real compulsion. The kind of behavior you would more traditionally associate with an addiction. Which means this is the best place for him. Him being here means someone is alive. You want to do carve-outs for mercenaries, too? 'Cause that wouldn't work out so well for Marines who switched over to private contracting..."

Booker involuntarily flexes the muscles in his forearms. I've gleaned that much about him from his shares, and he doesn't like that I have him pegged down to his branch. Marines are the easiest to spot, though; it's the bravado.

"... but we're all here trying to be better," I tell him. "So I think we should support Stuart, not tear him down."

"Whatever," Booker mutters, folding his arms.

I look at Valencia. The one I've had the hardest time figuring out, because she tends to speak the least. Booker is a Marine turned mercenary; Kenji was a Yakuza hitter. Stuart is Stuart. All I can tell about Valencia is she's Mexican, but she doesn't carry herself like military or police, so I figure she had something to do with the cartels.

"V, what do you think?" I ask.

"I think this is a little too much crosstalk," she says, staring past the circle and through the wall.

"Back to the meeting." I wink at Stuart. "What have you got for us, Stu?"

"Well," he says, still looking at the ground, now hugging

himself for support. "Last night, I went to this bar near my apartment, because I like their fries. Their burgers are sort of meh, but their fries are good. So I got a plate of fries, and the bartender, she was my type." His lips curl into a smirk, and I think all of us freeze a little at the word *type*.

The more Stuart talks, the faster his voice gets: "It's Astoria, so it's generally a quiet neighborhood after last call. I could have followed her home, found out where she lived. Or I could have talked to her and learned a little about her. I was always good at that. Getting people to open up to me. But I didn't. I finished my fries and I paid my bill and I went home."

Kenji claps, enthusiastically, and the rest of us follow with a little less verve. "Good for you, Stuart," he says. "How did that feel?"

Stuart tilts his head, digging the thumb of his left hand into the palm of his right. "I still wonder what her head would look like sitting in my fridge with an apple crammed in her mouth, but the important thing is, it's still on her shoulders, right?"

I can feel the discomfort snaking through the room, so I clap again. No one follows, but it doesn't matter. The silence is broken. "One day at a time, buddy," I tell him. "One day at a time."

Booker mutters something, but I can't make it out.

Kenji sighs and says, "Thank you, Stuart. Now, our next meeting is going to be a special one . . ."

A flush of warmth spreads through my body. Doesn't matter how far we make it in life, we're all just little kids who want a gold star from their teacher.

"Mark is a few days out from one year," Kenji says.

At this, everyone claps, much more enthusiastically than they did for Stuart.

Kenji has seniority here: five years and change. Valencia has four, and Booker is over three. Stuart, the new addition to the group, is still a few months in, which is a delicate time for people in recovery, and why I want to encourage him.

Everyone waits, offering me the space to speak.

"I almost can't believe it." I take my last prize—my six-month chip—out of my pocket. The inscription is barely legible, the hard plastic surface worn smooth from how often I need to rub it between my fingers and remind myself it's real. "I was thinking about it today, how that feeling never goes away. The muscle memory. And it made me think, can I really change? But I guess it doesn't matter whether I can or not, the only important thing is that I want to."

I look up and meet everyone's eyes in turn.

"I just want to say, I'm thankful for all of you. No one understands what taking a life does. How it screws you up, but then how even more screwed up it is that you get used to it, and then it just becomes a job. Then you go see a movie and it's like this noble profession, but the reality is we're just tools, so somebody with power can have even more power. I can say, with complete and total honesty, even though I still struggle with my programming, I don't miss killing. And that feels good. From the bottom of my heart, I'm thankful for you scumbags."

That draws a big, explosive laugh from Booker and a judgmental look from Kenji. Before he can say anything I put my hand up.

"I don't say scumbags because you're former killers. I say it because you always leave me alone to clean up after the meetings."

"Okay," Kenji says, with just the slightest roll of his eyes. "We've got some time left. Booker, would you like to share?"

They do, and the story remains mostly the same. Booker talks about the ghosts of past victims, the ones who follow him through the grocery store and stand by the foot of his bed at night. Valencia talks about wanting to be a mom, but not wanting to be a mom who kills people, and how one day she hopes to be worthy of the privilege. Kenji talks about the amends he made the other night, to the girlfriend of a man he killed in Kyoto.

There are no time limits. With only five of us, it can sometimes be hard to fill an hour. All it takes is for someone to be in a mood. But even on the nights we end up telling the same stories, I find comfort in being here. In seeing these people and knowing I'm not alone.

As I listen to them I consider the upcoming milestone.

One year since the biggest mistake I ever made, if you're not counting all the others.

Contentment courses through me, and at the end of the hour, when it's time to say the serenity prayer, I fold my hands together and speak in unison with the group, and it's like I'm saying it for the first time:

"Grant me the serenity to accept the things I cannot change, the courage to change the things I can, and the wisdom to know the difference."

ASSASSINS ANONYMOUS

With the room cleared, I close my eyes and take a deep breath. I like to bust on everyone for leaving me to clean, but really I enjoy it. It's meditative, allowing me space to process the events of the meeting. A nice little decompress before I head back into the world, where the lights and the sounds and the people put me back on edge.

For a few moments I feel safe.

There's a shuffle behind me. I turn to find Stuart, standing awkwardly on the other end of the room. His hands are clasped in front of him and the way he's looking at me, eyes unblinking, makes me think of a bug, like I turned on the light and caught him and he could bolt in any direction. Maybe I'm just uneasy because I know what he used to get up to in his free time. The silence between us stretches for a beat too long, so I ask, "How you doing there, bud?"

"What *is* the difference between hit men and assassins?" he asks.

"A hitman gets paid by a political or criminal organization to kill someone. An assassin kills for religious or political purposes, but they don't always get paid. The lines are blurry. Lee Harvey Oswald was an assassin, but there are guys and gals in this fellowship who changed the course of world events and you'd never know, and they got paid very well to do it. The terms are sort of interchangeable but sort of not. Kind of like how all bourbons are whiskeys, but not all whiskeys are bourbons?"

Stuart shakes his head. "I don't get it."

"Yeah, I pushed that one too far. It's the best I got at the moment, though."

"What does that make me, then?" he asks.

"A killer, same as me," I tell him. "Someone who belongs here, same as me."

Stuart takes a few steps forward, and I tense, and I think he sees it because he stops. One thing I've learned about him, and a thing I actually give him credit for, is that he's aware of the effect he has on people. "I wanted to say I'm sorry for interrupting Kenji's announcement," he says. "And thank you, for the thing with Booker."

"Booker sleeps in a bed made of sandpaper. At the end of the day he's not a bad guy. None of us are. We just have the luxury of recognizing that we've made mistakes."

"I like that," Stuart says, chewing on it. "The luxury."

"Don't give me too much credit. Kenji said it to me once."

Stuart looks down at the floor. "I get it, though. I'm not like the rest of you. Not really."

"Hey, Stu." I turn to him fully and wait for him to bring his eyes to mine. "It's good that you're here."

"Thank you," he says. "That means a lot, coming from you. Listen . . ." He looks down at the floor again, shuffling his feet, before looking back up at me. "I don't have a sponsor yet. Would you consider . . . doing that?"

A clammy wave passes over my skin as it erupts into goose bumps.

You don't have to have a sponsor in recovery. Kenji sponsors me, but he doesn't have one. Booker and Valencia sponsor each other. I never considered taking on a sponsee. Up until now I've been happy to defend Stuart—because if he can change, so can I—but taking an active role in his recovery is a different level of commitment. And not one I'm ready for. I'm still trying to handle my own.

"I need to think about that," I tell him. He nods, and then, without saying anything else, he steps through the darkened doorway at the far end of the room. With him gone, the air feels a little less thick.

A stew of complicated emotions mix in my gut. A little regret, that I might have hurt his feelings. A little relief, that I may have shut the conversation down.

Back in the day, I would have done the math, and the equation would be elementary—ending Stuart's life would have the potential to save so many others. Then I would slit his throat and leave him bleeding in a ditch.

I'm a different person now. Ultimately I do want him to succeed, but the sponsor/sponsee relationship is an intimate one.

I'm going to have to talk to Kenji about this. *He* might not think I'm ready.

One can hope.

As I'm about to dump the leftover donuts in the trash can next to the table, there's a squeak of a footstep behind me.

"What's up, Stu, forget something?" I ask.

As I turn, a boot smashes into my chest.

3

Pain don't hurt.
—Dalton, *Road House*

The Bowery
Now

Three times circling the block, watching for tails, then waiting ten minutes so I could slip past the doorman—I'm pretty sure the Russian is gone, but I still feel guilty about coming here. I bang on the apartment door with an eye on the end of the hallway. The pain is fading into a general numbness, so I don't feel *too* guilty. There's only so much blood in my body.

She may not be home. She may not live here anymore. But a shadow passes across the lens of the peephole. A chain rattles, a lock *shunks*, and the door cracks open.

Astrid is wearing a lavender silk bathrobe, which serves to accentuate her toned, athletic figure. Her long hair, the color of fall leaves, is still wet from the shower. Her face is smooth and makeup-free, so that I can better appreciate the years in it.

As always, the sight of her snatches the breath out of my chest. Everyone's got their own taste and preference, but to me Astrid looks the way a woman is supposed to look.

Not that I'd ever tell her that. Our relationship has always been purely professional, and I'm about to test how far that'll stretch. It's been so long it takes her a second to register that it's me. Then her face twists in confusion. "Mark? I'm meeting a friend in an hour and . . ."

She looks down at the jumble of bloody rags I'm pressing to my stomach.

"What the hell . . ."

"May I come in, please?" I ask.

She steps aside, mouth hanging open. I move through the sparse, tastefully appointed living room and consider the couch, but it's white leather. That could stain, so I head for the bathroom, which is a wreck—makeup scattered, used towels on the floor. I drop the mess of soiled rags into the claw-foot tub. "It's been a while. What's the going rate for a drop-in like this?"

Astrid is standing in the doorway, trying to regain her senses. "Six grand."

"I'll give you twelve," I say, pulling my shirt over my head and finally getting a good look at the angry, black gash on my abdomen. It's still weeping blood, but slower. Whether that means things are improving or I'm running low on gas, I'm not sure. The fact that I'm woozy isn't a good sign. I lower myself into the tub.

Astrid is standing over me now, clutching her robe tighter. "It's been more than a year since I saw you last. You can't just roll up without calling."

"I deleted your number." Something that looks like disappointment flashes across her face, but maybe that's me being hopeful. "I'm sorry. I truly am. But if I go to a hospital, I'll spend the rest of my life in prison or get killed on the way there."

She exhales deeply, then taps her phone and puts it to her ear.

"It's me. I'm sorry, I just had a family emergency come up . . . No, it'll be okay, but I have to cancel tonight . . . I'll call you soon."

She slaps the phone down on the sink and roots around underneath, hands me an orange pill bottle without looking at me. "Vicodin. It's not going to help right now, but you'll be thankful for it later."

I dry-swallow two. She makes quick work of setting out a medical kit, placing a clean towel on the floor to kneel on, and then washing and drying her hands. As she's pulling on a pair of blue latex gloves she asks, "How long was the blade?"

"Three, four inches," I tell her.

She uses cotton pads to clean the wound, then spreads orange antibacterial solution around it. She follows that with a needle, dosing small pumps to the perimeter of the laceration.

"Lidocaine?" I ask.

She nods. "I need to know if something got nicked. The best I can do is put a finger inside the wound and feel around. It's not foolproof and I could miss something." She holds up the needle. "This isn't going to help all that much."

"Better than nothing. Don't worry, I won't hold you liable if I end up dead."

She furrows her brow at me.

"And I'll leave when you're done, so if I do die, you don't have to move a body. I remember the drill."

She holds up her hand, fingers spread. "You ready?"

I open the bottle of Vicodin and swallow two more. It's going to be a while before they soak in, so no, not really, but what choice do I have? She hands me a small towel.

"Bite down," she says.

I do, and she doesn't wait. She slides a finger inside, and my vision explodes into a star field.

There was this boxer who used to say pain is information. Your shoulder hurts, you protect it. Your ribs ache, you cover them up. Process it like that, and you can deal with just about anything.

This, though—this just hurts.

I fight the urge to lash out, to scream, and I focus on staying still as her finger probes inside me. It slips and slides and feels like she's going to rip something out.

After a millennium of this, she withdraws her gore-covered finger and sniffs it. "Intestine seems intact. Doesn't feel like there's a ton of blood in the body cavity. Again, I can't be completely sure. I'll sew you up and then you have to go."

"Sure, sure," I say. I consider asking for a shot of something—she always has some nice whiskeys on her bar cart—but the alcohol on top of the Vicodin could make the bleeding worse. The lidocaine, at least, takes the edge off the needle and thread she snakes through the folds of my skin. Anyway, the pain centers in my brain are frayed and throwing sparks. At this point anything else just disappears into the din.

"Are you going to tell me?" she asks.

"Tell you what?" I ask, like I don't know.

The needle seems to get stuck and she resets herself, pushing it carefully through my flesh. "I knew you were in the business of hurting people, but you never said why or how, no matter how many times I asked."

"Safer that way."

"Now I want to know. It's the least you could do after barging in here unannounced."

"Twelve grand isn't enough?"

She takes her hands off the needle. "You can finish if you want. Makes no difference to me."

"I appreciate this, and I appreciate you," I tell her. "But I'm going to be really honest here: the less you know, the better."

"Is it going to blow back onto my doorstep?"

"I made sure I wasn't followed."

She smirks, seemingly satisfied, and resumes sewing.

"I thought you'd found someone else," she says.

"I got a pretty bad paper cut a few weeks ago but figured I could handle it on my own."

"Hmm," she says. That's it, "hmm." I'm left to wonder what it means. Instead of asking, I watch her hands. They're long and elegant and they work with the speed and precision of a concert pianist's. A few more minutes and she's done. The wound suddenly looks a lot less intense.

She pulls off the gloves, tossing them in the tub at my feet. "As long as it doesn't get infected or show signs of bruising, which would mean internal bleeding, you should be in the clear." She sits back on the floor, looking at everything in the room but me. I lower myself a little and try to get comfortable in the tub. We both take a moment to breathe.

I dig my boxy black cell phone out of my pocket and, after it registers my fingerprint, plug in my ten-digit access code. Astrid smirks. "Still got that hunk of junk? All the cool kids have iPhones."

"This hunk of junk," I say, thumbing through my contacts, "is unhackable and untraceable. Try to break in and the data wipes. You can roll over it with a tank. Now, I have to make a call. Can I have a moment?"

"No."

"What do you mean, no?"

Astrid fixes me with a hard stare. "I get that the less you tell me the better, but you're also not keeping me completely in the dark."

"Fine. I'm calling a friend. If he picks up, I can have him get the money from my apartment and meet us here. If he can't, I'll go get it."

Kenji picks up on the second ring. "Mark? Is everything okay?"

"Not really. Can you talk?"

He doesn't respond right away. He must be moving to a safe space. Kenji has a normal phone, so even given the level of encryption on mine, it behooves us to keep things short and obtuse. When he speaks, his voice is hushed. "What happened?"

"Got a surprise visitor after everyone left. Russian, tall, tattoo of five dots on his forearm. Very disagreeable. I'm safe for now, but I could use a hand. Can you pick some stuff up from my apartment?"

He pauses. "I'm indisposed. But I'm glad you're safe. That's the most important thing. Until we know what's going on, it's probably best to keep some distance. Maybe you should get out of town?"

"What do you mean, get out of town? I need to find out what's happening."

"You need to be safe."

"I don't run from fights."

"That sounds like something the old Mark would say."

I try to respond to that, but find I can't. "Okay, listen, can you check on the others?"

"I'll put out a draft, and I'll see if I can find anything about the Russian."

"Fantastic. Be safe out there, okay? Head on a swivel and all that."

"You too. Keep me updated."

I click off the call. Hopefully this is just on me. It has to be, right? It's either someone looking for revenge, or someone looking to keep me quiet. Could be a family member or friend of someone I killed, could be any number of people I used to work for, or against.

The notebook is the key.

Why did he take the notebook?

"Mark," Astrid says.

"Yeah."

"The money? Also, I'd love to get the bathroom cleaned up.

I can deal with a little mess"—she looks around and shrugs—"but this is a lot of blood."

"Yeah, yeah, sure." I get up slowly. The stitches tug, but they hold. "Let me get washed up."

As Astrid exits the room she says, "I have some clean clothes that may fit you."

"I'll go to my place, get the cash, and bring it back."

She reappears with some folded clothing. "I'd offer you a clean towel but I don't think I have any left. And take my number. I'm not letting you disappear on me again until I get paid."

It would be hard to impress on her that the reason I deleted her number is that I needed to put all forms of temptation behind me. Not having someone to tend to my more serious wounds made the idea of getting wounded a lot less appealing.

But it was sad, too. She was a big part of my life for a long time. Part of my routine. She saved my life more than once, and sometimes we'd share some laughs while she fixed me. It's why I'm one of the few clients who has her home address.

I miss the way she laughed: high and energetic, like a pop song.

What's the use of explaining that? Where would I even start?

"Okay," I tell her, and read off my cell. She calls me, then hangs up, so I have her number again. "I'll be back in a bit."

As I approach West Third and Sullivan, even with the windows closed, an acrid, chemical smell creeps into the cab's interior. That, coupled with the flashing lights, makes me think this night is about to get a whole lot worse.

We turn the corner and black clouds of smoke spill into the night sky from halfway down the block and six floors up.

See also: the approximate location of my living room.

I toss a fifty at the driver, yank the door open, and dive out. I nearly break into a sprint through the snarl of traffic, but the stitches demand I slow down.

I experience an immediate sense of relief when I make it to the crowd of people standing on the outskirts of the emergency response and find Ms. Nguyen holding a gray plastic cat carrier. She sees me approach and hoists the carrier above her head.

"We were afraid you were up there," she says. "He came down to my fire escape."

I take the carrier and P. Kitty shifts around inside, crying at the lights and smell and general disturbance. I place him down and throw my arms around Ms. Nguyen. She returns the hug with enough strength to make the wound on my stomach flare, taking my breath away.

I always suspected he snuck through the window and climbed down to hers for treats. I kiss the top of her head and tell her, "Thank you for not listening to me." Then I lift the carrier to eye level and peer inside. P. Kitty, in all his dumb orange furball glory, looks at me and offers a little hiss.

"Love you, too, buddy," I tell him. Then I turn back to Ms. Nguyen. "Is everyone okay?"

"Yeah, I think so," she says.

The other residents are lucky; there's a firehouse around

the corner, so the FDNY must have responded within a minute or two, minimizing the damage to the rest of the building. My apartment may be smoldering ruins, but it's just stuff. My money is safe, from both the fire and whatever damage ensues. I can always come back for it. But I can't get another P. Kitty and for that I owe Ms. Nguyen more than she'll ever know. Once I get into my safe I'll pay off her rent for the rest of her life.

My perception finally catches up with reality and I know there is no way this can be a coincidence. It must have been the Russian, or someone working with him. So I guess I can say, with some degree of confidence, this is personal. The air is that tight kind of cold that makes it hard to draw a full breath. Plus the Vicodin is kicking in. Within seconds my head is spinning.

Ms. Nguyen sees this and puts her hand to my chest.

"Just breathe," she says.

Four in, hold for four, out for four, empty lungs for four.

It helps, a little.

"You okay?" she asks.

Nope.

"Yeah."

"Good," she says, a smile creeping across her lips. "Because some of these firemen are pretty cute. I think I'm going to go see if any of them are single."

"Knock 'em dead, sweetheart. I have to take P. Kitty somewhere safe. I'll be right back, okay?"

She turns to the building, watching a firefighter atop a ladder spraying a burst of water into my apartment. I duck into the corner bar down the street and find that Tom is working. Finally, something works out in my favor.

Tom looks like an extra from a biker movie, with his barrel chest and thick gray beard. Half a life in Boston and half a life in New York has left him with an accent like a cartoon bear, and the Santa hat perched on top of his head makes him look like a dirtbag St. Nick.

He's also the only bartender in this joint who'll let me come in with the cat.

The Blinds is a tiny little corner spot mostly frequented by locals. No TV, so it doesn't attract a sports crowd. Right now, there are a handful of folks, most of whom I recognize, which offers me some level of comfort. No one at all seems bothered by the conflagration happening a few blocks down. I take a seat against the back wall, where I can see the front door but it's not as obvious that I'm here if you were to look in the window.

Tom ambles over with a glass of rye on the rocks. "That your building down there, Mark?"

"It's been a night," I tell him. "Not a good time for booze, but I'll take some of that jet fuel you pass off as coffee."

Tom shrugs and places the glass down in front of Mike, a former cop now employed at holding up that one particular barstool. He downs it without any acknowledgment.

"Coffee coming right up," Tom says. "Bowl of milk for the kitty?"

"He's good right now, thanks."

"Seriously, though," Tom says, "the owner will be back in a bit and she'll flip her lid if she sees him in here. We can argue extenuating circumstances, but I just don't need that kind of trouble tonight."

"I need a minute to get myself situated," I tell him. "Then I'll be on my way."

With the Vicodin in full effect, I'm feeling muddy, my brain full of wet sticks. Tom places a mug on the table and heads out for a smoke. The coffee is blazing hot and blacker than the void of space. Immediately my neurons fire.

So, I need twelve grand. My chief source of money is the pile of cash in my apartment, and that's going to be tricky to access if someone is watching. I've got a debit card for traveling and emergencies, which pulls from an offshore account on the Isle of Man, but I'm limited to a grand a day from ATMs. Which I don't like using because they tend to have cameras.

And I still need to find someplace to stay tonight. Preferably off the grid, and amenable to cats. I've got about six hundred in my wallet. I need a shitty hotel that'll let me pay in cash. P. Kitty seems to have settled now that we're inside, but he's going to need to eat soon.

The door opens and my heart leaps a little, but it's just Tom. Then again, he's got a look on his face. The kind of look I don't like. He comes over holding a folded piece of paper between two fingers and says, "Here's a weird one. Gentleman outside asked me to pass this to you."

"Must be mistaken," I tell him.

He places it on the table in front of me. "Described you perfectly. Russian accent." He must see the wave of panic that crashes into my face because he asks, "You good?"

"Honestly? I have no idea."

He tugs at the felt marker dangling from the collar of his sweatshirt and tosses it on the table. "Never leave home without one."

I take it and point it at him. "Thanks, man."

He tips his Santa cap to me and heads for the bar.

In his twenties, Tom worked security at one of the most notorious punk bars in Boston, and he said the marker got him out of more scraps than he could count. I've always appreciated that—for both the ingenuity, and, after going sober, the concept of a nonlethal personal defense. Something about holding it makes me feel safe.

I take another sip of coffee to keep from throwing up, then unfold the paper. Immediately this incredibly shitty night gets a hell of a lot worse.

In neat, block letters it says: SHE'S PRETTY.

I toss a twenty on the table and I'm gone before Tom even turns around.

Astrid is wearing a black turtleneck and blue jeans and a look of abject fury when she opens the hotel room door. She lets me inside and then shuts it behind her before laying into me.

"What is going on, Mark?" she asks. "You told me this wouldn't blow back. And why do you have a cat?"

"My apartment got blown up," I tell her, then kneel down to open the carrier. P. Kitty takes a tentative step out and surveys the room, as I'm doing the same. Last time I was here it was bedbugs and bloodstains, but they've classed it up since then. Now it's all soft corners and mirrors. There's even a complimentary bottle of lube on the nightstand.

It's the first place Astrid ever fixed me up, and luckily when I called she got what I was going for, telling her to leave immediately and meet me here, and only get the room if they let her pay cash. I figured it was safer to get her out the door than to waste time trying to go back for her.

I had to drop another hundred on the way in, paying off a panhandler to distract the guy working the desk so I could sneak in with the carrier. Which the panhandler did with a little too much aplomb, screaming about the quality of the coffee in the lobby and knocking over a table, but it worked.

"Am I in danger?" Astrid asks.

I dig out of my pocket a can of cat food I picked up at a bodega and place it down on the floor next to the carrier. P. Kitty goes to it immediately, though I'm sure after this he'll burrow under the bed until he gets acclimated to the new space.

"Yes," I tell her.

"Well, thanks for that."

She whisks into the bathroom and slams the door. I gently lower myself onto the bed and stare at myself in the mirror on the ceiling. The coffee only did so much. I'm a little high and very exhausted. Thinking makes the wound in my gut glow red.

I stick my hand in my pocket, feel the six-month chip.

I close my eyes, consider taking a nap, but there's still too much to do. P. Kitty nestles up to my good side and I stroke his head.

"Thanks, buddy," I tell him. "Glad someone here still likes me. Though I know that's only because I feed you."

He's a little wall-eyed, so usually I can't tell if he's looking at me or something else, but I like to think it's the former. He drops his head and purrs into my skin.

I click through my phone to the encrypted mail app and check the drafts folder. It's how the group communicates; emails can't be traced and read until they're sent. Leave them in a drafts folder and the only people who can see them are people with the password to the account.

There's a new draft from Kenji at the top:

Mark was attacked after group. Russian, tall, tattoo with five dots. If this sounds familiar let us know. Meetings postponed until further notice. Respond here to let us know you're safe. K.

Underneath that:

Don't know him. He better hope we don't find him. B.
    What are you going to do? Amend him to death? Will ask around on the QT. V.
    We got your back. S.

I type out a quick response:

Thanks, fam. M.

Seeing their messages only makes me a little misty.

Astrid is out of the bathroom now—I didn't even notice the door open—and sits on the edge of the bed. She says, "We need to talk about this."

That gauzy feeling makes it difficult to multitask. "And I need to figure this out. Pet the bunny closest to the bench."

"Isn't it 'kill the alligator closest to the boat'?"

"Productivity doesn't have to include killing."

"Fine," she says. "I'm hungry. We're ordering in and I'm adding it to your tab."

"Sure," I tell her. She uses the room's phone and has the front desk connect her to a pizza place, and then she's asking me about toppings, but I'm already lost trying to figure this out.

I have killed a lot of Russians. If the KGB knew who I was, my picture would be on dartboards all over Moscow. The list of people who'd want revenge is both endless and devoid of any jobs that spring to mind as likely instigators. There's a certain level where killing stops being personal. Usually it's just the money that matters, and money can be replaced.

Just because this guy is Russian doesn't mean he works for Russia. He could be freelance. He could work for the Agency, which has finally found me, and decided their lives would be made easier if I was dead.

So it seems like a stupid move, digging through my phone, searching for the encrypted messaging app that used to pay my bills. The one I should have deleted along with Astrid's number, and didn't.

But that's the closest bunny.

Just seeing the blinking blue cursor on the black screen

brings back a flood of memories of what using this app meant. None of those memories are good. This is the kind of triggering action I'd love to talk to Kenji about, but given the circumstances, I have to rely on the tools I've got.

This is not who I am anymore.

This is to protect me and the people in my life.

It's not a slip, it's the next right action.

I fire off a message that I'm not even sure will be read.

That part of me hopes won't be read.

Requesting meet
Rev 6:8

With that done, I navigate through the international sections of the *New York Times* and the *Washington Post*, looking for leads. When that doesn't pan out, I open up D@nt3, the secure web browser that anonymizes my presence on the web, and pull up the Via Maris website.

Another thing I haven't looked at in a year.

I key in my username: GJoubert, after the hitman Max von Sydow portrayed in *Three Days of the Condor*. I appreciated that he was both professional and kind: pursuing Robert Redford's Condor until his assignment changed, then offering his former target words of encouragement and a ride to the train station. I used to think the username was a cute reference, but now it makes me feel a little embarrassed.

The Via Maris was an ancient trade route that linked Egypt with northern Syria, Anatolia, and Mesopotamia. Now it's a darknet marketplace where you can find anything from an assassin to an M777 howitzer to a former doctor who takes cash and is comfortable operating in bathtubs.

It's how the people in my world communicate. It's also where I spent a lot of late nights, strolling through the message boards, to see what was really going on in the world, or to figure out where I might get sent next. Sometimes I'd look for local gigs—small-scale stuff that would earn me a little cash and scratch the itch until the Agency came calling.

The feeling of being back on the boards is both warm and cold.

The pizza arrives and I realize I should have said something about being lactose intolerant. Worse, it has olives on it.

"Who the hell puts olives on pizza?" I ask.

"I do," Astrid says.

"You're a monster." She mumbles something as I scrape the cheese off a slice and eat it so fast I can't even register if it's any good. I shift and realize P. Kitty is no longer nuzzled next to me. He's now sitting on Astrid's lap, and she's stroking his orange fur while chewing on a slice.

She catches me looking at them. "What's his name?"

"P. Kitty."

She laughs. "That's a ridiculous name for a cat."

"It's an awesome name for a cat."

"How'd you come up with it?" she asks.

I'm about to answer when my phone buzzes and I am immediately beset by a feeling of intense dread. Sending that text was the only thing I could think to do, but I just rang a bell that can't be unrung, and I have to hope that in the course of figuring out what's going on, I didn't just sign my death warrant.

Confirm identity

I comb through my memory for something that only Ravi will recognize. When it comes to me, I crack a smile. He'll appreciate this—assuming that hearing from me didn't cause him a stroke.

Gulab jamun

There's a lingering pause. Probably longer than it needs to be, as I imagine he's now making frantic phone calls, or checking the windows to make sure they're locked. The response comes in:

SIN
ASAP
Details TK

Singapore.
Of course.
A little more clicking around on my phone and I find a story from a few hours ago about Cho Jin-Su, a North Korean diplomat drowned in a hotel pool there. I poke his name into Google and find he has ties to their nuclear program. The man is forty-three and, from his picture, looks pretty fit. Pool

drowning makes sense. I would have done something similar. Deaths with the potential to start World War III are best made to look like an accident.

I put down my phone and wave at Astrid. "Do you have any friends or family you could stay with? Out of town? Like, very far out of town?"

She shakes her head before taking a few ruminating bites of pizza. "I have a sister in Portland, but we don't really get along. Why?"

"Because I have to go to Singapore."

"No, *why*, Mark?" she asks. "What is going on? I deserve to know."

She's not wrong. I don't have to tell her everything. But I need to tell her something.

"I'm an assassin. Someone's trying to kill me. I don't know who, and I don't know why. I have to figure that out."

"And the answer is in Singapore," she says.

"The person I need to talk to is in Singapore. It's a bit of a haul, but given the current state of things, flying halfway around the world sounds pretty appealing."

She puts down the uneaten crust of her pizza and strokes P. Kitty's head. He nuzzles back into her, closing his eyes and reveling in the attention.

"So you're like John Wick?" she asks.

I don't bother to contain the eye roll. "Being an assassin is nothing like *John Wick*."

"If he knows who I am now, too, wouldn't I be safer with you?"

I can't tell how she feels, asking it. She sounds annoyed, but

I think I can detect an undercurrent of fear in her voice. At this point, I don't know how to answer that question. Maybe? Or maybe whoever this is will lose interest if she disappears? There are too many unknowns.

Astrid scratches at a dried piece of cheese stuck to the top of the pizza box. "And I've always wanted to see Singapore. I've heard the shopping is incredible."

"Yeah, one of the malls has a river with a gondola in it."

She picks up another slice, takes a bite, and with a full mouth says, "Whatever's happening right now is on you. I don't want to get killed or kidnapped because you darkened my doorstep. So I'm coming with you and you're going to make this right. And I have conditions."

I hold my hand up, beckoning her to list them.

"You're paying me a retainer. Five grand a day."

"Only fair."

"And I want you to tell me the truth about who you are."

"That's going to be a lot of real heavy stuff."

Astrid nods. "I get that. But if I'm in this now, I want to know the scope of it."

The money, I don't give a damn about. It's the emotional honesty that feels like too steep a price. Especially because I spend so much time unpacking my past in program, it's nice to have time where I don't do that.

But I sense this isn't a negotiation. Or it is, and I've already lost.

"Fine." I get to my feet and my body feels like a concrete statue come to life. "I'll tell you more on the plane. Let's go get us some passports."

"I thought it wasn't safe for me to go home?"

"It's not," I tell her. "I have a guy."

She nods, then glances at the carrier. "Is the cat coming, too?"

I look at P. Kitty, now standing in the tub, peeking over the rim. When the smell wafts over I realize I should have gotten a tray and some litter, too, but at least he was smart enough to go in the tub. I peel off another hundred and leave it on the dresser for cleanup.

I could probably leave him with Ms. Nguyen, or at a shelter, but I don't want to. I want P. Kitty with me, where I know I can protect him. I don't say that to Astrid because she might be annoyed that I seem more committed to him.

But she's not the only one in this room who's saved my life.

"Yeah," I say. "We're taking him with us."

The copy store on St. Mark's Place is easy to miss. It's below street level, at the bottom of a short but treacherous flight of stairs, the stone grooved by time and foot traffic. The sign is battered, letters missing, and the door is half covered in plywood, someone having kicked in the lower pane of glass.

The inside is a jumbled mess, with a broken copier on the left wall and a counter dominating the rest of the space, behind which there are endless, haphazard stacks of unopened paper and cardboard boxes. The bald, heavyset Hawaiian man behind the counter is munching from a package of Oreos and reading a beaten Green Lantern comic. He barely looks up when we enter.

"Black-and-white copies only," he says, turning to the next page.

"Actually, I was wondering if you could help me," I tell him. "I've got this old Xerox, model 5052, that I'm trying to fix up. I'm in the market for spare parts. Specifically, the roller attachment. The hinge broke."

The man puts down the comic and slowly chews an Oreo as he looks me up and down, then Astrid, making sure to take his time on her. Then he glances down at the cat carrier but doesn't say anything about it.

Satisfied with what he sees, he flips up a section of the counter and squeezes past us to the front door, which he locks. Then he flicks off the lights, leaving us with nothing but the red glowing EXIT sign to navigate by.

He disappears toward the back, wending through a narrow pathway between the paper and boxes, where he turns on a small lamp. He uses a key to open another door behind him, which reveals a storage room full of more copier paper. He hands me two bundled reams.

"Put them anywhere," he says.

I place them down precariously on another pile. Astrid joins in and the three of us form an assembly line, moving paper until the man uncovers the edges of a doorway in the floor. He inserts another key and pulls it up, opening to a pool of darkness. Lights click on from somewhere down below, revealing a metal staircase. He turns around to take the stairs backward, bracing with his hands so he can worm his way through the opening, and Astrid asks, "Can we have a moment?"

He shrugs. "Need a few minutes to get set up." Then he's gone.

She turns to me and slaps me on the chest. "What is this, Mark?"

"We're getting passports and IDs. Fake names. Only way to travel."

She looks around at the stacks of copier paper. "Okay, this is some John Wick shit, though."

"And?"

"You told me it was nothing like that."

"Maybe it's a little like that."

"I don't feel good about this," she says, eyeing the basement.

"You were pretty gung ho twenty minutes ago."

"The reality is starting to sink in," she says. "I'm not waiting for the plane. You have to give me something right now."

She grabs my arm as she says this, digging her thumb into my skin. The look on her face is a mix of anger and—I think—desperation. I get it. This is a lot to ask of a person. I owe her something.

Unfortunately, there's only one thing I can give her to guarantee she understands the gravity of this.

I tell her: "They called me the Pale Horse."

She steps back. Her eyes go so wide I can see bloodshot white all the way around green irises. She shudders like she stepped into the cold night air. She keeps stepping back until she's against the far wall.

At this point I don't know what else to say, other than: "I'm sorry."

Her eyes fall to the floor and her shoulders slump. I want to cross the room to her, want to comfort her, but my hands suddenly feel the way they used to: sharp, designed to kill. Not at all appropriate for what she needs right now.

What she needs is for me never to have knocked on her door. Not tonight, not all those years ago, either.

I say it again—"Sorry"—and head down the ladder, giving her some space to process what I just told her.

4

At times, because of one man's evil, ten thousand people suffer. So you kill that one man to let the tens of thousands live. Here, truly, the blade that deals death becomes the sword that saves lives.
—Yamamoto Tsunetomo, *Hagakure: The Way of the Samurai*

Singapore
Fifteen Years Ago

The Millennium Hotel juts into the Singapore skyline like a giant domino: broad on two sides, thin on the other two, darkened glass gleaming in the harsh sunlight. The air is so humid it's like trying to breathe underwater, my blazer and khakis sopping up pools of sweat.

The Marina Bay neighborhood is bustling with a lunchtime crowd of locals walking with singular purpose toward lunch and tourists gazing like zoo animals at the sights. The concrete-and-glass architecture is just standard enough that this could stand in for any midsize American city's financial district. The only differences: no homeless people digging through the garbage or sitting by the curb, and no cops in sight.

Poverty isn't really a thing here. The only thing thicker than the humidity in Singapore is the money. And as for the cops, that's a mix of two things: self-policing rooted in national pride, and an Orwellian network of surveillance controlled by an authoritarian regime that enjoys liberal use of the death penalty.

The other main difference is the racial makeup: a preponderance of Chinese people, with a spattering of Indian and Malay, which is pretty representative of the country's demographics. As an average-looking white guy, I stand out. Not ideal, but not much I can do about it.

I finish pretending to smoke a cigarette and toss it into the waste bin next to me, which is a hundred feet from the front door of the hotel and conveniently located in a rare camera blind spot. The smoldering cigarette lands inside the paper bag I already disposed of, the inside of which I coated with nail polish remover. I don't wait to see if it catches, I just make my way up the stone path and through the heavy revolving doors into the lobby of the hotel.

The space is grand, just bordering on opulent, full of white marble and gold trim, a contrast to the shadowy façade. The focal point in the middle of the circular lobby is a gurgling fountain, filling the air with an ozone smell, surrounded by people in business wear. There's a banking conference in town, which brought out just enough white people, so I can blend in a little better. No one pays me any regard, which floods me with a tingle of excitement.

They have no idea what's about to happen.

By the time I make it to the front desk, someone outside is yelling. All around me, shoulders tense, eyes dart to the front, the tranquil space suddenly filled with tension. At the main desk is a young Malaysian woman in a cream-colored dress, a pastel-pink tudung wrapped around her head and shoulders. She offers a megawatt smile with no eye contact and holds a finger up before hustling to the front. I lean over the counter and slip the USB kill switch into the side of her computer monitor, tap the ENTER button on the keyboard, and pull it out. It's in my pocket before she's left the lobby. I walk toward the elevator bank and climb aboard.

The kill switch disabled the hotel's cameras and security and erased any video they had stored. It probably screwed up a bunch of other stuff, too. This thing is like dropping a rabid Tasmanian devil into the server room. It's effective but not discerning. It'll take a while for hotel security to find the problem and repair it. By the time they do I'll be gone, all without my face appearing on camera.

At the top floor I step into a quiet, blue-carpeted hallway and head toward the stairwell. I know the hotel is expensive because instead of handles the doors have actual doorknobs. Two more flights up and I find that the door to the roof is locked, but thanks to the kill switch, the alarm won't be enabled. I use a snake pick to sweep the tumbler, and after a few passes all the pins click into place.

The roof is forty stories up and completely exposed to the brutality of the sun, making it ten times hotter than the ground. The Marina Bay Sands looms in the distance, hazy in the heat. Probably the most signature building in the Singapore skyline, it looks like someone balanced a surfboard across the top of three identical towers. Beyond the Sands is the vast ocean, dotted by massive container ships, stretching out to a smattering of islands and the South China Sea.

From here I can see a good chunk of the country, a bucolic mix of man-made structures and verdant vegetation. Yesterday a chatty cabdriver told me he can bike the circumference of the nation-state in four hours. I'd love to try that, but I suspect I won't be staying long after this job is done.

I pull the nylon rope and grapple concealed inside my jacket, then shed my top layer, leaving me in a white button-down and khakis, a climbing belt and harness concealed underneath. I would have preferred tactical gear, but this operation presented a number of challenges.

According to the brief, Jonathan Campbell is a CDC biochemist looking to trade his expertise to the highest bidder in return for wiping out his gambling debts and giving him some more money to play with. Since his concentration is biological weapons, this could be bad.

The highest bidder so far is a splinter faction of Islamic jihadists who may or may not be—but probably are—tied to Hezbollah. They're keeping him in Singapore while they negotiate numbers and sort out the logistics of moving him. There are plenty of casinos to keep him busy and, presumably, enough security to keep him safe.

Campbell spends his nights living large with a battery of ten bodyguards. The buyers have built in a layer of plausible deniability. Instead of sending out men of their own, they've hired local Triads. That they've survived the sledgehammer of Singapore's law enforcement means they're tough. Though not the kind of tough I can't handle.

Still, I can't pull off a hit on a casino floor. When Campbell isn't in the casinos, he's sleeping it off here, in an executive suite on the top floor. Satellite imagery says there are rarely more than two men in his room, and the rest are in the adjoining rooms or a floor below.

As much as I wish I had more time to plan this out, or at least the cover of darkness, Campbell is only supposed to be here for another day or two. Ravi said the Agency classified this as an ASAP op. If it's so important, I don't know why they chose it for my first gig. Maybe it's a test.

As I stand on the roof, looking out over a foreign country that looks like a city sprung up out of a jungle, the wind whipping at my face, ready to rappel down into a hotel room and murder a bunch of people I've never met, I feel a tug in my gut.

This will be the first time I'm taking lives outside the haze of a battle. Shooting someone who's trying to kill you in the sands of some forgotten corner of hell, that's not only acceptable, you sometimes get medals for doing it.

There's something slightly distasteful about this. I feel like I'm hunting deer with a tactical nuke. But I get it. I did the math. Campbell is willing to sell off deadly knowledge and tech, which will likely be turned on Israeli civilians. Biological weapons don't discriminate between enemy combatants and innocent children. Taking him off the board isn't a question.

And yet.

When I was a kid, I wanted to be an astronaut.

It's funny, the thoughts that come to me as I peer over the edge, my stomach doing a drunken flip. The ground is five hundred feet below and I can feel the hum of gravity. Campbell's balcony is twenty feet down, but I need to land on the far side of it, out of view from the sliding doors. Which means the optimal target is really only four feet by four feet.

Too much to the left, they'll see me and be ready before I get my bearings.

Too much to the right and I'm going to spend the rest of my life regretting this decision.

All five seconds of it.

It's better to move than let fear make its case. There's a pipe at my feet, burrowed into the surface of the roof. I give it a yank to make sure it's secure, then attach the grapple, loop the nylon rope to the climbing belt, and dangle myself off the edge of the building.

I glance down one more time to situate myself and let go.

My stomach hovers for a moment before I connect with the balcony, and I fold down into a kneeling position to let the impact disperse through my body. I detach the rope and make sure it's hanging out of view, then reach down and press my fingertips to the rough concrete under my feet, appreciating the solid ground.

And I'm in the shade now, which is a value-add.

Now comes the part I can't control.

Ravi said that of the two bodyguards who stay in the room with him, one of them is a chain-smoker. The overflowing ashtray on the small patio table confirms this. So I have to wait until he comes out. I can neutralize him, which leaves only two people inside—one of them being Campbell, and he's not a fighter.

My knuckles crack as I interlace my fingers and stretch out my hands. Given the local government's delight in using the death penalty, the risk of walking around with a weapon is too high. Not that a gun would have been all that helpful; even with a silencer it would be loud enough to alert people in the surrounding rooms. But these can look like murders, not accidents—apparently someone in some office somewhere wants to send a message—so I don't need to worry about finesse.

I press my ear to the door. There's a low murmur inside that could be people talking or could be a vacuum cleaner. That's the best I can do. I take this as an opportunity to review the floor plan, which I spent the morning committing to memory.

The sliding doors open onto a living room. There should be a coffee table, a couch, and two easy chairs right in front of me. Across from that is a kitchenette, to the right of which is the entryway and a half bath. The bedroom is to the left, with a king bed and a full bathroom beyond that.

After ten minutes I'm getting worried, that maybe they went down to the pool or something. That maybe the hotel will sort out the camera problem before this guy has a nicotine fit. But then a man in a tank top and jeans comes out, his hands cupped to his mouth, from which erupts the familiar *scritch* of a lighter. He's Chinese, mid-thirties maybe, with a bodybuilder physique and a round, boyish face. He has a nasty-looking bowie knife tucked into a leather holster on his belt. He takes a deep drag, gazing out over the bay, basking in the breeze coming off the water.

The serenity of the moment.

I wonder what he's thinking about.

Does he have a girlfriend? A family? Kids?

I push those thoughts away. In this equation he's a remainder and I need to turn in a clean sheet. He's still in full view of the sliding doors so I move fast, slipping behind him and hooking my arms around his neck and his forehead. He goes tense, reaching up for me. But before he can get a good grip, I yank hard, separating the vertebrae in his neck with a crack that feels more satisfying than I would care to admit in polite company. As he falls, I slip the knife out of the holster and turn to pull open the sliding door.

At which point I realize our intel was not good.

There are five men in the room.

Two on the couch, one on each easy chair, one across the way at the kitchenette, making himself a cup of tea. They're dressed as casually as the man I just killed. The coffee table is littered with empty beer bottles and snack wrappers. They're watching *Pretty Woman*, the part where Julia Roberts and Richard Gere are shopping.

They all look at me in complete and utter confusion. I catch a glimpse of someone lunging from the bed to the bathroom—probably Campbell.

Adrenaline kicks in and time slows down, giving me a few nanoseconds to calculate the odds here. No one seems to be carrying a gun, but there are most definitely a few more knives in the room. Knife fighting in close quarters means you're going to have a bad day. I need to even things out. Lucky for me

I can see the angles, like they were drawn by a divine hand: what goes where to produce the maximum amount of death.

It's a little like playing pool.

Scumbag, corner pocket.

The biggest threat is the man by the kitchenette. He's farthest away from me. He could leave the room to alert others, or find a more useful weapon in the melee. So before anyone can get to their feet I flip the stolen knife in my hand and send it sailing across the room and into his chest. It buries to the hilt and he goes down without a sound, trying to pull it out, dead before he gets a good grip.

Four.

As I'm doing this, the other men shout at each other in Mandarin and get to their feet, so I throw a kick into the easy chair closest to me. The man getting up from it falls into a tangle and crashes into the glass coffee table, sending shards of glass spilling across the floor. His head hits the frame at an odd angle and kinks hard to the side. He doesn't move after that.

Three.

There's a heavy glass vase on the table next to me, so by the time the closest thug gets to me, I've got it in my hand and arcing toward his head. It connects and shatters, water and petals spilling across his face, the shock traveling up my arm. His eyes dim. Good chance I split his skull like an eggshell.

Two.

The final combatants have had enough time to square up. Both of them are young, buzzing with anger and masculinity, ready to prove themselves. The closest is a slight kid with a shaved head, his body covered in tattoos. He takes out a switchblade and clicks it to full length. I move to my left, putting them in a line so I can focus on him first. He waves the knife around like a kid showing off a lollipop. I throw a hard kick into the side of his knee, snapping it. He goes down yelling and I put my hand on the back of his head and throw him face-first to the ground, then stomp the top of his spine. The yelling stops.

One.

This last guy is tall and slim but carved out of granite. He puts his hands out, palms up, and keeps his distance, marching in little steps that suggests he's trained in Muay Thai. Just as I set my guard, he lunges forward and snaps a kick at my head, which I barely manage to block. He's fast. I hop back a little to create some space and figure out the best way to engage him, when something slams into my back, throwing me toward the couch.

I somersault onto the remains of the shattered coffee table, slipping on the glass. There was a sixth man. Probably in the bathroom. He yells for the kickboxer to get help. The man nods and runs for the door.

Great.

I push myself to my feet, ignoring the glass slicing into my palms. The sixth man is older than the others. Long gray hair hanging wild around his head, stout but athletic, and a neutral look on his face like he's waiting in line for coffee.

Which means he's the only one of these knuckleheads who's dangerous.

He pulls out a blade—a short tanto, essentially a shrunken-down samurai sword. I reach out blindly behind me, hoping to grab one of the beer bottles that fell from the shattered coffee table. But I end up with a cushion from the easy chairs, which I hold out like a shield.

He looks at it and laughs, advancing on me, so I throw it at his face, which causes him to instinctively put his arms up. I leap over the couch and throw a swift kick into his midsection. He hits the wall and I follow as hard as I can, throwing my shoulder into his stomach as I grab his arm and control the sword, then slip under him and angle it up to slice open his neck.

He makes a drowning sound, and a geyser of hot, sticky blood sprays both of us. A little gets in my mouth, which ignites something dark and animal inside me. My blood converts to steam and I want to tear his flesh off with my teeth.

No time for indulgences, though.

I grab the tanto and stalk into the bathroom, feeling like I should be wearing a black cloak and carrying a scythe. I find a man cowering by the toilet with his hands up. He matches the picture in the brief—tall, forties, silver hair, skin gray from spending too much time in basement labs.

Campbell.

"I'm sorry, please," he says, his voice quivering. "I can pay."

It may not be the field of war, but the man on the balcony, the other men in the room, they were Triad. They were in the game. The potential for death in this life assumed. This man wasn't in the game, but he decided to join. The knowledge he put up for sale could shift geopolitics and end a lot of lives. Painfully.

"Sorry, bud," I tell him. "The math isn't in your favor."

I grab him by the hair and yank his head up. He squeals like a cat. I sever his carotid artery. He grabs his neck, trying to keep the blood inside. It doesn't work, spilling between his fingers. He chokes and gags and dies.

There's shouting from somewhere outside the door. The knob on the front door jiggles. It flies open and the kickboxer comes in, now carrying a gun, and there are more men behind him.

My exit plan—strolling through the front door—is no longer an option. Climbing back up to the roof will take too long. They'll be on the balcony and aiming comfortably at my ass before I'm halfway up.

Only one way out now.

I make for the sliding doors as bullets slam into the wall behind me. I hope that pipe is strong. I grab the rope and loop it a few times around my hand, and before my brain can take the chance to weigh in, I jump out from the balcony, soaring over downtown Singapore.

Laughter explodes from my chest.

I wonder if the laughing is meant to cover up the fear. But I do a quick inventory and don't find any. I feel shot through with god-energy, like I can bend the universe—life and death itself—to my will.

It feels good to be good at something.

Then my arm almost yanks out of the socket when I hit the end of the swing and start coming back. I grip the rope with both hands and swing straight for the sliding door of the room one floor below. I kick as I connect with it, shattering it, and tumble inside, landing hard, shards of glass slicing my skin.

The adrenaline is doing a great job, keeping the pain at bay. Tonight's going to be a rough one, though.

There's a heavy, older white man lying on the bed, his body milky white except for his face, which is beet red. A young woman with bronze skin and dark, cascading hair is riding him. The two of them immediately yell and pull at the covers.

"Sorry," I tell them. I climb to my feet and head for the door. Before I open it, I reach into the closet and pull out a black blazer. The man is much bigger than me so it'll work to hide some of the blood. I take a quick look in the bathroom mirror. My face is a little cut up and I can't do much about that.

As I open the door to the hallway there's a man running past with a gun. I throw a kick and take him clean off his feet, throwing him into the other wall and crumpling him to the ground. I yank the gun from his hand and put a bullet in his head—no sense in playing it safe at this point—then turn toward the end of the hall and see two more men coming at me, guns drawn.

Two more bullets and I'm alone again.

Those guys just came off the stairwell. I bet the rest are headed that way as well. It's faster. I dive for the elevator and slap the DOWN button. The doors open just as my suspicion is confirmed and the stairwell on the other end of the floor bursts open. I jump onto the elevator and press the CLOSE button as many times as I can, praying they don't make it.

They don't. The doors close. The other elevator was on the ground floor. No way they're going to cover thirty-something flights of stairs in time to catch me. Which gives me a head start. I can't go through the lobby, police will be either here or close by. I hit the button for the pool, on the third floor, and figure I can improvise.

It's only now I realize I'm not alone; there's an old man in the elevator wearing khakis and a polo, with sunglasses and a bucket hat on his head. White, definitely American, with that kind of terrified wonder you see in people from the Midwest. I'm still carrying the gun, and the oversize jacket I stole isn't hiding the blood as much as I'd hoped.

I tuck the gun in the back of my waistband. I want to say something to him but I have no idea what. I think back to what Ravi said. The idea was to be invisible. People will see your face; let them forget it. One of the many reasons I was picked, he said, was the fact that there's nothing particularly remarkable about me.

Average-looking white guy.

Still, should I kill this guy? Cameras are still out. I could.

But that doesn't seem fair.

"Give me your wallet," I tell him.

He fumbles for it and passes it over. I pull out the license. Franklin Reynolds, with an address in Kansas City. I hand him his license and pull a wad of cash out of my pocket, then gesture to his ring. "Go to the bar. Have a drink. Don't volunteer to talk to the police. If they talk to you, you didn't get a good look at me. Don't even tell your wife about this. You understand, Kansas City?"

He nods. The doors open and I step off into an empty hallway. I hustle to the men's locker room, the pool visible through floor-to-ceiling windows on an outdoor deck. There are people changing in the locker room, but nobody looks up, everyone more concerned with their own modesty. I grab a complimentary bathrobe, strip down to my boxers, and shove my soiled clothes into a garbage can. Then I go to the sink and make use of the free toiletries, wiping off as much blood as I can.

The guys protecting Campbell are bottlenecked. And anyway, they don't give a damn about him. He was a job and now the job is off. They'll be looking to scramble for the shadows, not get revenge.

The locks in here are all cheap and flimsy. I manage to work through three until I find a change of clothes that fit, and I'm just pulling on a pair of slightly-too-tight jeans when the door opens and a Chinese man walks in wearing a black suit. He juts out his chin and raises his voice to be heard throughout the space. "Everyone, there's been an emergency. We need to ask you to evacuate the building for a few moments." He repeats it in Mandarin and then Tamil.

I join the men streaming out of the locker room, eyes on the ground, and stroll calmly toward the elevators.

With nightfall comes relief from the choking humidity. My stolen jeans don't feel so oppressive, and there's even a nice breeze coming off the bay.

The stone steps leading down to the water are filled with

tourists milling about under a darkened sky, waiting for something to start. It's just dark enough that my injuries aren't as apparent, so I'm less worried about hiding my face. My body is creaking and groaning like a piece of farm equipment left in the rain. I can barely raise my arm above my shoulder. Despite this, I'm still a little high after mainlining that much adrenaline. Ready to go another few rounds if necessary. I weave through the crowd, bouncing on my toes, looking for Ravi.

It doesn't take long to find him, leaning against a railing, away from the crowd. He's wearing a white polo shirt, cargo shorts, and sandals. He's scruffy and his black wavy hair, shot through with the odd strand of gray, is stylishly unkempt. His outfit makes him look like a dad, but his sharp features and sly grin make him look like the kind of dad who hits on his kid's second-grade teacher. He looks out over the bay like he looked at me when we first met, like he looks at the entire world: everything is a spreadsheet. Just data to process and put in its place.

I lean on the metal railing next to him. He looks me up and down, and for a fleeting moment his eyes widen. He tries to distract me from that by holding a brown paper bag toward me. Inside are deep-fried dough balls.

"I got a dairy thing," I tell him.

"They have milk powder in them, but they're cooked. Can you have milk products that are cooked?"

The answer is usually yes but sometimes no. Whatever, I haven't eaten since breakfast. I'll pick up some Lactaid just in case. I pluck one out. It's sticky and smells like a rose. I shove the whole thing in my mouth. It's so sweet my teeth ache, but that might be trauma from earlier.

Did I get hit in the face? Maybe I got hit in the face. I don't remember.

The city's skyline glitters across the bay, the buildings tall and almost leaning toward us, a rainbow of colors giving off *Blade Runner* vibes. We're just far enough from the rest of the crowd that we can't be heard, but he speaks low anyway.

"You're alive," he says, his voice as flat and as calm as the dark water stretching out below us.

"You seem disappointed."

He doesn't say anything to that.

"What are these?" I ask, reaching out to take another dough ball.

"Gulab jamun," he says. "They're all over the place in Little India."

"Your intel sucked," I tell him, chewing slowly. "There were six men in the room, plus Campbell."

He shrugs, takes out a ball, examines it closely, and takes a small bite. "Earlier in the day it was eight. There was some scuttle about an attempt on his life, so they circled up."

The way he says it, completely unperturbed, makes me want to slap him. "You couldn't share that?"

Ravi takes another small bite.

"So it was a test," I tell him.

He offers me a little side-eye and a smirk. "And you passed."

"Bullshit," I tell him, a little too loud, then look over my shoulder to make sure no one is close enough to hear. "I could have gotten killed."

"We thought you might die, or at least get arrested, at which point you would have been dead before you saw the inside of a cell," Ravi says. "That was the interview. And this is the job. The stakes can be anything from a pile of money to the end of the world, and the only requirement is that you're the best. The fact that you're standing here tells me you'll do just fine."

I take two dough balls at once and shove them in my mouth. Think back to three months ago, getting pulled into a blank room at Coronado, Ravi sitting at a table, regarding me like color-coded cells on a computer screen, trying to figure what they added up to, his hand on a folder in front of him that he never opened.

He told me he worked for an organization called the Agency. I asked if he meant the CIA, and he told me, no, the CIA was peewee football and he was with the NFL. The best I can tell, it's some deep-state shit—a clandestine group made up of various government agencies and financial and industrial leaders, all with a goal of keeping the planet spinning the right way.

"I'm impressed," he says now, throwing away the now-empty bag in a trash bin next to him, and taking a wet wipe out of his pocket to clean his fingers while I suck mine clean. "For every seven people we recruit, one makes it. The first assignment usually isn't so hard—generally you at least get a gun. But the fact that you went in there unarmed?" He looks me up and down again. "Impressive. Really impressive."

He's trying to flatter me.

As much as it annoys me, it also works. I didn't join the

SEALs thinking I'd be using my words. And what I did today, that's not something just anyone can do.

"Why me?" I ask.

It's the question I'd held back until now, but it feels important.

"No family, no real ties to civilian life," Ravi says. "High test scores, glowing recommendations. You have an ear for languages. You have the right temperament. Plus the military is full of militia nuts who sleep with their AR-15s, or guys who have a pair of plastic nuts on the back of their pickup truck. You're neither of those things. We have some other metrics, but ultimately, you were exactly what we look for."

"And how am I supposed to trust you?" I ask.

Before Ravi can respond, the sound of delicate, haunting Chinese string instruments swells up from unseen speakers, and the water in the bay explodes into towers of mist that are filled with tendrils of neon light, shifting into shapes like flowers and mandalas. They grow larger and get closer until there's condensation on my face. The crowd oohs and aahs.

It's beautiful, but hard for me to appreciate.

Ravi takes off his glasses and cleans them on his polo. "You're not supposed to trust me. You're just supposed to help me keep the world running."

He replaces his glasses and offers me his hand.

I think about becoming an astronaut.

I think about the man I killed on the balcony—the crunch of delicate things shredding in his neck and the way his body went limp when his soul left.

I think about how good it felt to jump from a tall building and be saved by my wits.

I think about how good it feels to be good at something.

I think about mainlining adrenaline for a living.

And I shake Ravi's hand.

"You need a handle," he says.

"What, like a nickname?"

"You need it from an operational standpoint," he says. "But as time goes on, that name will serve as a deterrent. Something that'll shut down certain situations without you having to raise a hand."

"I'll leave that to you," I tell him. "Feels like an asshole move, naming myself."

Flashbacks to grade school, seeing *Predator* for the first time and thinking that maybe if I had a cool nickname like Dutch, I wouldn't get bullied.

It didn't work.

Ravi gazes at the water, at the neon shapes shifting in the mist. "'And I looked, and behold a pale horse, and his name that sat on him was Death.'" He smiles, satisfied with himself. "I've been wanting to use that one for a while. But like I said, one in seven. Okay, Pale Horse." He slaps his hand on my shoulder and leaves it there, giving it a squeeze. "Hezbollah won't want any fingerprints on this. To them, this never happened, so no one's looking for you. There's a flight booked home for you tomorrow night under the name you flew in on. In the meantime, visit the food markets. The Maxwell Food Centre on Kadayanallur Street is my favorite. Get some chicken rice. Some char kway teow. Enjoy yourself."

He removes his hand and, without another word, leaves me there. I watch him move through the crowd, multicolored lights illuminating his white polo, and then he's gone. I turn back to the bay, watch the water and the light dance and grow bigger, forming greater and more complicated shapes as the music hits a crescendo.

And I looked, and behold a pale horse, and his name that sat on him was Death.

I'm not a Bible guy but I know how that verse ends. Johnny Cash's gravel voice sings it in my ear.

And hell followed with him.

The music stops. The lights go out. Water rains back into the bay, and the crowd is enveloped by darkness.

5

> The lion cannot protect himself from traps, and the fox cannot defend himself from wolves. One must therefore be a fox to recognize traps, and a lion to frighten wolves.
> —Niccolò Machiavelli, *The Prince*

Singapore
Now

A flight attendant who is clearly smiling through exhaustion offers me two blank customs forms. I pass one to Astrid and click the overhead light, casting a yellow glow in the darkened cabin. Astrid places the form down on her seat tray and taps the red-lettered, bolded words: WARNING: DEATH FOR DRUG TRAFFICKERS UNDER SINGAPORE LAW.

"Should we be worried?" she asks.

"We're speaking again?"

"I'm serious," she says, casting her eyes downward at the carrier under the seats, where P. Kitty has barely moved for the duration of the nineteen-hour flight.

Fun fact: pets can't overdose on CBD. Though I did take the time to dump the treats out of the branded bag and into a Tupperware container, so as not to jam us up with TSA. I didn't know what the rules were and didn't care to look them up.

"I think we'll be okay," I tell Astrid, shifting around in the seat, trying to get my blood circulating. My body is stiff and sore, but at least the volume of the discomfort is turned down. In the concert hall of pain, I've moved from next to the speakers to the back of the venue.

Her tone isn't exactly warm, but it's the most we've spoken since we got our passports, and I consider that progress. The cab ride to the airport, then the two hours we spent waiting for the flight—mostly she just stared off into space. Since she wasn't feeling chatty, I popped a handful of Vicodin before the flight took off. I made it through most of the trip asleep or in a haze.

I pass a few more treats through P. Kitty's cage, and he doesn't swipe at me, so he must be in some twilight space, too. Good for him.

"I didn't think you were real," Astrid says, digging a pen out of her purse.

"What do you mean?"

"I patch up bad people," she says, filling out the form, careful to match everything to the information on her new passport, looking back and forth between the two. "People tell stories. Sometimes people tell stories about the Pale Horse. Like he was some kind of supernatural creature."

Can't help but feel a little rush at hearing that.

She looks at me out of the corner of her eye. "You look like the kind of guy who takes off his wedding ring at the bar before he hits on me, and when he flames out, drives his minivan back to his family on Long Island. You don't look like an assassin. Jason Statham looks like an assassin."

"First off, thanks for all of that," I tell her. "Second, Jason Statham is a movie star who happens to play a lot of assassins. He looks like he chews glass for breakfast. He walks in a room and you know someone's about to get hurt. I don't. That's kind of the point." I give her a little smile, afraid of how it might look, but it's the best I have to offer. "Anyway, stories are stories. They grow in the telling. I'm just a guy who was good at his job."

"Was," she says. "What did you do, quit?"

Part of me wants to tell her everything. The program, a year sober, all of it. But as much as I trust her, which is a fair bit more than most people, I can't really trust her. Not with this. I think back to the fight with the Russian. If I were at full capacity, he'd be dead and I wouldn't be here. Instead I'm fighting with a hand tied behind my back. Invoking the name of the Pale Horse might keep me safe for a little while longer. It's not exactly living in my truth, but my reputation is the best shield I have.

"I've been focusing on my golf swing," I tell her.

She finishes the form and passes me the pen. I fill out mine, almost putting down *Mark* under NAME. I manage to fix it without making it look like I tried to. "What did you do while I was sleeping?"

"Watched a lot of movies," she says. "Ordered dinner for both of us, then ate both of them."

"Watch anything good?"

"Rewatched *When Harry Met Sally*. Love that movie so much."

"That's a top five all-timer, easy."

She squints at me. "Would have figured you as more of an action movie guy."

"I prefer classics, rom-coms," I tell her. "My life has enough action."

She rolls her eyes a little at that—totally fair—but then her expression goes flat. She leans toward me and lowers her voice. "So do you have, like, a code?"

"A code?"

"A code. Hit men always have codes."

More movie bullshit, but that said, I guess we all do have a set of morals that act as our North Star. "I don't think I'd kill anyone under eighteen, but also never had to test that. You just . . . you have to be in the game and the math has to work out. Balance the scales in some way. Sacrifice one life to save others."

"Have you ever killed a woman?"

"A few."

I let that hang in the air. After it settles she says, "I need to ask you a question. And I need you to be completely honest with me."

I put the pen down on top of the half-finished form and turn my body toward her. Showing my belly. A little vulnerability.

"I've seen your face," she says. "I know who you are. Do I make it to the end of this?"

Ah. That's why she wants to know about codes. She's had time to think and she's wondering, when we get off the plane and closer to customs, when we're surrounded by security, if she should run screaming for help.

"I promised you I would protect you, and I will." She seems a little unsure. "If anything, as someone who saves lives, the math is in your favor."

"But I've saved some pretty bad people."

"Then you're Switzerland. I have no interest in going to war with Switzerland."

It's truth by default. A year and a few days ago I would have considered the possibility. Remainders complicate equations. I hate myself for thinking that. Old programming. But the way her body relaxes, she seems to accept it as sincere.

She stares at the screen on the seat back in front of her, playing an advertisement for the airline. "So what's the plan?"

"Once we land, I should have instructions on where to meet my old handler, which I will ignore, and then I'll go find him," I tell her. "We post you and the kitty up at a hotel. I'll hit an ATM and get some cash. I'll see what I can figure out. Then I come back to you and we decide on the next right action."

I've got one more errand to run, but I don't want to tell her about that one. I'm still trying to convince myself that now isn't the right time. But I'm flying across the world—when else might I get the chance?

"Dump me in a hotel," she says. "Like a glass figurine you don't want to break."

"Astrid, the people I'm dealing with are serious."

"Here's the thing about the people you deal with," she says.

"They all end up coming to me to fix them, because at the end of the day they're just scared little boys who want their mommy."

"The hotel is safer."

She sits back and folds her arms. "The hotel better have a nice spa."

"I'm gonna hit the head."

She digs in her purse and passes me a small zipped case. "Clean it up, apply a fresh bandage. Simple enough, right? You don't need help?"

I wave the case at her. "Thanks."

As I move toward the front of the cabin my body cracks back to life. I pick an empty bathroom, which is spacious enough to move around in. One of the few perks of international flights. I splash some water on my face, try to wash away the fuzziness. I take a piss and wash my hands and pull my shirt up.

The stitches have held. It still looks pretty gnarly, but no redness or bruising. I give it a poke around the edges. Hurts, but normal parameters of pain. I open the case and clean the wound and put a fresh bandage over it, and when I'm done and everything is put away I turn to the mirror and stare at myself.

I'm still not sure if bringing Astrid along was the right call. Maybe I should have gotten my hands on some cash and sent her off to points unknown before I left for the airport. Now she wants to help? I don't begrudge her the impulse, but the last thing I want to do is put her in the line of fire.

I scratch at the two days' growth of stubble on my face and

wonder what it'll be like to see Ravi again. I never had much of a family. The Agency became something adjacent to that. Ravi being the dad who sometimes sent you to knock down a hornet's nest with a stick while he drank beers in the living room.

By the end of my reign, just invoking the name Pale Horse was enough to make people drop their weapons and run. I walked on water. I was a god. Hell followed with me. Now the one thing I was good at, the one thing I was better at than nearly anyone, is something I can't do anymore.

What if this is his game plan? Flush me out, drop the hammer.

The Agency could be behind this. There's a reason their employment plan doesn't come with a 401(k). You die, or you survive long enough to run and hide. Could be there's something buried in my head that the Agency needs, or doesn't want someone else to know.

But I still can't shake the feeling that this is personal. The Russian took the notebook. The list of everyone I need to make amends to. He took it like he was looking for it.

I've got a lot of questions right now, and not a lot of answers, but that doesn't bother me. The thing that bothers me—that downright scares me—is whether Ravi is going to see it in my eyes when we sit across from each other. That I'm no longer willing to kill. That I can no longer protect myself.

I've got to sit down with the lions and hope they're not hungry.

Which is the problem with guys like Ravi.

They're always hungry.

I need something to give an edge. Just a little bit of assurance. The idea comes to me quick, because it's a bit cliché, but sometimes the clichés are that for a reason—they work. I exit the bathroom and head back toward my seat, get close to Astrid, and tell her, "Maybe there is a way you can help."

She smiles and says, "I'm listening."

I had hoped that, since it's winter, it wouldn't be as hot as the last time I was here. But no, as soon as we stepped outside the airport, the humidity hugged me like that weird uncle you try to avoid: way too tight and in all the wrong places.

It's a little cooler inside the Maxwell Food Centre, free from the sun's judgmental gaze, with an army of ceiling fans pushing the air around, swaying the garland and tinsel strung from the rafters that thinly acknowledge the holiday.

It's near lunchtime, so the place is packed with people lined up at the various food stalls. The sound of pots banging and woks scraping, along with the smell of sizzling meat. Not many white faces, so again, I stand out.

Singapore used to be like Thailand—street food anywhere it could fit. In order to make conditions more sanitary and the streets safer for traffic, vendors were moved into food halls like this. Each stall serves only a handful of dishes. Each one has a specialty, whether by dish or region. A plate of something delicious costs a couple of sing, which translates to only a few bucks American. I remember the chicken rice at Tian Tian being pretty transcendent. My rule in these places is to find the longest line and get on the end, then just order whatever dish most people are walking away with. Hasn't done me wrong yet.

But I'm not here to eat.

I weave around tables with orange and green plastic tops, each one surrounded by six low-slung yellow stools bolted into the ground. Some of the stools have packages of tissues on them, the local sign of "I'm waiting on a line; this seat is taken." Some people leave behind purses or phones. Another testament to the country's low level of crime.

Ravi is sitting toward the back of the center where it's a little more quiet, a table to himself. White polo, shorts, sandals. I walk past a stall that has its cutlery laid out in the front and manage to swipe a fork and a knife without anyone noticing. Then I stand across from him until he notices me.

Before him is a geometric assortment of plastic cafeteria trays—red and orange and green, all laid out at precise right angles, the gaps between them uniform. Each tray has a different plate on it. I recognize the char kway teow, a stir-fried dish of wide rice noodles and Chinese sausage and prawns and blood cockles. Then there's the chicken rice from Tian Tian—a plate of boiled chicken covered in a brown sauce, next to another plate with a dome of rice, along with three dipping sauces. Then a whole bunch of other stuff I can't identify.

Ravi looks older, almost fully gray now. I can't decide if I want to hug him or punch him. I don't know which would hurt more.

Finally he looks up at me, his face twisting from surprise to fear to equanimity.

I sit on the stool across from him and stab my fork into a piece of chicken and pop it in my mouth. It's room temperature, but soft and tender and juicy. How in the world they make lukewarm boiled chicken taste this good is beyond me.

"You're alive," he says.

"Déjà vu."

I take a forkful of rice. He stabs his fork into a stir-fry I don't know the name for and puts it in his mouth. The two of us chew as we watch each other, slowly, like there might be sharp things hidden in the food.

"If you're waiting for your bodyguards, they're both indisposed," I tell him.

"Are they alive?" he asks.

"One is in a stall in the bathroom on the south wall. The other is in a storage closet on the east wall. I'm not here to burn bridges."

He nods. "We weren't supposed to meet until tonight."

"And give you a chance to prepare?"

He smiles. The two of us falling into old patterns. Me trying to impress him, him being impressed but trying to hide it. He doesn't ask how I found him. He doesn't want to insult me like that. The truth is, I know he likes to eat and I know this food hall is his favorite. It was a sensible but lucky guess.

Still, just being here, sharing space with him, the psychic static of what we used to do together brings back the old programming. The food trays, his water glass, they're all plastic. But the cutlery is metal. Not strong metal, but sturdy enough to pierce an eye or ram through a neck. There are thirty-seven people within a fifty-foot radius of me. Twenty men and seventeen women. Exits in every direction, but I'd choose the left, because the crowd is thickest and there's a massive metal contraption along the path, laden with finished trays of food that could be tipped over to block the way behind me. Plus a mop in a bucket against the wall, which could be snapped off into a makeshift weapon.

Electricity crackles in my fingertips. For the first time in a long time, I feel like me. The me who dealt in life and death like they were playing cards. I take a bite of char kway teow and a sausage explodes in my mouth.

He puts down his fork and folds his hands in front of him. "We assumed you were dead. That's how these stories end. Most assets either get killed or they run. I didn't peg you as a runner."

"I need a favor," I tell him.

He smiles at this, his eyes going wide.

The audacity of this ask.

"We did have something planned for you at the meeting later," he says.

"Was it cupcakes? Please say it was cupcakes."

"It was not."

"Too bad. So listen, I was attacked by a Russian. Tall, Mohawk." I hold up my forearm. "Five dots, like a die."

Ravi opens his mouth like he wants to say something, then stops and resets. "There's always a Russian, isn't there?"

"Do you know him?"

"That's not much to go on. The tattoo is popular among

Russian criminals. It's supposed to mean they've spent time inside. The dot in the middle is him and the four dots surrounding it are guard towers." He pauses, his eyes drifting around the crowd. Whether he's looking for a person or the right words, I don't know. Then he says: "Frankly, I'm surprised whatever went down between you two ended with him still on this side of the dirt."

I consider my box breathing, but even that feels too vulnerable.

"I skipped breakfast that morning," I tell him. "I'm still good enough to subdue two men in a crowded place without being noticed. Still good enough to find you in a country of five million people two hours after stepping off a plane. Has there been any chatter about anything related to me? Any reason someone might come for me?"

He sits backs, picks up his fork, and resumes eating. "Not that I've heard. Now, I'm sure as you can imagine, I told the Director that we made contact—"

"Snitch."

He arches an eyebrow. I put my hand up for him to keep going. Ravi says, "He was surprised. That surprise gave way quickly to anger. This isn't a job you just disappear from. He wanted me to mobilize Azrael."

Ravi does love his biblical references. Although I never met Azrael, his reputation looms like a storm cloud. The Agency's second-best hitter, and I'm sure once I was gone he stepped in to fill the void.

"Sending a squad of goons after me is one thing," I tell him.

"You want to send another pro? That's like stopping a hurricane with an atom bomb."

"I don't want to start a war," Ravi says. "The Director has calmed down a bit. He's willing to make you an offer."

"What's that?"

"Come in from the cold, full debrief on the past year. The Director will want to extract some kind of price, to prove you're still loyal. Knowing him, the pound of flesh could literally be a pound of flesh. But I'll sweeten the pot. We'll help you find and eliminate the Russian. Then you're back to work the next day. You're going to be on a short leash for a while."

I consider it.

It's not great that I consider it.

It would be so easy, like slipping on an old pair of shoes. It would mean safety and security, not just for me, but for Astrid, and P. Kitty, and my home group.

If this is even a real offer. This could be something to get me through the door so they can swing the ax. I grip the blunt butter knife a little tighter. That god-energy coursing through me.

Maybe this is who I am, and who I am can't change.

Then I think about what Kenji would say: *Let go and let god.*

I loosen my grip on the knife and put it on the table.

"You ever heard of Kurt Gödel?" I ask.

"He was a German mathematician," Ravi says.

"Correct," I tell him, picking up my fork and taking a bite of an egg dish. "He developed something called the incompleteness theorem. Math is supposed to be an absolute system of truth, because one plus one always equals two, right? I won't get into it now because I probably won't explain it right, but the incompleteness theorem states that any set of rules you could provide as a foundation of math will inevitably be incomplete. There will always be true facts about numbers that can't be proven by these rules."

"What is this supposed to mean?"

"Math is an imperfect system." I toss down my fork and stand up from the table. "See you around, Ravi."

"Why'd you quit, Mark? Was it a woman? Just like there's always a Russian, there's always a woman."

"I took some time off."

He's smiling now. That smile snatches the breath out of my chest. "I knew there was something different about you."

He sees it. I wonder what gave it away. Doesn't matter. I reach up and scratch behind my ear. The sign Astrid and I agreed upon. A few seconds later a red glowing dot appears on his chest.

"You got something on your shirt there, bud," I tell him.

He looks down and laughs. "I've seen this movie. Like you didn't pass someone a few bucks and a laser pointer as, what, an intimidation tactic? Please." He makes a show of brushing at the red dot with the back of his hand, like he's wiping away a mote of dust.

I put my hands on the table and lean down close enough that he can smell what I just ate.

Channel that most savage part of me.

"You want to bet on that?" the Pale Horse asks.

His eyes go just the slightest bit wider. Spine gets a tiny bit straighter. Whatever he suspected a few moments ago has dissipated. He remembers what I'm capable of. He knows I could have a bullet pumped into his heart and be well away before anyone shows up to stop me or save him.

I turn and disappear into the crowd before he has a chance to overthink it.

Astrid peeks around a food stall, the laser pointer already in her pocket. I grab her hand and we make our way toward the blaring sunlight outside the food hall.

"That was fun," she says, an edge of excitement to her voice.

There's something about the reaction that doesn't sit well with me, but I don't want to waste time unpacking it.

Pink and blue neon signs light up the Geylang neighborhood. It's just north of the central business district, but it could be an entirely different country. Gone are the skyscrapers and tourists, replaced by shophouses and sex workers. There are a lot of eyes on me. I'm the only white face I've seen since I got off the train, still standing out like a cat in a dog park.

I cut away from the crowds on Geylang Road, onto the lorongs—the side streets where the hustle recedes a bit. There's the occasional brothel, where women sit on folding chairs or stand by the sidewalk in small clusters, wearing sheer, skimpy outfits, smoking cigarettes. When I catch their eye they give me a subtle wave, but when I keep walking they don't call after me.

Singapore is in a strange sort of gray zone with sex work. Prostitution isn't illegal, but public solicitation and running a brothel is. Mostly the authorities tolerate it. Plus in this neighborhood you can walk past a handful of brothels, turn a corner, and find a row of small Buddhist temples. So you have to navigate the area with caution, and in the face of silent spiritual judgment.

But if you want to find the little crime that exists in Singapore, this is where you do it. It's tucked into the shadows, but I know where to look. Astrid protested, a little high on the success of her assignment with Ravi, but this thing I have to do on my own.

It's insane that I'm even still here. The Agency will have mobilized a small army. But they'll dump their resources into the airport, train stations, and bus terminals. They expect me to run, not wander. That buys me a little time.

Unless they've accessed the local surveillance network, which I'm sure they most likely have. Even here, there are bulbous CCTV cameras everywhere, hanging from streetlights and nestled into corners. I know to duck my head away from them so they can't get a full scan of my face, but there are too many to account for.

Working for the Agency comes with perks. Fingerprints, facial recognition, family and employment history—all of that is wiped from existence. If someone goes looking for it, they might see a faint shimmer, but that's it. That's been great up to now, but the Agency flipped off the switch, which means they can turn it back on. They may have started when I first messaged Ravi, but no one was waiting for me at the airport, so that's a good sign.

Ravi.

His offer to come in from the cold is tickling my ear.

That's why what I'm doing right now is necessary. Take a step forward, get a little further from the fork in the road I came upon a year ago. Lucky for me, even though the Russian took my notebook, the information it held is still etched across the inside of my chest.

It suddenly sinks in, how alone I am right now. How I could very well be strolling down a quiet street to a death sentence. I pull out my phone and dial Kenji. He picks up on the first ring.

"You're okay," he says, almost surprised, which only hurts my feelings a little.

"How is everyone?"

"Safe. And you?"

"Found my old boss. He doesn't know anything about the current acquisition. But he did offer me my old job back."

"How did that make you feel?" Kenji asks.

I pause long enough that I don't need to answer.

"It's okay that you considered it," he says. "This is not a perfect process. You're not perfect. What do I keep saying? Let go . . ."

He gives me the space to finish. ". . . And let god."

Not that we believe in god. Not after the things we've done. One of the core tenets of Alcoholics Anonymous is surrendering yourself to a higher power—whatever you determine that higher power to be. For us, though, we thought of ourselves as gods. Because we did what gods did. Dealt in death, decided who lived. To *let go and let god* is Assassins Anonymous–speak for: *You are not a god, you are a human being, and what you did, you did to other human beings.*

This is exactly the moment where I need to chew on that, even if it's getting stuck in my teeth.

"In other news," I tell Kenji, "I'm about to make my first amends."

"Mark, you're not ready to move into the ninth step," he says. "First, we're supposed to sit down and review the list, and you and I decide who's best to make a direct amends to."

"I traveled all this way," I tell him. "And honestly, given a whole lot of factors, it feels a little like providence. I think I need to do it. Get the ball rolling. I told you about that one. My first on the job."

He sighs. "It's going to be uncomfortable. Be careful. Don't linger."

"Thanks, pal."

"Mark?"

"Yeah?"

"I'm proud of you," he says, enunciating slowly, making sure each word lands.

They do.

"I love you, too," I tell him.

We click off the call as I'm approaching my destination: a boxy, dilapidated apartment building that stands out in a long row of three-story row houses.

The Fuji Majestic.

Also known—not to most, but to me—as a base of operations for the local Triads.

Inside, if the intel I gleaned from the Via Maris is correct, is one of their lieutenants: Xie Yang, who goes by the name Billy. His dad was Wen Yang, a Triad enforcer who, a very long time ago, stepped onto the balcony of a room at the Millennium Hotel for a cigarette and had his neck snapped by an American assassin.

The apple, it seems, landed right next to the tree.

Which is why I said this feels like providence.

One, because I don't want to do this, which is always a good reason to do something related to recovery.

Two, because my first amends may as well be with the first guy I murdered as an Agency hitter.

There's a man smoking by the front door. Mid-twenties, shaved head, neat goatee, neon-pink tank top. Not Yang. I suspect I'll see a version of his dad when I lay eyes on him. I walk up to the guy at the door and get close. Not too close to disrespect him, but close enough to show I'm not afraid of him, either. I tell him: "I'm here to see Billy."

The man takes a deep drag on his cigarette, flicks it into the street behind me, and folds his hands in front of him, all without taking his eyes off me.

"Tell him it's about his father," I say.

The man stares at me for a moment longer, then slips through the front door.

He probably understood me. English proficiency in Singapore is high, especially among younger people. I watch through the metal security gate as he walks down a poorly lit hallway and gets on an elevator.

I wait, walking in circles. Thinking about what I want to say. Nothing really comes up, so maybe I'll just wing it, which I'm sure is a terrible idea, but hey, this is a learning process.

The man returns and opens the door, nodding for me to

follow. He didn't have a weapon on him before, but now he sports the telltale bulge of a gun at his waistband, clumsily tucked into the front of his pants. That's so dumb. You'll never get a clean draw. Why do people do that?

The answer is: movies. Always movies.

We ride the elevator in silence, then walk down a long hallway. Thumping music rattles one door. A baby cries behind another. I am having second thoughts. Maybe I should have run as soon as I left the food market.

The man leads me to a door, which he opens, letting me step inside first. I don't like that he's behind me now. I expect it to be an apartment, but the living room is like an office, decorated by a grown-up who enjoys the aesthetic of a teenager.

It's lit by purple recessed lighting, with framed posters on the wall for classic kung fu and action movies. *Drunken Master, Five Deadly Venoms, Iron Monkey, Master of the Flying Guillotine, The Killer, Infernal Affairs.* A few I don't recognize.

There's a massive wooden desk against the back wall, so big it looks impossible to have gotten through the door. Behind the desk is a glass display case of Chinese weapons: hook swords and tai chi swords and a beautiful, gleaming pair of butterfly swords. Sitting at the desk, which is covered with rolling papers and sloppy piles of pot and a shiny silver Taurus 856 revolver, is a young Chinese man wearing white Nikes and a red tracksuit.

In my mind, I see his dad. They have the same boyish softness, though that barely works to offset the hatred in his eyes. This is a wound he did not expect to have opened tonight.

On the wall to his left is a poster for the movie *Hard Boiled*.

I nod my head at it. "Classic. Chow Yun-fat. The Chinese Tom Cruise, am I right?"

"Who are you?" he asks. "And what do you know about my father?"

"Look," I tell him, glancing at the guy behind me, who is slowly moving his hands toward his waistband, like the amateur he is. "I think it would be best if we could speak in private."

I can hear the man behind me, the skin rasping against the metal of the gun as he wraps his hand around it. All that old programming—it's not even like it's coming back to me, it's just immediately present. I don't think this guy is really going to shoot me, so I let him pull the gun out and press it to the back of my head. Maybe it'll make him feel better.

Billy smiles as he watches this unfold.

Problem is, the man with the gun, he did the dumb thing, which is: he got too close. The safest minimum distance to hold someone at gunpoint is twenty-one feet. Anything under that, all bets are off. Guns can misfire. Adrenaline screws with fine motor skills; not everyone has the close personal relationship with that hormone like I do. Aiming and getting a shot off is harder than people think. If he were a professional, he would have taken a few steps back, at least.

I stand still, unbothered, and make sure they can both see that.

"I'm not here to hurt you," I tell Billy. "Just something I think you ought to know. My goal is to have a respectful conversation, and it can't really be respectful like this. So I'm going to ask once, and I'm going to ask nicely. Could you please tell your friend to put the gun away and give us five minutes?"

Billy was curious, to a point, but he's grown bored with this. He looks around his pristine office, and I'm not surprised at all when he says, "Take him down to the basement or something. Just not in here."

"Okay, then," I say, and before the guy behind me can fully process the command, I dip my shoulder and step back, pushing his gun arm toward the ceiling in case he fires, which he doesn't. I sweep to the side, pulling the gun from his hand, and disassemble it, dropping the pieces to the floor.

Billy puts his hand on the Taurus and I yell, "Hey."

He freezes and looks up at me.

"I promise you I will take that one, too. Five minutes, then I'm gone."

Billy stops. Sighs. Then he waves the other guy away.

Once we're alone I cross the room and sit in the free chair in front of the desk. Twenty-two feet. He should have taken the shot. Billy leans back, slamming his Nikes on the desk and leaning back, trying to exude power.

Trying to hide the fact that he's spooked.

"I barely knew my father," he says. "He died when I was twelve. Even then I hadn't seen him in years. What do you have to tell me that I would need to know?"

"I killed him," I say.

As soon as the words leave my mouth, I feel an enormous amount of relief.

Like, that's all it took? I can just say the thing? Easy as that?

But then Billy launches himself over the desk, knocking me to the ground, and drives his fist into my face.

In the tumble, he manages to avoid the wound in my stomach, and for that I'm grateful, but he sets himself on his knees so he has proper leverage and whales on me. Wordlessly swinging, over and over. Thank god the carpet is thick because the way my head is bouncing off it, it doesn't feel good, but it could be worse.

I seek the serenity to accept a thing I cannot change: I killed this man's dad and now he wants to kill me.

My nose breaks. Blood fills my vision. Before I came here I left the concierge at our hotel an envelope with my ATM card and my PIN, and said if I wasn't back by morning to give it to the woman staying with me. Astrid will be fine. Even if I'm dead.

Billy grabs my collar, looping his hands in it, and pulls me toward him. He holds his fist up. It's coated in blood, vibrating with power, and I feel like this might be the one to knock me out.

After that it's down to the basement.

"Tell me your name," he says. "So I know the name of the man who killed my father."

I see an opportunity to be honest.

And maybe save my own life.

If I try really hard, maybe I can convince myself that's all I'm doing.

"Mark," I tell him. "But I was known as the Pale Horse."

Billy's grip goes slack and he drops me to the floor, my head bouncing off the carpet again. He scrambles off me, backing himself into a corner like a frightened animal, looking for an exit, but afraid to try to pass me to get to the door. I get to my knees and feel along the ridges of my broken nose, then bear down and push it back into place, crying out as bone scrapes cartilage.

"You . . ." he says. "You . . ."

"Yeah," I tell him, breathing through the pain. "That's me. So, anyway, can I finish saying what I have to say?"

Billy looks at me with complete and utter confusion. He moves to his chair and sits, holding his head in his hands.

He thinks he's going to die.

God, the power this holds over people.

The power I hold.

No. Not anymore. Don't think like that.

I sit on the chair across from him, my face aching, and say, "Your dad was part of a crew protecting a guy trying to sell dangerous intelligence to dangerous people. I broke his neck. I thought I was saving the world and used that as an excuse to end his life. I can't sit here and say I wish I could do it differently. I'm not sure that I do. What I can tell you is that I'm sorry for whatever hurt that put on you. I can't make it up to you. Killing me won't bring him back and I promise, it won't make you feel better. But you need to do what you need to do."

"You . . . you're the Pale Horse," he says, still not looking at me.

"We established that, yes."

"So . . ." He finally makes eye contact, and his face bursts into a broad smile. "I just kicked the shit out of the Pale Horse."

That, I was not expecting. "Sure, if you want to call it that."

He claps his hands and gets up, pumping his fists as he jumps around the desk. "And my dad was killed by the Pale Horse! Do you know what this is going to do for my reputation?"

It's so absurd I want to laugh. He crosses the room to a mini fridge and pulls out two bottles of Tiger beer. He uncaps them and places one of them in front of me.

"And now I'm having a drink with the Pale Horse," he says, shaking his head and taking a sip. "*The* Pale Horse. You're a legend." He looks me up and down. "Thought you'd be taller. More built, though. Like Jason Statham."

I suppress the sigh, pick up the bottle, and take a swig. The beer is ice-cold and takes a little edge off the pummeling I just took.

Billy takes a long pull and wipes his mouth with the back of his hand. "Look, man, I didn't really like my dad. He wasn't good to my mom. He pretty much abandoned us. I guess in the moment . . ." He goes searching for what he wants to say, staring off into the distance, before snapping back. "I figured I should hurt you because that's how it's supposed to be, right? But I guess I'm just more amazed that you're here."

The god in me is the thing that saved me.

This is terrible for my recovery.

"Revenge never ends up feeling the way you think it will," I tell him. "It sounds great until you have to sit with it. I know that just sounds like me arguing in favor of my life, but that's what I've come to learn."

He eyes me as he takes another long pull from the bottle.

"I don't know that it's worth killing you," he says. "For the mess alone."

He's getting bold now. I have to give him a little credit for that.

"That's very magnanimous of you," I tell him.

"Magnanimous?"

"Kind."

He nods. "So what now?"

"You have a story to tell. Enjoy it for whatever it's worth. If you're really not going to shoot me in the face, I guess my next step is figuring out how to get out of this country alive."

He gives me a quizzical look and I shrug.

"My old employers want me dead. They know I'm here."

He scratches the back of his neck slowly, then says, "I'll make you a deal."

I put my hand up, beckoning him to proceed.

"I can get you on a boat, no problem. We have a route between here and Jakarta."

"What do you want in return?"

"I get to tell people that I messed you up. That you killed my dad . . ."

He pulls out the drawer on his desk and goes rooting around in it. The deal tastes sour on the back of my tongue. The Pale Horse doesn't get slapped around. He doesn't leave people alive. He wouldn't let some kid one-up him and walk away.

But that's not me anymore. That's just a story I told myself, and I've been trying to change that story. What does it matter if the narrative spins in a different direction?

"And," he says. "I want a souvenir."

He places on the desk a Damascus steel dagger with a pearl handle.

"Nondominant hand is fine," he says. "Even though my dad was an asshole, it seems like a pretty fair price, right?"

Four seconds in, hold for four, out for four, empty lungs for four.

He places his hands palm down on the desk and smiles, waiting for me.

I stand and take the knife. Feel the weight of it, get a good grip, then spin it in my hands and slam it down into the wood, between the ring and middle fingers of his left hand.

"Your souvenir is you get to live," the Pale Horse says.

He blanches at that. I offer him my hand. He shakes it with a blank expression.

"It's not just me that needs to get out of town," I tell him. "I'm with someone. And we have a cat."

He pulls out a piece of paper and scribbles on it, his hands shaking, then passes it to me. "Be at this address in two hours. Ask for Xiao."

I drain the rest of my beer, put the bottle on the desk, and tell him, "Thanks."

As I'm headed for the door he says, "Seriously, man, I feel like I need you to impart a little wisdom on me before you go. I'm twenty-six and I run the Singapore Triads. What would you tell yourself if you could talk to your twenty-six-year-old self?"

I think about it for a few moments and then tell him, "Go be an astronaut."

I leave without seeing how he reacts to that.

Raindrops tap the windshield of the cab as it pulls to a stop in front of the hotel. I hand the driver some sing, get out, and watch him pull away, leaving me alone on a quiet, tree-lined street next to the highway.

I hope Astrid has calmed down a bit. She did not approve of the accommodations—it's a two-star hotel, flung far from the city center. There is no spa. As much as she wanted to get a room in Marina Bay, the surveillance network is too tight.

But something broke our way: it's a ten-minute stroll to Jurong Port, where we're supposed to meet Xiao, if he exists and Billy isn't planning to show up with an army of Triads. I doubt it, though. I think I succeeded in both impressing him *and* scaring the piss out of him.

I tilt my head back to the sky and let some raindrops fall onto my face.

What I did, dropping into my old persona, I did to survive.

I ignore the tingling in my fingertips. The floating feeling in my chest.

The fear in Billy's eyes as I plunged his dagger an inch deep into that desk.

That god-fear.

I call Kenji. He doesn't answer. It should be . . . noon there? He must be waiting for me to check in. I made my first amends. This is a big deal. Maybe he's busy. He'll call back in a few. He always does.

The lobby is empty, besides a pretty Indian man with a blue vest standing behind the desk, a pair of felt antlers on his head. He barely glances up when I walk in. I dig around in my pocket for the key card as I step onto the elevator. We've got an hour until we have to be at the port. Wish I had enough time for a shower, but just to be safe, after leaving Billy, I rode the train to the far west side of the country before taking a cab back. If I had a tail, I would have seen it, or lost them in the process.

I get to the door at the end of the hall and give it two knocks, then one, then two, so Astrid knows it's me. After a moment she knocks back.

Three times.

It's supposed to be twice.

Which leaves me with a fast decision to make. Someone's in there, but the Agency can't be here in full force. There would have been a Taser in my neck the moment I stepped out of the cab. I don't want to abandon her, so I open the door to find her standing by the beds with a look on her face not dissimilar from the look on Billy's after I drove the knife into the table.

There are two men at the far end of the room, dressed all in black. Both have scowls that look practiced, and the kind of bulk that comes through the tip of a needle. That's the first thing that pegs them as B-team material. The guy on the left has a shaved head the same circumference of his neck; the guy on the right has a Viking beard and long brown hair tied into a ponytail.

They're not like me, more like blunt instruments. Strong enough to do some damage but not always smart enough to get away with it, so ultimately expendable.

The guy with the shaved head—the Neck—is resting his hand on the gun holstered at his waist, finger on the trigger guard. "The rest of the team is on its way. Won't be long now."

"Are you hurt?" I ask Astrid.

She shakes her head. P. Kitty is nowhere to be seen. His carrier is in the corner and empty. He's a smart cat. I mean, he's not, he's burned his tongue five separate times chewing through electrical wires. But he probably had the sense to seek refuge under the bed.

I close my right eye and tell Astrid, "Everything's going to be all right."

She lowers herself to one of the free chairs. This is a micro hotel, so the room is longer than it is wide. There's a small table and two chairs to my right. To the left, a small kitchenette and TV. Beyond that is a raised platform with two beds almost directly next to each other, the heads pushed against the right wall. There's barely a foot of clearance on the left side.

The two men are standing at the far end of the room with their backs to the window, against the fully drawn, light-blocking curtains.

I reach up and rub my closed right eye.

"Hey," Ponytail says. "What are you doing?"

"What am I doing what?"

"Your eye."

"Got something in it. Some dust maybe."

The Neck takes his gun out and holds it to his side. "Don't you move, chief. Orders are to bring you in alive, but shit happens, you know? Being the one to cap the Pale Horse might mean a promotion."

There's a toiletry bag on the table that Astrid must have picked up. Not ideal, but I can work with it.

Ponytail clears his throat. "So you're *him?*" Just a touch of awe in his voice.

"In the flesh."

"Don't look so tough to me," the Neck says.

Though *his* voice has a little rattle.

I keep gently rubbing my eye. "Stories get bigger in the telling. Truth is you two look pretty tough, so I'm not going to do anything stupid."

"Ought to knock the living shit out of you for what you did," the Neck says. "Though it looks like someone already did."

It takes me a second, then I remember: Billy.

"You should see the other guy," I tell him. "Not a scratch on him."

"Don't worry," the Neck says. "Before this is through, I'm going to get my licks in. You deserve that much."

"Probably in general, but sure, why specifically?"

"Because I woke up with my face in a squat toilet."

Ah. They were Ravi's goons at the food market. They went down so quick I barely registered what they looked like. Telling them that would probably not endear me to them.

"Yeah, man, I can see how that wouldn't be pleasant," I say. "It wasn't personal. Honestly, I'm sorry about that."

Astrid is twelve feet from me and out of the line of fire of the man with the gun. The man on the right hasn't drawn yet. The two of them are nineteen feet from me. Not great for them.

I slump my shoulders forward, keeping my hand over my

eye. "I don't even care," I tell them. "I'm just so tired. Tired of running. Tired of living like this. Tired of always being afraid. Like your life could end at any moment, right? People think being the Pale Horse is all fun and games, but it's *hard*. Living up to that expectation."

The Neck laughs. "You big baby."

"Hey, Astrid?"

"Yeah."

"Where's P. Kitty?"

"Under the bed."

"Ah. Smart. Hey, you guys don't know all that much about pirates, do you?"

Before they can answer I snap out my hand and hit the switch on the wall next to me. With the curtains drawn and no other illumination in the room, we're plunged into darkness. But taking a few minutes to close my right eye gave it time to adjust. Not fully, but more than anyone else in the room.

I close my left eye and open the right, and I can make out the faint outlines of the men across the room. All they're seeing is black. Astrid dives to the floor. I grab the toiletry kit and wing it at the Neck, since his gun is already out. It strikes him in the face. I make a running leap, vaulting myself off the first bed and crashing into him with my knees out, knocking him hard against the wall. Ponytail is searching the room for me but still can't see. As soon as I land and brace myself, I swing my foot into the side of his knee.

I turn to the Neck, who's slightly hunched over, and slam my knee into his head a few times, smashing it into the wall. He drops the gun. The drywall cracks and breaks. Then I throw another side kick at Ponytail's shoulder, knocking him down, preventing him from getting his bearings and reaching his gun. I have to be careful not to knock either of them through the window—we're eight floors up and that's a death sentence.

The Neck slumps to the floor. I turn and hammer my fist into Ponytail's stomach. It bounces off the plated ballistics vest under his shirt. Feels like punching an overfull heavy bag. It gives him a chance to throw himself forward and smother me with his body in the tight space. He gets me in a headlock, so I twist until I've got an opening and drive my elbow up and into his jaw.

He staggers back, about to fall against the window, but I manage to grab him by the collar and pull him forward. Then I snap a kick into his knee, and as he's going down, I put my knee in the side of his head.

Hands wrap around my throat. The Neck breathes into my ear. "Gonna enjoy this."

Before I can consider which way to break the hold, he cries out and falls backward onto the bed. He's reaching for the back of his knee, screaming, as Astrid brings her foot up high, like she's executing a ballet move, and brings it down hard on his forehead. She grunts with a surprising level of savagery as she does it. The Neck goes limp, and Ponytail isn't ready for round two, either.

"Didn't see that coming," I tell Astrid. "Can you hit the lights?"

After a few seconds of scrambling and grunting, the room illuminates and the blast is harsh enough to make me squint.

I blink it away and then check the two men to make sure they're still alive; they're both groaning in sloppy piles. The Neck has a bunch of heavy-duty zip ties on his belt, so I use them to bind their hands and ankles before patting them down and relieving them of their belongings. I fieldstrip the guns and bend the recoil springs so they won't go back together right. Phones get stomped on, and cash goes in my pocket.

"Mark, what the hell is going on?" Astrid asks.

I hit the floor and find P. Kitty cowering in the corner under the bed. I really have to stretch to grab his leg and pull him toward me, and once I've got him close enough, I scruff him, which gets him to go limp. Then I cram him in the cat carrier.

"Sorry, bud," I tell him. "No time to be polite. I promise I'll make it up to you."

"Mark, I—" Astrid starts.

"Grab your stuff, we're going."

As I'm giving the room a quick scan to make sure there's nothing else I need, static crackles from one of the slumped figures. A male voice says, "Echo, check in. Do you have eyes on the target?"

I dig around in Ponytail's vest and find the radio. "Not yet," I say.

"We've cleared the Marina Bay. Sending you backup. Report in ASAP if he arrives."

"Copy. Over and out." I switch off the radio and smash it.

"What now?" Astrid has her belongings assembled into a small backpack we picked up in the airport, and she's holding the cat carrier.

"We go for a little boat ride," I tell her.

"Where to?" she asks.

"Jakarta."

We opt for the stairs instead of the elevator. As we descend, all I can think is: I should go back and kill them. Leaving them alive is a mistake. They could get free and come after us. They could alert the Agency teams, who'll get here quicker. They could have hurt Astrid and P. Kitty. It's not just that the math isn't in their favor. There's a tug at the core of me, this feeling in my body like something is missing and watching the life leave their eyes will fill it.

Meanwhile, Astrid is looking at me like she can't decide if she should thank me or drive her fist into my nuts for getting her tied up in this.

"Pirates?" she asks.

"It's thought pirates wore eye patches so one eye was adjusted to the darkness. They could transition more easily between above and below deck."

"And what the hell happened to your face?"

"My face?"

"You look like raw beef."

"That was a completely separate situation with a different person who wanted to kill me. It's been a day. Where'd you learn to fight?"

"Why would you assume I can't?"

There was an efficiency to her movement that makes me wonder how much more there is to this story, but I don't have time to dig. It's comforting, at least, that my back is better protected than I previously thought.

The door opens and the lobby is empty. I don't bother

checking out; I don't want anyone to clean the room and let the goon squad out with time to notify anyone. I feel a twinge on my stomach. There's some blood seeping through my shirt. Great. Must have torn a stitch. Something else to worry about.

Before we hit the door, I hear "Mr. Joubert?" The desk man in the felt antlers is walking toward us, his hospitality smile shining. "Are you checking out?"

"Uh, no, just moving some stuff to the rental car. We're headed back up to the room in a few."

He eyes the carrier but shrugs, then holds out a folded piece of paper. "Someone dropped this off for you." He hands it to me and goes back to the desk. Astrid peeks over my shoulder as I open it.

I CAN FIND YOU ANYWHERE YOU GO, KOTENOK.

I honestly do not know what's worse. The fact that the Russian was in this hotel and seems to delight in screwing with me, or the fact that, when we get outside and I check my phone, Kenji hasn't gotten back to me.

6

> Bowing is an expression of gratitude and respect. In effect, you are thanking your opponent for giving you an opportunity to improve your technique.
>
> —Jigoro Kano, the founder of judo

Prague
Five Years Ago

I cup my hands to my mouth and blow into them. Should have brought gloves. The snow is coming down heavy and the awning I'm tucked underneath is barely keeping it off. It's beautiful, really, the way the snow, illuminated in the yellow sodium-vapor lights, transforms a quiet industrial park into something luminous. I breathe the cold air into my lungs and try to enjoy the tranquility of this moment.

Which will, very shortly, be interrupted by mayhem.

I pull the tablet out of my coat and check the feeds I placed around the inside of the dilapidated warehouse this morning. Still only a handful of thugs, smoking cigarettes and playing cards. No sign of the target: Daisuke Sakai, a kumicho—or supreme boss—in the Yakuza.

Sakai is here to sell a shipment of weapons to the Nationalist Social Club, a neo-Nazi group that's mostly based in the

United States but has recently been stirring up shit in France, Hungary, and Germany. Agency intel says they're planning something big and violent, and NATO back-channeling has determined that, given the NSC is a homegrown group, this is America's problem to clean up. In more ways than one, because the weapons were procured from an Afghani dealer and, of course, were originally sold by the United States.

What a tangled web of bullshit we weave.

And I'm the one who has to untangle it.

Sakai, along with a group of his men, plus about a dozen neo-Nazis, should have been here by now, but there wasn't snow in the forecast this morning.

My phone buzzes with a message from Ravi.

RAVI: Sitrep?

ME: Our friends are running late.

RAVI: Probably the weather.

ME: Thought so. Hey, where should I eat after this?

RAVI: La Degustation. Michelin-starred. Classic Czech cooking. Unbelievable.

ME: Thanks, bud. Hey, do you get your meals expensed?

RAVI: No, but I'm not married and don't have kids. What else am I going to spend it on?

RAVI: Your flight leaves tomorrow but I can push it back a day.

ME: Think it's safe?

RAVI: You worried?

ME: Nah. I'll try to book a table. You want to join?

RAVI: I went yesterday but I'd happily go again.

I click through to the restaurant's website. Nothing open

for dinner tomorrow, but there's a table free at one thirty p.m. I book it under the name George Joubert and pass that information along to Ravi.

That'll be fun. Ravi will tell me what a good job I did here and then he'll pick up the tab. That's never a bad way to end an assignment.

Then I wait.

A lot of this job is waiting.

The snow continues to fall. I pull out the tablet again, quadruple-checking the status of the kill switches that'll put out the lights, the triggers on the flash-bangs, and the relay on the gas canisters that'll pump the space with BZ. I can barely contain my excitement about that.

Also known as 3-quinuclidinyl benzilate, it's a gas that induces cognitive dysfunction, delirium, and hallucinations. It's usually a little tough to track down, but we're in Eastern Europe, where it's a buyer's market for shit like this. I've been wanting to try it forever. Intel suggests there could be up to twenty men, and I'm not too worried, but my job gets a lot easier if they're all tripping and disoriented.

Satisfied that everything is set up and ready, I check the cameras again—still no sign of the rest of these idiots—and go back to blowing in my hands. The air is still, that quiet so loud you can hear the snow hitting the ground. All that quiet, almost turning into its own layer of sound, so I nearly miss it: the soft crunch of snow underfoot.

It came from my left. I pull my trusty SIG Sauer P365 from my hip and swing around the side of the stairwell enclosure I've been tucked behind, where I find a dark figure crouched and waiting. I notice him a moment before I notice the long silver katana he has pressed to the side of my neck.

"Anatahadare?" the man says.

Who are you?

He's dressed head to toe in black, a balaclava wrapped around his head. He's older, fit, left-handed, obviously Japanese. I don't think he's part of this crew. First, because he's sneaking around on the roof. The guys downstairs are sloppy—I did a pretty good job hiding all my gear, but they didn't sweep the space like they should have.

But also, I recognize the look in his eyes.

It's the same look I see in the mirror.

He's a professional.

So I gamble a little. It's a hell of a gamble because he's positioned himself so that even if I get the shot off, the drag and weight of his body will take the katana clean across my carotid artery, which I suspect will give like wet tissue paper.

"Watashi . . . wa karera . . . to issho ni imasen?" I respond.

I'm not with them.

I hope that's what I say. My Japanese isn't great.

"American," he says.

"I'm here for Sakai."

The man pauses and I wonder if this is the moment. I tense my finger on the trigger a little—not so much as to alarm him, but enough maybe it'll give me an edge. If I step back and . . .

The sword comes off my throat. He's still holding it up, but it's lower now. I bring my gun down in response.

"I am also here for Sakai," he says.

"I don't know if that makes this a lot more complicated, or a whole lot easier."

The man looks around the roof, making sure we're still alone. I've been listening for the telltale sounds of cars and voices that would indicate we have company. Nothing.

"Who do you work for?" he asks.

"An interested party," I tell him. "That's the best I can tell you. How about you?"

"I am here to settle a debt," he says.

I want to laugh, but he's still holding a sword in my general direction. "Look, buddy, I don't care which one of us kills Sakai. All I have to do is make sure he's dead before I leave. You can have him. But I spent a better part of my morning setting up some cool traps and shit, and I'd hate to see them go to waste."

The man leaves his fighting stance, drawing himself to full height, still a head shorter than me, and sheathes his sword.

"I must be the one to deliver the killing blow," he says.

"You don't have to negotiate for anything," I tell him. "I agree to your terms."

We both look around the roof, unsure of what to say next. I've never worked with anyone who wasn't Agency before, and never with another professional. Usually I just get a bunch of dummies for backup who can't spell their last names without peeking in their underwear.

"So what do I call you?" I ask.

He stares at me for a few moments. This is like talking to a cat. Is he going to nuzzle me or scratch at my eyes? I get it, I'm on guard, too. Then he peels up the bottom half of his mask to show me his face. He's older than I would have expected.

"Kenji," he says.

"You got a stage name?" I ask.

He squints his eyes and tilts his head. "Stage name?"

"Yeah, like a nickname. Code name. Whatever."

He nods. "The Baku."

"Oh, man," I say, bursting into a smile, and then feeling a little sheepish for it. "I've heard of you. Baku is a demon that devours nightmares, right? That's cool. Wasn't there this big Yakuza dustup in Osaka two years ago? You walked into a room of thirty men, unarmed, and walked out without a scratch?"

He gives a small smile. "There were a few scratches. And it was twenty-four."

"Well, these things always get bigger in the retelling."

"What about you?" he asks.

I almost don't say it.

Almost.

But the truth is, I don't get to indulge in this very often.

"Mark," I tell him. "But I go by the Pale Horse."

Kenji's body freezes. Then he drops to his knees, bows his head, and presents his katana to me.

"Jihiwokou," he says.

Mercy.

"I did not know it was you," he says.

Well, this is a little embarrassing, actually.

"C'mon, man, we're good," I tell him.

He looks up from where he's kneeling, confused. My head

just grew a few sizes. It's hard not to feel a certain type of way about this.

But as good as I am, this guy nearly got the drop on me and I have to respect that, so I try to play it off a little and put him at ease. "Starting to wonder if we should find a place to wait inside or something. My fingers are going to break off when I start pulling the trigger."

He gets to his feet and leads me to the other edge of the roof, where there's an alcove better blocked from the wind. There's a smattering of footprints in the snow. This is where he must have been waiting. Which is a little funny. I wonder how long the two of us have both been up here.

There's a black sack on the ground. He reaches in and pulls out a small gel pack, cracks it, and tosses it to me. A hand warmer. I hold it between my palms and he takes out a thermos and offers it to me.

"Kanpai," he says.

Steaming-hot green tea snakes through my body and immediately warms me. I hand it back to him and as a show of respect he doesn't wipe the rim before he takes a long sip.

"My name is Kenji Sakai," he says.

"Ah, family shit."

Kenji nods as he puts the cap back on the thermos. "My brother. I do not agree with his decision. Selling weapons to these people. Money should not matter more than honor."

"Money tends to get in the way of most things. But that probably means after this you don't get to go home."

"I'm not planning on it," he says. "My brother's life will be the last one I take."

"Really?" I ask. "Getting out of the business?"

"I'm tired," Kenji says, leaning against the wall, gazing into the distance. "May I ask you something?"

"Sure."

"Does it ever weigh on you? The accumulation of it?"

He doesn't have to say what *it* is. I know what he means. I follow his gaze with my own, over the barren industrial area, like there's some kind of answer written on the horizon. "It's all math to me. I balance equations. Your brother, all those people who are going to show up here, they're planning to do some bad things. We take them out, those bad things don't happen. Overall, it's a win."

"And do you sleep at night?" he asks.

"Like a baby."

Kenji gives me a little look that says he does not. "I believe that every time we kill," he says, "we lose a part of ourselves, and gain a part of that person." His eyes take on a soft haze of sadness. "I feel like I have lived a very long time, and I am ready to rest."

"Geez, man, you're not gonna off yourself when this is through, are you? We don't really know each other, but I'm not sure that's the answer . . ."

"No. There is a group of people like us, who have laid down their weapons. A support group, to help us transition into a new life. One without killing. After I kill my brother, I will drop my sword and seek them out. See if I can make another life for myself."

I reach into my coat to check the tablet. He side-eyes me

and his hand reflexively goes for the blade. "Checking the cameras." He nods and relaxes. The party has yet to arrive.

"So what is it?" I ask. "Like AA for killers?"

"Exactly that."

"We're not really addicted to this, though, are we? It's not like heroin."

"It's a pleasure-reward system," Kenji says. "You do your job. You do it well. You earn money or praise. Your brain produces dopamine. You get used to dopamine, so you look for more." He side-eyes me again. "You know what I mean."

Not a question.

Because yes, I do.

It feels good to be good at something.

"It doesn't have to be a drug to be addictive," he says. "Sex is addictive. Gambling is addictive. The thrill of winning. The risk of losing. The danger. There was a study in which they found people who kill, people like us." He taps his head. "We have deficiencies in the prefrontal cortex of our brains. That affects judgment, decision-making, self-control. Many of those same things are present in addicts."

Never really thought of it like that. Or gave it any thought, ever. What I do is what I do and I learned to stop parsing it while midair in Singapore.

"Do you think you'd ever stop?" he asks.

"Always figured it would be nice to have a farm one day. A dog. Something quiet. Sleep in every morning. But to be honest, this is the only thing I've ever been good at. It's hard to think of not doing it."

"The program is not just about *not* killing," Kenji says. "It's about surrendering the ego. The idea that we're granted the right to make decisions that aren't ours to make. I would like to do that. And maybe, one day, make amends for the things I've done."

"Amends?" I ask. "Like, sit down with the families of all the people you killed and say you're sorry? Jesus, man, I'm not passing judgment on how you want to live your life, but that just sounds humiliating."

"The difference between humility and humiliation is willingness," Kenji says. "Ultimately, it's not for them. It's for me."

There's a crunching sound in the distance. Tires. I check the cameras. The men inside are scrambling so they look like they haven't been goofing off for the last hour.

"Showtime," I tell Kenji. "You don't have a gas mask, do you?"

"I do not."

Damn it. Only brought one. I was really looking forward to using the BZ. Oh well, have to do this the old-fashioned way. I take the HK417 assault rifle off the holster on my back and give it a quick check. "Sakai is yours. I imagine we're not getting drinks after this, but it was nice to meet you."

He presents me his hands, one cupped underneath the other.

Perched on his palm is a small, intricate paper crane, folded from white paper.

I pick it up. I consider sticking it in my pocket but don't want to damage the delicate beauty of it, so I place it inside the case I brought the HK in.

"If you ever decide you would like to find that farm," Kenji says.

"Thank you," I tell him, not entirely sure how I mean it. It's a kind gesture, and I'm happy to know he's finding his own peace. But I don't feel like this will be anything other than a really good story and a cool souvenir.

Because I'm not addicted.

I can stop any time I want.

There's a shout from down on the street, and the sound of a gate rolling up. I check my rifle one more time and say, "Let's go kill a whole bunch of people."

7

> It isn't the mountains ahead that wear you down.
> It's the pebble in your shoe.
> —Muhammad Ali

London
Now

Astrid fiddles with her phone by the front door of the basement flat as I keep an eye on the street. There aren't a lot of people walking by, and the ones who are don't pay us much attention.

"It was like a year ago, I think," she says, muttering under her breath, more to herself than to me. "I'm sure I still have the email in here somewhere . . ."

London makes me nervous. Same problem as any major city—the surveillance network. The more time passes, the more time the Agency has to upload my image to law enforcement databases around the world. Sooner or later just stepping outside is going to be dangerous.

Which is why, if this works, it'll be a pretty big win. The short-term rental site listing shows the flat isn't available, but the lights are out and there's a pile of moldering leaves on the mat that hasn't been cleared. So far we've struck out on finding a cash-only motel that wasn't out in the sticks, and we need to get off the street.

And we could both use a shower. Billy's man came through and got us on a fishing boat. Seven hours later we were in Jakarta, and he even handled the entry passport stamps so we wouldn't get hassled on the way out. Couldn't find a direct flight to New York, but Astrid said she might have a connection in London that could be useful.

"Got it," she says. She keys a code into the lock on the door, and we get lucky. It opens onto a very small, very European apartment. White walls, tight space, IKEA furniture, faux-wood flooring, weird plugs everywhere.

"This thing sucks, by the way," Astrid says, pocketing her new burner phone. "You really think this guy is tracking me?"

"He's tracking something."

Which dawned on me halfway through the ride to Jakarta, which is why both of our phones are now at the bottom of the Java Sea. I miss mine already, feeling naked with a regular old smartphone, but I can still access my secure email and I was able to get D@nt3 working for the Via Maris. I don't redownload the messaging app that I used with Ravi—no sense in letting him drip poison in my ear.

Before we enter I pull out my phone and check the Wi-Fi networks. One of the network names looks a little funny—a long, unintelligible string of numbers and letters. I check the locking mechanism on the door one more time. It's not sophisticated enough to transmit a signal. I put P. Kitty down and tell Astrid: "Wait here."

Given it's a basement flat, it's pretty dark already, so I don't turn on any lights. I use the flashlight on my phone to sweep the place, moving extra slow around the bed, the light fixtures, the electrical outlets. There's a good bit of dust, so that's encouraging, that we won't be disturbed. In the bathroom I catch a glint coming from the vent. I yank it off and find a little black box that fits neatly in my palm. There's even an electrical outlet installed inside the vent, so the wires aren't visible. I bring it to Astrid.

"Camera," I tell her. "Wi-Fi enabled. Doesn't look motion-activated. The owner probably isn't monitoring it if no one's been here."

"That creep . . ." Astrid says.

"I suddenly don't feel so bad about breaking in."

Now that we're settled, I set up P. Kitty's stuff—a can of cat food, a bowl from the cabinet I fill with some water, and a litter box, which, helpfully, this apartment already has, because it's pet-friendly. I take P. Kitty out of his carrier and he lolls around for a minute, taking in the new space, before heading for the food. Little guy must be ravenous.

I grab my bag and head into the bedroom, figuring I can jump in the shower after Astrid, but I find her naked from the waist up, her back to me. There's a nasty scar down her back, like someone inserted a meat hook and dragged it down diagonally from her left shoulder.

We clock each other at the same time. She puts her arms up to cover her breasts but doesn't know which way to turn—whether her chest or the scar is more intimate. I jump out of the room to give her privacy.

"Sorry, sorry," I call around the corner.

"We're both adults, I guess," she replies. "I've seen you with your shirt off."

"That's a hell of a scratch. Can I ask?"

She comes out of the bedroom barefoot, in jeans and a white T-shirt. She looks me up and down, deciding how she wants to answer. She settles on: "Not everyone I've worked with over the years is as nice as you."

The old me would have offered to pay whoever did that a visit. Part of me still wants to, but I feel like Astrid wouldn't take it as chivalrous. Not that it would have been; it just would have been an excuse to hurt someone.

"Seriously," I ask. "What's your story? You handled yourself pretty well in that hotel room."

By way of answering, she makes her way to the kitchen and pulls out the coffee maker, filling it with water and then picking a pod out of the tray underneath. She looks toward me expectantly and I nod. She starts the first one brewing and pulls a stool underneath her, then takes the first steaming mug of coffee and passes it to me. I set it on the counter to cool while she sets up hers.

"So what's the plan, boss?" I ask.

"The plan," she says, "is I go out and talk to my friend. And hopefully that friend tells us where to find the guy we're looking for."

"And how do you know this guy is even here?"

"Because I do," she says. "Again, you boys love to brag. I'm good at listening."

"Are you sure it's safe?"

"I'm not a damsel."

She takes her mug and turns to the sink, where she splashes in a little water to make it cool enough to drink. As she touches it to her lips and peeks at me from over the rim of the mug, I am struck by how incredibly attractive she is.

Not that I didn't notice before. You always notice a woman like Astrid.

But there's something about this moment, where we can breathe, where we can enjoy a drink together, where she's putting me in my place, that I feel safe with her. I want to tell her the truth about me. I want to lie down with my head in her lap. I want to kiss her and feel something other than this mix of broken glass and battery acid in my stomach.

Which means what I really need is a meeting.

Twice now I went to speak and the Pale Horse's voice came out. I'm slipping back into old patterns and routines. It doesn't feel good.

That's the thing I keep trying to convince myself.

And I'm doing a bad job at it, so I need a meeting.

"You do your thing, and I have some errands to run myself," I tell her.

"I'll text you when I've got something."

"Ten-four," I say, and go to the bedroom, where I pull out my phone. Still nothing from Kenji, which is making me nervous. I texted him the new number and figured he would have gotten back to me by now. Something is up. If the Russian was in Singapore, then he couldn't be causing trouble back home. Anyway, Kenji can handle himself.

Still, I pop into the secure email account and leave a note in the drafts folder:

K, could use a check-in. M.

I include my new number, in case the other message didn't come through. Then I hop onto the Via Maris and navigate to the discussion boards. This is where you go to get into long discussions about the pros and cons of bump stocks, or the best way to dissolve a body, or reviews on survival gear. Nearly all the forums are public, except a few, including Paper Cranes. I input the password and scroll through the list of cities until I land on London.

A thread pops up with just a username: 1DayUK. It's otherwise closed to comments. I send a private message:

In town and HALTing.

HALT is the AA acronym for hungry, angry, lonely, and tired—because when those needs aren't being met, we're particularly susceptible to relapse. I hope they use the same acronyms over here, because I am currently all four of those things.

I jump in the shower and let the hot water sear my skin, then soap up and rinse the wound on my stomach; Astrid repatched it on the boat, and it doesn't seem too bad. It hurts, but so does the rest of my body. I haven't been this tired since Hell Week. Five days, twenty hours a day of PT, two hundred miles of running, four hours of sleep a night. Cold, sandy, hungry, and someone screaming in your face the whole time.

I'd trade that for this in a heartbeat.

Which is why I spent most of the trip here alternating between rest and trying to figure out the value of the notebook.

The whole thing is written in code, but anyone with a bit of time and half a brain should be able to crack it. I remember most of it and it's easy enough to eliminate the small-time jobs. Whoever's doing this is a major player. Which leaves any number of government officials, oligarchs, oil-rich terrorists, and other sundry wealthy psychopaths.

A day later and I've got nothing that feels like a solid lead, which is so frustrating I want to scream, so it brings me a modicum of comfort that, when I get out of the shower and check my phone, there's a meeting and an address waiting for me.

It's a different church and a different basement, but cool water fills my veins as soon as my shoes squeak on the linoleum floor.

Some people think of recovery as a destination. Really, it's a path you travel for the rest of your life, and the finish line is perpetually over the horizon. You have to learn to be happy with the journey. To *be* the journey.

As I enter the room, a bear of a man turns to me from a folding table that I expect to be holding coffee and donuts but is in fact holding scones and tea, which is kind of neat. He has sandy hair, a thick beard, and a face that's taken a lot of punches.

"You the chap who messaged?" he asks, his working-class British accent so heavy it could sink in water. I wonder what brought him to this room; he doesn't strike me as the MI6 type, more local leg-breaker.

"That's me," I tell him.

He opens his arms like he expects a hug, but I don't know

that he really wants one. "Welcome home, brother. American, yeah?"

"What gave it away?"

He waves me over to the table. "New Yorker, too. You got that dry sort of attitude down tight. Kenji still running that meeting?"

"That he is."

"He's a good egg, isn't he?" The man offers me his hand. "I popped in, I dunno, three or four years ago, when I was in the States visiting my daughter. I'm Ray."

We shake. His hand is huge and feels cast out of concrete. I wonder what kinds of things he did with this hand. "Mark."

"Mark. We don't often get visitors, but they're always welcome. I'd ask what brings you to town, but the thing I've learned doing this is, the less questions the better, am I right?"

"You are right. But I'm struggling today and I'm glad the timing worked out."

"How long you got?"

"A few days out from a year."

"Little over eight myself," he says. "Good on ya, that first year is a big one. Now let's go get you a day closer."

He gestures me toward a circle of chairs, in the center of which is a small table holding the same kind of sound-dampening device Kenji uses to keep our meetings private. As I take a seat, another man enters. He looks like a boxer—cauliflower ears, bald head, thick in the shoulders but still light on his feet. He gives me a hard stare and then glances over at Ray, who nods.

"All right," the man says in a soft and lyrical Irish accent that belies his demeanor, "new faces today then that we've got?"

A woman enters next. She's tall, lithe, her black hair in a short pixie cut. Japanese, I think? If so, probably not Yakuza because that's a boys' club, so maybe she's a freelancer. She gives me a brief nod as she whisks herself into a seat and folds her hands in her lap.

There are eight chairs set up but when the third man enters, Ray says, "That's everyone. We'll get started in a moment, so grab yourself a cuppa."

The temperature of my skin rises, like a spotlight has swung onto me.

The man who entered, his black hair is going gray, his nose is sharp, his eyes hard as coal. There's a scar on his chin, peeking out through a few days of stubble. He has the lean body of an Olympic swimmer. His name is Jean Lavigne. He's a French assassin, code name Noire, which may lack the panache of Pale Horse, but it is very French, so there's that.

Our paths have crossed.

Six years ago, a group of Algerian Islamic militants set off a bomb filled with nails and gunpowder in a train station in Lyon. Four killed, dozens wounded. Lavigne was sent to kill Zain Hassan, the group's leader. Problem was, Hassan had information vital to America's national security, so I was sent to stop Lavigne.

It wasn't a job I felt good about. The math was sloppy. Lavigne was a professional and he was doing his job. Hassan was a piece of shit; two kids were disfigured in the bombing. But according to my calculation, taking him alive would save more lives down the road, so it had to be done.

Which is why I didn't kill Lavigne, I just slowed him down. He was closing in on Hassan in Qatar, so while he was en route to Hassan's last-known location, I took off his ear from five hundred feet with a scope. That gave the Agency team enough time to go in and scoop up their target.

Lavigne looks me up and down before sitting across from me. He knew it was the Pale Horse who did it, and I know he was looking for revenge. He put feelers out, trying to find me. He got close once, too, in Morocco. But he never saw my face. I try not to stare at the knob of pink, mottled skin where his left ear should be.

"All right, everyone," Ray says, taking his seat with a steaming paper cup of tea. "As you can all see, we got ourselves a new one today. All the way from the U.S. of A. Why don't you introduce yourself to the group, friend?"

"Hi, I'm Mark," I say, trying not to pay too much attention to Lavigne so as not to tip him off, "and I'm a killer."

The group claps for me.

"Hello, Mark," Ray says.

The meeting starts. The Irish boxer, Liam, reads the literature. Once we get through everything, Ray asks if anyone wants to share, and he seems to gesture to me, out of deference to me being a guest, but Lavigne raises his hand.

"I'm Jean, and I am a killer," he says in a sloping, breathy French accent. "I haven't killed anyone in three years. I am having a very difficult day today." He pauses and stares down at his hands folded in his lap.

This is the exact opposite of what I came here for.

He continues: "I was in the supermarket yesterday. There was a little boy . . ." He takes a deep breath. "I heard him say to his mother, 'Mommy, what happened to that man? Is he a monster?'" He tilts his head down like he can hide his ear. "I don't blame the child. There are still days I want to find the man who did this and show it to him. I have worked very hard to leave that life behind. We carry things in here." He touches his chest. "But it is the outward reminder, the thing I see in the mirror every day, that I struggle with. It says to me: 'You can never change. You will never be whole.'"

He bends forward, the processing of this emotion making him smaller.

I realize he should be on my amends list, and he isn't.

Which makes me wonder how many people I left off.

How many more people I hurt.

Will the process ever end? Or will I spend every waking moment until the day I die trying to make good on things I can never truly make good for?

"I apologize," Lavigne says to me. "As a guest, I should have let you go first, but I just needed to get that out. You understand?"

I nod slowly, not really sure how to tackle this one. Part of me wants to say: *It was me. I'm the one who took your ear.* If he tries to attack me, presumably the other people in the room will stop him. Maybe this is the safest place to do it, where we can talk it out with witnesses.

I want to do that. Except for the burning feeling in my chest. The reminder of the ways that I've left hurt in this world. This man just wants to be better and I make it harder for him every day.

"All good, buddy," I tell him, as I take the six-month chip out of my pocket and turn it over in my hand. "Not sure how you do it over here, but my home group does a chip for one month, six months, and one year." I hold up the six-month chip. "I'm having a hard day, too. I'm a few days out from replacing this one, and it felt like such a big milestone. Now some things from my past have come back to haunt me. And I just feel it all coming back. The way I used to be. The worst part is, I kind of like it. I miss that feeling. Killing people makes life a lot easier, you know? Then the problem goes away. And maybe that's why recovery is so hard. We never learned how to sit with the things we did. We just put them in the ground and moved on. We never had to have the hard conversations . . ."

The rest of them are nodding along. I don't know if there's a time limit here—Ray didn't say anything, but again, there usually isn't—so I keep going.

"I made my first amends . . . a day ago?" I gesture to my face, and the cuts and bruises left by Billy. "It was weird. He beat the shit out of me, but he also seemed to forgive me. It was a little complicated. Point is, I thought it was going to make me better. Encourage me to stay the course and keep going with this. Instead there's a part of me that just wishes I had killed him on the spot, so he can't come back and cause trouble for me."

More nods.

"It's hard to let people live," I say. "It's hard to live."

I glance up at Lavigne, who holds my gaze.

I did it.

It was me.

I'm sorry.

Just say it.

"I understand the feeling, my friend," he says.

That word, the way it comes out of his mouth, it scorches my exposed skin.

Friend.

I tumble into a dark hole of self-hatred, interrupted by the Japanese woman, who raises her hand.

"Hina," Ray says, gesturing to her.

"The Pale Horse, no?" she asks.

My heart slams to a stop in my chest and I look up at her, but she's looking at Lavigne.

"Yes," Lavigne says. "He was the one who did this."

"I'm afraid to say this, but I think I have to, in the interest of being honest with myself." She looks down and closes her eyes. "He's the one person I would throw this all away for. I would kill him if I had the chance. Without a second thought."

"That's a tough thing to confront," Ray says. "Thank you for sharing that."

What? I don't even recognize her.

Ray clasps his hands in front of him. "Harboring hatred for the Pale Horse is like drinking poison and hoping it kills him. It doesn't do any of us any good. We have to remember he's sick and suffering. What you have to focus on is what you're doing today."

As he says this, he glances at me, thinking maybe this is helping.

It is not.

The rest of the meeting passes in a thick mist and ends with the serenity prayer, even though I'm not feeling very serene. When it's over I head for the food table to grab a scone on the way out. I don't want to bolt—that would look suspicious—but I don't want to linger, either. Anyway, I need to find Astrid. I need to check for word from Kenji, and . . .

"Mark."

I turn to find Lavigne with his hand proffered to me. I can't tell anything about the look on his face, his demeanor, because all I can see is that nub on the side of his skull. I reach for his hand and we shake. "It is good that you came," he says. "We need each other on days like this, no?"

"We do," I say, holding my scone, wanting to run, wanting to tell him who I am, and why I did what I did. I was following orders, which is all any of us are doing, but the truth is, that wasn't an excuse. I made my decision. And after I sighted him in my scope and pulled the trigger, when I saw his head jerk, as he looked around frantically before diving for cover, I was a little disappointed that I didn't put the bullet into his cerebellum.

The Agency had said to stop him, so killing him was on the table. In a moment of professional solidarity, I figured it best to wing him, but later I felt like it was a sign I'd gone soft.

"I do not know how long you're in town for, but would you be interested in grabbing a drink?" His eyes duck away from mine a little before meeting them again. "No shop talk, if you don't want. We don't have to talk recovery, either."

Jesus.

He's hitting on me.

This just keeps getting worse.

He's a handsome man. And that accent. My taste for men is a little narrower than it is for women, but he's definitely in my wheelhouse. As I'm playing it out in my head, he senses my hesitation. "Sorry, what is it they call this? Thirteenth stepping?"

Old-timers hooking up with people who have less time in recovery. It's generally frowned upon, but it happens. If not for the insanely complicated psychosexual component of this, I might have considered it. It would certainly take my mind off everything that's going on.

But then I can never make amends to him.

After he bared his soul, and I just sat and listened and didn't say anything.

"I'm sorry," I tell him. "I would. But I'm meeting a friend and things are a little complicated for me right now."

He puts his hands up and takes a step back, showing me some deference. "Of course. Perhaps if you stay in town a little longer and things settle down . . ."

"I'm sorry about your ear."

Lavigne draws himself to full height, puffing his chest out a little. "Thank you. But you do not owe me an apology."

"Yeah, well . . ." I start, and then I see the hundred ways this can go wrong. "Just, sorry, is all."

He shrugs. "It woke me up. It helped get me to this room, and . . ."

"Holy shit."

We both look across the room to Hina, standing with her

phone in her hand, staring at the two of us. If not for the intervention of a few tendons and some muscle, her jaw would be on the floor. "I just got a text . . . there was a video posted on the Via Maris . . ."

No.

She raises a finger at me. "It's him. The Pale Horse."

Lavigne turns to me, his eyes raging, and he says, "You . . ."

The second his shoulder twitches I have my arm up to block the swing. My lizard brain is calculating the angles—slip right, hook to the ribs, uppercut to the jaw—but I push down the instinct and shell up, going straight to defense. I don't want to hit back. Part of me wonders if I should drop my hands and let him take his shots. So I let him hit me, absorbing the blows and hoping it brings him some modicum of peace.

He lands a few but suddenly they stop, and Ray is holding him in a bear hug. Lavigne is half of Ray's size, and Ray is still struggling to hold him in place. Liam, meanwhile, is standing in front of Hina, his hands up, saying, "Not for him. He's not worth it." She's trying to duck around him and he's moving to block her path and I don't know how long that's going to last.

"You bastard," Lavigne says, trying to break free from Ray's grasp. "You just sat there with a straight face?" He spits in my direction.

"You better go," Ray says to me. "Now."

I don't wait to argue or make my case. As I reach the door I hear Ray call out, "And don't come back, ay? This particular group maybe isn't for you."

Turns out, Billy's office had a camera in it, and I guess he saw an opportunity to build some cred. So he posted a clip of him whaling on me, with the message: **Getting revenge on the PALE HORSE for killing my dad. I let him live—and I doubt he'll be coming back.**

Which raises a few issues. First, the video very clearly shows my face, which will mobilize a whole lot of people who want to kill me. Worse is the chatter on the discussion boards. Some people assume it's not true; no way would the Pale Horse take a beating from some kid and let him live.

But if he did, they say, he must not be as tough as the stories said.

I knew there'd be a price for that boat ride. Didn't know it'd be this.

Astrid asks: *"Grosse Pointe Blank?"*

"Huh?"

"What about *Grosse Pointe Blank*?"

"Oh." Snapped out of my funk, I toss my second emptied Americano into a bin. "Never saw that one."

"Really? It's a classic."

She knows about the video. I made it clear it wasn't a topic for discussion. If this is her way of taking my mind off it, fine. "I don't buy John Cusack as a hitman," I tell her.

She nods slowly, thinking. "Okay . . . *Collateral*."

"That the one with Tom Cruise?"

Astrid nods.

"I buy Tom Cruise as a killer, definitely. But kidnapping a

cabdriver and icing him at the end of the night? Needlessly cruel. Cabdriver's not in the game."

"How about *The Professional*?"

"That's a good one. Jean Reno is great. But it has to be the international cut, not the American one. American one lost twenty-four minutes of footage."

"Because of all the creepy Natalie Portman stuff?"

"Yep, but it's the best depiction I've seen of the assassin's life." The thing I don't want to say is that what resonated most with me was Reno's quiet sadness and loneliness.

"*In Bruges*?" she asks.

"Really funny. Brendan Gleeson, man. I'll watch him in anything."

"*Mr. and Mrs. Smith*?"

"Saw it. Don't remember anything about it."

"And we've established you don't like the John Wick movies?"

"I didn't say I didn't like them. I said they were fantasy. Keanu Reeves is a national treasure. But people stabbing each other in Grand Central during rush hour and no one notices? C'mon."

"Do you have a favorite?"

"I like Joubert. The assassin in *Three Days of the Condor*. He was a pro."

"Okay, but that's a thriller. I mean a favorite hitman movie."

"*Le Samouraï*."

She nods, takes a long sip of her tea. "Never seen it."

"French film from the sixties. Very cool. I wouldn't say no to Alain Delon, either."

"Thought you didn't like action movies."

"I didn't say I didn't like them. I just said I don't prefer them."

"Okay," Astrid says, as a smile stretches across her face. "Favorite movie of all time."

I know the answer, but it's not an answer I want to give, so I offer a worthy runner-up. *"Willy Wonka and the Chocolate Factory."* Then, tired of this line of questioning, I nod up at the building in front of us, reaching into the overcast sky like an obelisk. "You sure about this?"

"He works here, and he's inside," she says. "He's not, like, the top guy. But he's near enough to the top."

The building contains the headquarters to a bank. Apparently our man works for said bank. Apparently he's an introvert who doesn't spend a ton of time socializing outside home or work, and he lives nearby, so the plan is simple: wait for him to come out, follow him home, then pop in to see what we can brace him for. Our flight to New York doesn't leave until late tonight, so it seems like a decent enough lead to chase down.

It's just after five, so I have to figure he's leaving soon. Still, I'm antsy and I have to piss. Astrid is bundled up in her little bubble jacket next to me and all I want in this world is to show her the maelstrom swirling in my chest. Maybe if someone else witnessed it, it'd lessen the intensity. But I can't. Can't tell her what I'm feeling because the second I do that, I'm admitting to the things I used to be, and the things I no longer am.

She hasn't asked me about my errand and I haven't asked her how she found this guy. I don't really need to know the origin of it, I just need it to work. I don't even know what this guy can do for us, but it's better than plan B, which is to go home and pour a glass of whiskey and cry into it while I pray for all the people who want me dead to get distracted and move on to something else.

Which is unlikely to happen.

We're surrounded by people, and even though nobody knows who I am, I feel like there are eyes on me. Any one of these faces could be a person prepared to shove something sharp between my ribs.

Astrid, meanwhile, is slurping down a cup of tea and grinning. This is a blast to her. If she only knew. I think she's falling into the thrill and romanticism, thinking this is a game. It's not. It's a terrible stupid thing and I hate this and I hate myself and I hate everything.

I glance into the bookstore behind me and figure if I can't find a little serenity, at the very least I can find a bathroom. But also, me and Kenji did agree to exchange gifts. A book would fit well within the spending limit. It's something to do. Replacing the bad memory with a good one. Maybe this can count as a little recovery.

I tell Astrid, "Bang on the window if you see him?"

She nods at me without taking her eyes off the entrance. "*Raiders of the Lost Ark.*"

"What about it?" I ask.

"My favorite movie of all time," she says. "Not that you asked."

"My apologies. That's a good one." She mutters something under her breath, but it's lost as I duck inside, the warmth of the bookstore and the smell of the paper enveloping me. The girl behind the register is drowning in a fuzzy beige sweater and maroon wool cap. She has a barbell nose ring and heavy black gauges in her ears. She smiles at me when I enter, then goes back to the book she's reading.

After hitting the bathroom, I roam the aisles, thinking: What do you get someone who used to murder people for a living?

If we were still assassins, it'd be easy. A knife is always nice. If he had a favorite rifle, I could get him a new scope—one of those really nice ones, with a ranging reticle that allows for bullet-drop compensation. But his go-to weapon was a katana. Maybe there are katana accessories? Like a nice cloth to clean it with? Then there's dark clothing, always a plus in this profession. And snacks. You spend so much time waiting for people to show up that a stash of protein bars or some trail mix really takes the edge off.

Except, that's the old programming.

Who is Kenji today?

He drinks tea. When we get dinner, he tends to go with the vegetarian option. We once had a very long discussion about Akira Kurosawa's filmography. His favorite is *Yojimbo*, mine is *The Hidden Fortress*. I think we both appreciated that neither of us said *Seven Samurai* or *Rashomon*. One time I met him in the park and he was reading an Agatha Christie novel.

I poke at the book spines as I pass them. Agatha Christie seems like too safe a bet; what if I get him one and he's read it? I could get him something in Japanese, or by a Japanese author. I want to find someone that he's never read. Someone new and surprising. Of course, it doesn't help that I spent more of my life killing than reading.

Damn it. Stop thinking like that.

This feels like an exercise in futility, until I stumble across a long row of Dostoyevsky novels. A little bell rings in my head. Something familiar. I pull *Crime and Punishment* off the shelf. A nice modern hardcover edition.

This is a book I read, a long time ago. It's about a man who decided that he was a superior person and that meant it was okay for him to murder his landlord? I think that was the gist. But I'm pretty sure the message was that killing is bad. That could work. I don't want to get him something where killing is an okay thing. I did take up reading a little after I went sober, just to do something with my time, and found that too many modern thrillers wrote off murder as an acceptable means to an end, with no thought to the real-life impact.

Doesn't matter how "bad" a person is—likely there was someone somewhere in this world who loved them, and that person has to live with a whole lot of pain in the aftermath. That's why I moved away from action movies, too. I found myself mourning all the henchmen getting mowed down in the background.

I take the book over to the counter and go fishing for my wallet.

"Oh, that's a good one," the girl says. "Loved it."

"This is a weird question, but the main character doesn't get away with it, right?"

She squints a little. "No, he ends up in prison. Sorry if that's a spoiler."

"The book was written a hundred and something years ago, I think we're past the point of it being a spoiler," I tell her. "Just wanted to make sure the guy gets what he deserves."

"Well, that's the question now, isn't it?"

I rack my brain for a witty rejoinder. Nothing comes to me.

"Don't worry, there is both crime *and* punishment." She smiles as she puts the book in a plastic bag. As she's handing it to me, there's a pounding on the front glass. Astrid is waving her arms, beckoning for me to come outside.

The second I'm through the door she takes off, not even waiting to see if I'm behind her. We cut through the crowd, but there are so many people on the street I'm not even sure who we're after. Two blocks later we're hustling down the stairs of the Leicester Square Tube station, and then running through the turnstiles, down the escalator, and onto a waiting car, where the doors are just about to close.

It's packed shoulder to shoulder. I find a place that I can grab a handrail and Astrid leans into me and whispers: "Gold jacket."

There we go. He's not easy to miss. A stocky Black man with close-cropped hair, a gold bubble jacket, black jeans, and gold sneakers. He has a heavy set of expensive noise-canceling headphones strapped over his head, bopping in time to music.

His name, Astrid said, is Gaius.

No one knows who runs the Via Maris. It's a small operation. Probably only a handful of people, which is how they do it without being caught. The site looks like it was designed and set up twenty years ago, but something like that doesn't need flash. It just needs to work.

The person at the top is someone who goes by the handle Hannibal Khan. Whether that's a mash-up of the serial killer and the *Star Trek* villain, or the conquerors, I don't know. It's a pretty cool name, though. Better than GJoubert.

It's amazing Khan has evaded capture for so long. The Silk Road, the original darknet marketplace, went bust after two years. Ross Ulbricht, who went by the name Dread Pirate Roberts, got nabbed by the feds, but not before making hundreds of millions of dollars. Had he not gotten caught, he was on track to make billions.

Hannibal Khan, meanwhile, seems to be a bit more clever. The Via Maris has been around for twelve years now, and I'm sure law enforcement is all over it, but so far, it's still up and running.

And Gaius, according to Astrid's source, is the man who runs the tech end of things.

We nearly miss it when his stop comes up, because he nearly misses it. He's lost in his phone and bolts off at Earl's Court at the last second, and Astrid and I muscle through the crowd just in time. He's still oblivious to our presence, and it's not like we're keeping too far back, so he's definitely not a pro. That'll make this whole thing a lot easier.

We follow him up the escalator and down two streets, where he stops for some Indian takeout, and then finally to his apartment complex. It's a newer building, fancy, all sharp angles and floor-to-ceiling windows, which means it probably has decent cameras, so even though Astrid follows right after, I grab her arm and hold her back.

"C'mon," she says. "He won't even notice us slipping in."

I point at the doorway, and even from across the street, the black dome-shaped camera is visible above the doorway. "Hold on," I tell her.

We stand and wait and watch, and I hope for a little luck—which comes when a light goes on in a window at the end of the fourth floor. Now we just have to get inside without ending up on video. No sense in leaving a trail of bread crumbs for the Agency or the Russian or whoever to find.

We passed a hardware store on the walk over. I lead Astrid in that direction and duck inside to buy a can of spray paint.

Hardware stores, a hitman's best friend.

We head back toward the building, and as I step into the vestibule, I pull the scarf up over my mouth and shoot a little blast of paint onto the lens. Because the dome is black, the paint isn't apparent unless you look close. Then I buzz an apartment on the second floor.

An angry voice comes back, "What?"

"Delivery for 5B. Just trying to leave it in the hall."

The door buzzes. We take the stairs to the fourth floor and head toward the end. There's only one apartment it could be, and no cameras on the way. We get to the door and knock, and after a moment, a soft voice comes from behind it. "Yes?"

"Delivery," I say, putting on my best faux-British accent, which I'm sure sounds terrible.

There's a pause, and a shuffling behind the door. Probably Gaius looking through the peephole, but I've positioned myself so he can only see a small portion of my body, and Astrid is standing against the wall.

"Leave it, please."

I pull the felt marker out of my pocket. "Gotta sign, mate."

Astrid rolls her eyes at me. I shrug at her. The thing I want to tell her is: *I used to be pretty good at this, so let's leave the judgment outside.*

There's a heavy sigh from behind the door and a chain unlocks. As soon as the door opens, I push my way in. Gaius is wearing a heavy robe, flannel pants, and a look on his face somewhere in the valley between surprise and terror. I grab his shoulder and press the felt marker into his ribs. Not too hard but it works its magic, knocking him off balance as he arches his body away from it, enough that I can move him against the wall. I tell Astrid, "Make sure we're alone."

I'm assuming we are, but she disappears down the hall to sweep the apartment. Gaius is surprisingly calm; I think he figures if he plays along he'll be okay. "Listen, man, I have money. Cold cash, under the mattress. Take what you want and go and we're all square, right?"

"Just be a good listener and everyone walks away healthy."

He nods and puts his hands up. Astrid appears at the end of the hallway and throws me a thumbs-up. I lead Gaius to the living room. It's cramped but tidy; a massive TV on the wall, every video game system I can name plus a few I can't, an expensive velvet couch. The glass coffee table has the takeout he just picked up, as well as his expensive headphones and a closed laptop. The TV is paused, Chewbacca frozen mid-scream.

I push Gaius toward the couch and he sits. "You ain't cops," he says, "but I'm not sure if that's much of a relief."

"We're not going to hurt you unless you give us a reason to," I say. I move into the kitchen—also clean and sparse, like it's never been used, besides a massive pile of rinsed and neatly stacked takeout containers next to the sink. I grab a chair from the small table and drag it into the living room, then place it on the other side of the coffee table. Astrid is standing by the hallway, unsure of what to do with herself.

Now that we're settled and Gaius gets a good look at me, his eyes go wide and he moves back into the couch. "Shit. You're him."

"You saw the video?"

"'Course I saw the video. Everyone's seen the video, bruv. Site's got more traffic than it's ever gotten." He puts his hands up in a peaceful gesture. "Look, just, before you do it, let me call my mum, okay? I won't tip her off, I just haven't spoken to her in a while, and it's weighing real heavy on me in this particular moment, that I ought to at least tell her I love her one more time—"

"Stop it," I tell him. "I'm not here to hurt you."

He squints, confused. "Then what are you here for?"

"Can you take the video down?"

He shrugs. "Maybe. Won't be a point in it, though."

"Why the hell not?"

He gives me a look like I just asked him why the sky is blue. "It's been shared and screenshotted from here to kingdom come. Toothpaste doesn't go back in the tube. Not even for you."

"Okay, then. What can you tell me about *me*? Who's been talking about me? Who's been looking for information on me? Someone's after me and that's where he must have researched me, on the Via Maris. There's got to be some trace of that."

"I don't dip into the site that much. I just run it."

"Would Hannibal Khan know anything?"

"Maybe. No idea. You know how the site works?"

"Sort of, but I see you want to explain it, so go ahead and explain it."

Gaius smiles a little. Even when it puts them at risk, people like to brag. Especially when they don't often get the opportunity.

"Okay, so, it's darknet," he says. "Not cataloged on any search engines. Only one way in: with a direct address, through D@nt3, which is sort of like Tor, but better. With Tor you enter the internet in one place, then your signal bounces between about seven thousand relays around the world, right? Makes it impossible to trace. We use about a half million relays, randomized every time. So, impossibler."

"I don't understand what any of that means, starting with 'impossibler,'" I tell him, figuring the more I can get him to talk, the quicker we get to something useful. "But how secure can it really be? The guy who ran the Silk Road got caught."

"Yeah, he did, and you know why? Some old message board posts with his email, and he had counterfeit documents sent to his house. Even after all that, the fuzz had to set up some elaborate sting to catch him physically logging into his computer to really prove it was him. We've been at this long enough I'd say we know what we're doing."

"Yet here I am, sitting in your living room," I tell him.

He exhales hard. "Yeah, kinda curious about that, bruv."

"Where is Hannibal Khan?"

"Never met the man myself. All I do is provide tech and support."

I pick his cell phone off the table and slap it down in front of him. "Call him."

"You think Khan is just someone you call on the phone? We message through an encrypted app. I never even met him."

"How does he pay you?"

"Same way you pay for everything on the Via Maris. Crypto. Which also can't be traced. You think this is some schoolyard bake sale we're running here?"

This is proving to be unfruitful. There's got to be more he's not telling me. I'm wondering what angle to take next, when he gives a little laugh.

"What?" I ask.

"I mean, I don't participate, but I know who you are. Always figured you'd be more of a Jason Statham type . . ."

Astrid giggles behind me.

"You have to remember something," I tell him, scooting forward a little on the chair, and the springs in the sofa squeak as he leans away from me. "I've had a bad day, on top of a bad week. This conversation we're having right here"—I gesture back and forth between us—"so far it's been polite, correct?"

He nods.

"Don't make it not polite," the Pale Horse says.

His breath gets stuck in his chest. Then he leans down and opens his laptop. "Okay, look, okay. So, I'm not supposed to say this, but, it's starting to sink in, the gravity of this, right? What I tell you now can't leave this room . . ." He taps at the computer and makes a face. "Actually, first, something weird here. I monitor broadcast signals around the building. Personal security measure. You know, make sure I'm not being surveilled. And I'm catching a weird GPS signal in here right now. Like, right here, in this room. One of you is carrying something that's broadcasting."

I look at Astrid and she shrugs. "We got new phones."

"Not phones," Gaius says.

"What if that's not how the Russian was tracking us?" I ask.

"We'd notice if he tagged us with something," she says.

"GPS devices are getting smaller," Gaius says. "Seen some as big as a five pence, and that's for the civilian market. We get into military application, could be even smaller."

I get up and check the bathroom. No electronics, it's within view of the living room, and the window is too small to wriggle out of. I come back and tell Gaius, "Go in there, close the door. Wait for us. Leave your phone."

Gaius puts his hands up and stands, happy to leave the room. As soon as I hear the door close and lock I run my fingers through my hair, then pull my shirt off.

"What are you doing?" Astrid asks.

"Making sure he didn't stick something on me," I say. "Seems far-fetched but at this point we can't be too careful. Can't be in my clothes. I dumped everything I was wearing that night."

She nods and pulls her shirt off, too.

"What are you doing?" I ask.

"Making sure he didn't get me," she says. "This guy is good, right? He was able to find me. Maybe he passed me and I didn't notice."

The two of us face away from each other and continue to

strip. I check my skin the best I can, but eventually realize there are spots I can't be sure of.

"Think we need to be a little more thorough here," I say. "Like you said, we're both adults, right?"

"This is turning into a tick check, isn't it?"

I turn and she's already naked. I try not to notice the subtle and gentle curves of her body, the way her hip is cocked out a little. She glances down at my crotch and then looks up fast, pretending she didn't.

"Well," she says, "let's get down to some very awkward work."

The two of us comb over the intimate areas of each other's bodies, looking for anything that might be attached to our skin. As she's checking my groin region I practice my breathing, careful not to get too excited. I do, a little, and she pauses, but she doesn't say anything. This is the first time I've been naked in front of a woman since Sara, and just by acknowledging that, my heart develops a dry crack across the surface.

When we're done we both pick our clothes from the floor.

"Nothing," I say.

As I'm pulling my shirt on she focuses on the bandage covering the knife wound on my stomach.

I look down and wonder if I pulled a stitch. I keep forgetting about it; the pain has subsided to the point where I barely notice it unless I move the wrong way, or I cough. But the bandage is clean, and . . .

"Oh shit," she says.

It hits me, and my blood turns to ice. "You stuck your finger in there . . ."

"If it was small I could have missed it," she says. "I told you it wasn't foolproof. How is that even possible?"

He stabbed me. Stuck it in, pulled it out, didn't even offer to buy me dinner first. How the hell could it leave a GPS device behind?

Then it hits me.

"A WASP knife," I tell her.

"A what knife?"

"WASP. It's nasty, made for hunting. It injects a bubble of carbon dioxide into the body cavity. It freezes and explodes. Maybe this was a modified version, just made to deposit something." The thought of an electronic device inside my stomach makes me a little nauseated. "What are the options, besides exploratory surgery in this guy's bathtub?"

Astrid shrugs. "Exploratory surgery in this guy's bathtub."

We throw our clothes back on and call to Gaius, who comes out of the bathroom. Astrid tells him, "I need a sharp knife, alcohol, some boiling water, as many towels as you have. Do you have any prescription painkillers?"

"Woah woah woah," Gaius says. "What did I miss?"

I pull up my shirt to show off the bandage. "The guy stabbed me. I think the tracker might be in here. Which means this guy might be coming here. As much as I don't want to do this, we need to get this out of me as quickly as possible."

"All right, hold on, you absolute lunatics," he says. "Give me a minute."

He disappears into the bedroom and we hear drawers opening and muttering, and finally he comes back with a small black device that looks like a walkie-talkie, with a thick black antenna on the top. He plugs it into his computer.

"Signal jammer," he says. "It'll block the signal as long as it's within twenty feet of you. But it's going to interfere with your cell phone, too. You can turn it off to make calls, but I suggest you don't. Soon as you do, this guy will have your location."

I move to the window and peek outside, scanning the street. It's decently crowded with pedestrians and I figure, maybe I'm overthinking this.

Then I see him.

The Russian is standing across the street. He's wearing a green military jacket and smoking a cigarette, leaning against a lamppost like he's waiting for a bus.

"Mark?" Astrid asks.

"How precise is this thing, Gaius?"

"Not to the spot. Probably a hundred-foot radius."

He must know we're in the area and we've stopped moving. So he's waiting for us to show ourselves, or he's just hanging back to keep an eye on us. I move away from the curtain before he can look up. "And how long is this going to take?"

Gaius hits a few keys. "Done."

I peek around the curtain, careful to keep myself mostly obscured. The Russian finishes his cigarette and takes something out of his pocket that looks like a phone. He stares at it for a moment, then looks up, scanning the block, confused.

"What's wrong?" Astrid asks.

I duck away from the window. "Seems timing was on our side. He's across the street. But it looks like the jammer worked."

She steps toward the window, but I grab her elbow. "Don't look."

"Right, sorry."

Gaius glances up from his screen. "Even with the signal dropped, he'll know you're somewhere in the vicinity. You can go to the roof, climb across the buildings, exit on the other side of the street. Probably the safest way."

I sit down on the couch next to him and put my head back on the cushion. "Yeah."

"I'm sorry, bruv, I'm not gonna lie, this is pretty cool, though."

"I'm happy you're impressed. Meanwhile I'm probably going to end up with some kind of rare metal poisoning. Back to what you're saying about the site?"

"Right, right." He shakes his head and sighs. "So, there's this thing called god mode, where I can access pretty much anything as long as it's on the site itself. Can't really look up where posts came from, but I can see if people are trading private messages."

"How does that help?" I ask.

He shrugs. "Give me some users to look up and we'll see."

I whip out my phone and pull up D@nt3 and go through the forums. Astrid does the same. Gaius, presumably, does as well. We all get lost for a little bit, looking for something that might be useful.

There's an entire forum now dedicated to talking about the Pale Horse, so I start there. Lots of people saying a lot of things. That they're coming after me. That I must be off my game to slip like that. A lot of talk about revenge. Some folks who want to meet me. A woman who wants to sleep with me. Nothing useful. Nothing encouraging.

Nothing that makes me feel very good about myself.

The whole time we're doing this, it feels like there's a sword dangling over our heads. I still want to go out there and confront the Russian. Except I've taken a few beatings in the last couple of days and I have a gaping wound in my stomach that Astrid has already had to repatch once. I'm not on the top of my game. And I'm still in the dark about exactly what's going on.

There's something else. This feeling I never really felt before. So brand new it took me time to feel out the edges and find a definition for it.

I'm afraid.

Because I don't know how to beat this guy without killing him.

"Hey, I found something," Astrid says.

She passes over her phone. It's a post from someone with a randomly generated username, a string of letters and numbers, that says:

The Pale Horse was not nearly as tough as I thought. I left him bleeding on the floor. Just a scared little kitten. Wait until you hear where I found him . . .

Kotenok. Kitten. That's what the Russian called me. At least he's keeping the recovery angle to himself for now. Once word gets out on that, I'm dead for sure. I have to figure he assumed I would see this.

Mind games. He's playing mind games. Maybe he doesn't even want the notebook. Maybe he just took it to screw with me.

"How'd you find that so quick?" I ask.

"There's a search function," Astrid says.

"'Course there's a search function," Gaius says, a little insulted.

"Okay, guys, cool. Thanks. Gaius, who posted that?"

He looks at the phone, then turns to his computer. "That's the user's only post. Give me a minute . . ." He taps a little more, watches the screen, then says, "The account is new, created a month ago. But there is some activity. Messages traded with another user recently, too."

"Doesn't seem very ethical that you can track private messages," Astrid says.

Gaius offers a long stare and a little laugh. "This *is* a criminal enterprise." He pokes at the keyboard and says, "I can't read the messages. But I can see that they were delivered, and to whom. He's been swapping love notes with a user named Sanjuro. Want me to see what I can find on him?"

The room spins. I lean forward and put my head in my hands. The two of them, Astrid and Gaius, fall silent. I'm searching for something to say, anything to say.

"Should I . . ." Gaius starts.

"No," I tell him. "I know who that is."

Sanjuro was the name adopted by the ronin—the masterless samurai—in *Yojimbo*.

Kenji's favorite Kurosawa film.

Which is why he chose it as his username.

8

Your worst sin is that you have destroyed and betrayed yourself for nothing.
—Fyodor Dostoyevsky, *Crime and Punishment*

Midtown Manhattan
Two Years Ago

It's three minutes past eight. She should have been out here by now. I check my phone and, finding nothing, return to watching the glass doors of the building. The security guard at the desk hasn't looked up from his phone in the eleven minutes I've been standing here, which means he hasn't noticed me. Which means he sucks at his job.

People stream past on the busy Midtown sidewalk. I pull my scarf over my face a little because it cuts against the bite of the wind, but also it makes me feel a little more secure when people can't see my face.

I'm hungry. Should have eaten something earlier. Always a mistake, not eating beforehand.

My phone buzzes.

So sorry. Meeting ran over. Headed down now.

I respond back: No problem.

I scroll up through the previous texts from Sara.

Me: What are you in the mood for?

Sara: There's a holiday thing over at Bryant Park. How about some hot cocoa?

Sara: Maybe some ice-skating?

Me: I don't know how to ice-skate.

Sara: There's a trick to it. I'll show you.

Me: Oh yeah? What's the trick?

Sara: You'll have to wait and see. I have a meeting until 8. Ok to meet after?

Me: Perfect.

Since I'm already in my phone I click over to the dating app where we connected. The first picture that comes up is her sitting in her office, presumably upstairs. She's wearing a blue and pink and gray flannel shirt. Her auburn hair curled and tousled, she's flashing a brilliant, nearly blinding smile.

Her likes include science fiction, spirituality, and eating out, as well as power exchange, group play, and ethical non-monogamy. Which is why I love this app. It's geared more toward kink and hookups than it is long-term dating, which means the important cards are on the table as soon as you sit down. When we matched and started chatting, two things were clear from the jump.

First is, neither of us was looking for anything serious, and that suited me just fine. We both wanted a regular friend-with-benefits type of situation, where we could get together and do some weird shit, but also maybe catch the occasional movie or go to a museum. When I shook Ravi's hand on that pier in Singapore I accepted that a nuclear family and white picket fence wasn't in my future. Which is fine; you can't be wistful for a thing you never had. But after years of one-night stands and escorts, I'm yearning for something a bit more.

Not for someone to know me, but maybe someone I can know a bit.

The second thing, which came across even in our messaging, was that talking to her was like touching the tip of a live wire. We spoke with the comfort of old friends, slipping into a rapport that felt fast and sexy and even a little sweet.

This is still a risk. I don't mind taking risk onto myself; that's my job. It's the risk I could be exposing her to. But I cling to the hope that I could protect her from anything. There aren't that many people on this planet dumb enough to mess with me.

"Mark?"

Sara is outlined against the light pouring out of the building's lobby, giving her a warm, golden aura. She's wearing a blue knit hat and a dark overcoat with a fuzzy black collar that swaddles her neck. The wind seems to stop the moment we lock eyes, causing the ambient temperature to come up a few degrees. All that rush of Midtown traffic and pedestrians suddenly goes silent.

"That's me," I say, trying to sound suave.

She smiles and tilts her head, and the way she looks at me is like she recognizes something. Then her eyes dart down to my crotch and she raises an eyebrow. "Your fly is down."

I spin around and zip it up in one motion, then turn back to her. "Not the kind of first impression I was hoping to make."

"It's okay," she says, stepping toward me, and I smell lavender. "How about that hot cocoa?"

We've only just met—some texting and one video chat—but she turns in the direction of the park and hooks her arm into mine. It feels adorably old-fashioned. There's a magnetism drawing me toward her. It would be unsettling if it weren't so soothing.

The branches of the trees surrounding the park reach into the sky like skeletal hands, cradling a heavy full moon in the indigo sky. We wend our way through the tables, the space lit by twinkle lights, the ground wet from melted snow and crunchy with salt, and head for the truck offering hot cocoa. It costs ten dollars a cup and takes five minutes to make. The line would move faster if fewer people were taking selfies at the front.

"New York exists in a quantum state," I tell Sara.

"Oh yeah?" she asks.

I nod toward a young couple throwing up peace signs for selfies with their cups of cocoa, blocking the next group of people from placing their order. "Simultaneously the best and worst city in the entire world."

She looks at the lights strung around the park, cranes her neck to watch the ice-skating rink, then turns to the tables filled with people talking and laughing.

"I don't know," she says with a smile. "I think it's pretty great."

Well, then. The way she punctured and deflated my cynicism makes me feel sheepish. But I don't mind it, either.

And that smile. I struggle with how to approach describing that smile.

Like she has it figured out, all of it, and she's patiently waiting for me to join her so she can celebrate my success.

We wait in a little pocket of silence, the line slowly inching forward, when she asks, "So what do you do, Mark? You never said."

"Data analyst," I tell her, which is my go-to. There's a kernel of truth there—my job is math-based, in a way—but it sounds broad and boring enough that it doesn't invite follow-up questions.

"Tell me how you got into that," she says.

Except now, I guess.

"I've always been a numbers guy," I tell her. "Math is how I make sense of the world. Makes me feel like I have a purpose. It's not what I wanted to do when I was growing up, but hey, who gets to do that?"

"And what did you want to do when you were growing up?"

"Astronaut."

She moves her body closer into mine to stay warm, fitting into the grooves like a puzzle piece. "Why?"

My pulse ticks up a few notches. I'm not used to people asking me questions about myself. I can't remember the last time I had a real conversation with another human being that wasn't related to my job. And those conversations tend to be brief or unfriendly.

The real answer is that I wanted to escape this earth and with it, my childhood, an unsettled and insecure series of foster homes. But that feels too intimate to share, so I tell her, "I wanted to see the stars."

Her smile tells me she knows I'm not telling the whole truth.

We take our hot cocoa and find an empty table—it's flimsy and the seats are small and cold but they're dry, and we sit and sip and stare at each other and something significant is happening. My brain is always passively taking in the surroundings, at some level of alert, even now when there's no present danger. It's just this constant hum: *Where are the exits? How many people are around me? What can I use as a weapon?*

And right now it's like all I have is this tunnel vision with her at the end of it. My perception is working in stops and starts. More than that, I feel like I should be worried, like I'm off my game, like it's not good to be distracted.

"So you said you were in the nonprofit world," I say.

She takes a sip of her cocoa and rolls her eyes back. "Oh, that's good . . . Yeah, I help run a group that organizes food pantries around the city. I wanted to be a princess when I was a kid, but part of the reason for that is I wanted to be a benevolent ruler where no one in the kingdom starved, so, it's on brand, at least."

I take a sip of my cocoa and she's right; like drinking a melted chocolate bar. This might have been a mistake, but I have some Lactaid in my coat. I nod up toward the skyscrapers looming over us. "And you sort of work in a castle."

"Right, but no scepters or fancy dresses," she says. "Astronauts analyze data, you know?"

"Yeah, but I don't get to go to the moon," I tell her. "It's fine."

"Stressful?"

"Some days. A lot of the time it's just, you know, killing the alligator closest to the boat."

She makes a face. "I hate that phrase."

"Some days are like that, though."

"Right, but why does productivity have to be about killing things?"

"What should I be doing to the alligators instead?"

"Petting them?"

"I'd lose a hand."

"Then make them . . . I don't know, bunnies."

"Bunnies?"

She nods. "Pet the bunny closest to the boat."

"Wouldn't the bunnies drown?"

She sticks her tongue out at me. "Pet the bunny closest to the bench."

"That's cute. I like it."

She places the hot cocoa in front of her and puts her legs in my lap. Immediately I start massaging her calf muscles. "What about family?" she asks.

"Don't have much of one. No siblings. Parents passed when I was a kid."

"I'm sorry."

"It's okay," I tell her. Seeking to put a period on the topic, I ask, "What about you?"

"My parents live in Phoenix, which is where I'm from. I have a brother who lives upstate. He's a prison guard. We're pretty close, but I don't see him as much as I'd like."

"Prison guard. He must be tough."

"He likes to think he is. If you ever meet him, he'll probably threaten you, do the whole 'big brother' thing, but don't worry, he's harmless."

I laugh at the thought, but also, the idea that I might meet a member of her family. That's new. I take a deep sip of my cocoa, racking my brain for something other than family to discuss so we don't stumble back onto my lack thereof, when I catch sight of a familiar face behind her.

Antonio Amato.

"Tell me a little more about how you got into the food bank thing," I say.

And I listen with one ear while I run the math in my head.

Sometimes I flip through open contracts on the Via Maris. Just something to pass the time between Agency gigs. Local jobs don't tend to pay as well, but they're way easier to pull off because I'm not infiltrating a government building or figuring out how to eliminate a major security system. Some of it is bullshit; a guy wants his wife killed because she's having an affair, someone wants their neighbor killed for mowing the lawn at seven a.m. every Sunday. I don't mess with stuff like that.

But two nights ago, I saw a contract for Amato and filed it away in the back of my head.

The empire lorded over by the Five Families may have crumbled to dust, but there are still pockets of mafiosi around, and Amato is apparently a big player who managed to piss off another big player, and that other big player is looking for someone to take him out.

Amato is wearing a tan coat, his graying hair slicked back. He's built like a linebacker who let himself go a bit. He's sitting a few tables over with an attractive young woman. College-aged. Maybe a mistress. The two of them talk and sip cocoa and I tell myself I shouldn't try to pull double duty on a date, but it's hard to say no to a hit of the adrenaline.

Sara finishes up what she's saying about helping people and I tell her, "That sounds like a really rewarding job."

"It is," she says, her eyes narrowed at me. "Sometimes I volunteer in the pantries. It's a good workout. We can always use a strong back. Mostly the volunteers are seniors. We need someone for when the fifty-pound bags of potatoes come in."

"That could be fun," I tell her.

She puts down her cocoa. "You okay? You seem like you're somewhere else."

Weird, I'm usually better at multitasking. Amato gets up from the table and moves in the direction of the restrooms, so I tell her, "Yeah, this is a little embarrassing to share on a first date."

She raises her eyebrows and takes another sip, like she's waiting for a hammer to fall.

"My stomach is a little wonky." I hold up the cup. "I got a dairy thing."

She sighs out a stream of relief. "Jesus, I thought you were going to tell me you were married or something. We could have gotten something else, you know."

"Yeah, but your heart seemed set on this."

She leans forward and pats my arm. "Everybody poops, it's okay. Do you want to use the bathroom in my office building?"

"Nah, bathrooms here are pretty nice. I'll be back in a few, okay?"

"Ice-skating after?"

"I told you I don't know how to ice-skate."

She gives me a smirk and a wink. "I told you there was a trick."

I put down my cocoa and get to my feet. "I'll consider it."

She leans back in her chair and crosses her legs in front of her, then whips out her phone, promptly disappearing into Instagram.

The bathrooms are at the far end of the park, and I make my way over, hoping I'll get lucky. On the way, I pull out my phone and hunt for the original post, find it, and text the number attached:

Accepted, will report back shortly

By the time I make it to the bathrooms, I get a response.

Picture plus payment info

Normally I'd say who I was and ask for the whole payment up front—no one ever says no—but I don't feel like getting into that now. Sara seems pretty understanding about the potential of intestinal distress, but the longer I'm in here, the more it may chip into my chances of taking her home tonight. Some mental images can't be unseen.

The bathroom is a trailer with a loud humming generator. Two doors, one for men and one for women. There's a traffic cone nestled in some brush, so I grab it and drop it in front of the door as I step into the men's side. Amato is standing at a urinal. I give a quick peek underneath the stalls and don't see any feet. There were no visible cameras on the walk over, since we're in the park, far from the street.

I lock the door. The *shunk* of it is loud and Amato spins around, his fly still down. Considering he has a contract on his head, I'm sure he knows exactly what's going to happen. I know I'm right when he charges at me. I try to sidestep but get blocked by a sink; the space is too tight. He grabs me around the waist and whales on my side, aiming for my kidneys and liver. Despite his age, he's a brawler, and brawlers do well in tight spaces.

I get a knee up to create some distance and consider head-butting him, but that could open a cut on my head, and head wounds bleed like crazy, which would be complicated to explain, so instead I throw a fist into the side of his throat. The human trachea has the same tensile strength as a soda can, and you can't fight if you can't breathe.

He chokes a little and backs up, his eyes wide.

"Please," he says, gasping. "Whatever they're paying you, I'll pay more."

I don't know what he did. I usually know what people did before I kill them. It helps to know sometimes. But I have to figure whatever got him a $25K contract on his head wasn't good.

"Sorry, bud," I tell him. "Math, you know?"

I snap my foot into his stomach, but he grabs it and wrenches it to the side. I go tumbling and hit my head on the sink. Get up and press my head and feel blood. Exactly what I didn't want. I get to my knees and throw a hard fist into his stomach, which doubles him over, and I grab him around the neck and yank, hard. His spinal column cracks and his body slumps to the floor. I flip him over and snap a picture with my phone, then send it along with my crypto account to the number from before.

I realize I have to pee but I feel like I've been in here too long, and sooner or later someone is going to disregard that traffic cone. My head is swimming and I check it in the mirror; there's a nice gash on my forehead, oozing blood. I grab a bunch of paper towels and press them to the wound, then crack the door open to make sure the coast is clear.

When I get back to the table, Sara is still on her phone. She looks up at me, confused for a second, and then her eyes go wide. "Are you okay?" she asks.

"Yeah," I tell her. "Slipped on some ice."

She motions me to sit and puts her hand on mine, taking the wad of paper towels, and winces at the sight of it. "We should get this looked at."

"Nah, it's not deep. It'll stop bleeding in a few."

"It's deep enough."

"What about the ice-skating?"

"We can ice-skate another day."

"Yeah," I tell her. "But you promised to tell me the trick."

She smiles that knowing smile again and sits back. "Let's just go up to my office, okay? It's right here. There's a kitchen and a first-aid kit."

"Sure."

We stand and she locks arms with mine. We're walking back the way we came, when a scream slices through the tranquility of the evening. It's the woman who was sitting with Amato.

"Someone, please, help! My dad!"

Oh.

Sara looks over—the woman is running back from the bathroom. "Maybe we should help," she says.

But there's already a handful of people rushing over. "I . . . I'm feeling dizzy," I tell her.

"Okay," Sara says, and we head back to the office, but the energy of the evening has shifted. What felt playful is suddenly fragile, like glass gone brittle in the cold.

Usually I walk away from a job a little high. That god-energy shot through me. I did the thing I was good at. I lived, the other person didn't. I would be rewarded. But I thought the woman was a girlfriend or a mistress. I don't know why that made it okay, but it did. Something about it being his daughter, and then Sara witnessing his daughter's grief, and now we're just walking someplace for her to clean me up and she doesn't know that I'm the one who caused that pain, makes me feel ashamed of what I did.

I've never once felt like that.

"Hey," she says, "are you okay?"

We're in the elevator, gliding up to her office. I don't remember walking through the lobby. What is happening?

"Yeah," I tell her.

We make it to her office and she leads me to a small kitchen and sits me down in a hard plastic chair, then disappears, returning with a white plastic first-aid kit. She opens it and lays out wipes and antibacterial ointment and butterfly strips, then goes to the sink and washes her hands.

Something about her doing this makes me feel worse.

Like I don't deserve it.

She comes back and opens a wipe, dabbing it around the wound on my head, cleaning away the blood, and I ask her, "What's the trick?"

"Hmm?" she asks.

"The trick to ice-skating?"

"Oh," she says. "Don't slip."

I laugh, and it cracks something open inside me, and I have to force myself to keep from crying. She stops what she's doing and looks me in the eyes. But she's not just looking at me, she's plucking through the strands of my life with her gentle brown eyes.

And she asks me, "Are you happy?"

I don't need to answer.

She knew it before she asked.

She puts down the wipe and leans forward and kisses me, and in that moment, I find a thing I never even knew I was looking for.

I feel safe.

9

A man's friendships are one of the best measures of his worth.
—Charles Darwin

Bushwick, Brooklyn
Now

The ringtone stops and the call times out. Kenji didn't answer when I got off the plane and he's not answering now. I still don't know what I'm going to say to him, or precisely why I'm calling, but it's something to do with my time, other than disappear down a dark little hole in my head and never come out.

I stick my phone in my pocket. I want to believe he wasn't involved, but I'm having a hard time. After he went against the Yakuza, killed his brother, and dishonored himself—the worst transgression someone in his position could commit—he fled to the States, unable to return home, unable to access anything from his previous life. He showed up in New York with the money in his wallet and the clothes on his back. I admired that about him. I sometimes wonder if I would have stuck with the program this long if I didn't have fat stacks of cash to keep me warm at night. I don't have to work another day in my life—even if some days it's hard to enjoy that comfort when I think about where it came from.

Is that why Kenji seemed cagey when we last spoke? I thought it was because we were trying to obscure our conversation. Was it something else? Did he hire the Russian, or just sell me out? Why would he toy with me like this? None of it makes sense. Hearing the word *Sanjuro* felt like a sledgehammer on my heart, and the psychic pain of it is still ringing through my body.

I thought he was my friend.

I take the six-month chip out of my pocket, turn it over in my hands. He gave me this. He was so *proud* of me. He was so excited for me to trade it in for the next one. It feels different now, like the weight of it has changed. It feels lighter. Cheaper. Fake.

"What's that?" Astrid asks.

I shove it back in my pocket. "Nothing."

"Whoever this is, I hope they show up soon."

The concrete steps leading up to Valencia's apartment are freezing, but at least the ground is dry. I could get us inside easily, to wait where it's warm, but surprising killers is never a good idea, even if they're reformed.

I've been here before. One night, maybe six months ago, after a meeting, we went out for drinks. She talked about the desire to be a mom, and we both got drunk enough that she decided I had good genes and it'd be cheaper than going to a sperm bank. We got here and were nearly naked when she stopped and looked me in the eye and seemed to recognize something and hit the brakes. She didn't say why, but I respected it and knew it was for the best. Preserving the safety and sanctity of the meetings was more important than getting laid, and I figure she was thinking the same thing.

If I had a choice I'd be here alone, but when I suggested finding a hotel for Astrid and P. Kitty to hole up in, she flipped. Told me she wouldn't be the woman in the hotel. Bringing her with me compromises both Valencia's identity and anonymity, but I couldn't think of a good way to explain that.

So here we are.

P. Kitty yowls in his carrier. I reach a finger through and scratch his head.

"We'll be inside soon, buddy," I tell him.

"Two days to Christmas," Astrid says.

"Did you have any plans?"

She shrugs. "Dinner with some friends. FaceTime with my sister, though we don't exchange gifts. What about you? How does a hitman celebrate Christmas?"

I think back to last year.

The tree. The popcorn. The presents.

The blood. The screaming.

"Alone," I tell her.

Valencia appears at the end of the block. She pauses when she clocks us, then resumes her pace. She's wearing a flannel jacket with a fur collar and hood hiding her face, carrying a grocery bag. I put up a hand and wave. She stands at the bottom of the steps and says, "Hey, Astrid."

"Hey, Valencia."

I look back and forth between them. "You two know each other?"

"Of course we do," Astrid says. "How'd that GSW heal up?"

Valencia's hand drifts near her left thigh. "Pretty good. Minimal scarring. You did nice work. Now, why are you both here?"

"Can we go inside?" I ask her. "It's important."

She walks past us and opens the door, and we follow her up the creaky staircase to her apartment. We get inside and drop our coats. She takes her bag to the kitchen and unloads meats and vegetables into the fridge. "You can free the cat," she says.

I open the carrier and P. Kitty waddles out, taking small, tentative steps around the living room. Poor guy has lived his entire life between a bodega and my apartment and now he's been halfway around the world. I pick him up and hold him, try to comfort him, but he squirms out of my grasp and sets about exploring the space.

"Fine," I tell him.

Valencia steps back into the living room. "I'm guessing we should talk in private. Astrid, help yourself to anything in the fridge. Mark?"

She leads me down a long hallway to the bedroom, and she closes the door behind us. The room is pretty simple: a queen bed with a crushed green velvet comforter, a vintage dresser, a nice standing mirror.

And a bulletin board, on which there are pictures of several men.

There's not much in common between them. Ages, races, and body type all vary. Each photo has an index card underneath with neat handwritten notes in Spanish, which, like a lot of languages, I can speak pretty well but have a tough time reading. My assassin brain says this setup looks like a series of targets. Before I can ask, Valencia says, "Don't worry about that. Did you kill Rubén Espinosa?"

I turn to find her laying into me with a razor-blade stare.

Espinosa. It takes me a second. Is that sad, that it does? Probably.

A compound in some sand-swept section of Mexico. Sneaking through at night to deliver a dose of ricin into the cocktail of a rebel seeking to destabilize the housing market. He was recruiting followers to destroy new developments and had orchestrated the killings of a dozen security personnel.

"I guess you saw the video," I tell her. "Yeah, that was me."

Her mouth is a flat, furious line. "Figured."

"Look, I don't know who he was to you, but he was a bad guy—"

"No," she snaps, taking a step toward me. "The bankers and government officials inflating the Mexican housing market by thirty percent were the *bad guys*, Mark. Espinosa may not have been perfect, but he was on the side of the people."

"And why do you care?"

"Because I was trying to protect him."

"I thought you were into cartel stuff."

She squints at me. "You think because I'm Mexican that I was affiliated with the cartels? That's a hell of a stereotype, Mark. I was Special Operations Group. You know what that is?"

Oh shit. "The covert paramilitary arm of the CIA."

"Yeah." She turns away from me and sighs with her whole

body. "That housing scheme screwed over a lot of people. Kept them in poverty. All so some asshole could afford a second yacht for when his first one broke down. We got the assignment to stop Espinosa. I was feeding him intel, keeping him a step ahead. Because whatever he did, he was doing for the right reason. I guess I did too good a job because they brought you in."

"Look, I was just doing my—"

She turns back to me, nearly shaking with anger. "Don't say you were doing your job. Bunch of brown people get uppity, try to fight back, so they send in the white Terminator to take care of them. Though I guess that's a tale as old as time."

"Hey..."

"What?"

"...I killed a lot of white people, too."

As soon as I say it, I realize it was a stupid thing to say. She puts her hands on her face, takes a few breaths in and out. I join her: in for four, hold for four, out for four, empty lungs for four. It's a little funny, how just a few years ago, this showdown could have played out very differently. I want to laugh, point that out to puncture the tension, but I don't think she's at the laughing stage yet.

"I always wondered," she says. "The hit was too clean. Now I know, at least."

"So we don't have to fight this out?"

"No, you dope. I can be angry and upset and still forgive you. That's the whole point of this program."

"Okay. I'm sorry. And sorry about the cartel thing. I was stereotyping."

She sits heavily on the bed. "Just tell me what's going on."

"I think Kenji sold me out."

Her face drops. She blinks a few times. "That doesn't sound right."

I give her a rundown of everything that happened in the past few days: the Russian, why I'm with Astrid, our trip to Singapore, the Agency on high alert and threatening to send Azrael after me, Gaius, and the connection to Kenji. She takes it all in with a stone face, slowly nodding along at points where I guess she has a sense of what's going on. When I'm done, we hang there in a long stretch of silence, sorting through the puzzle pieces.

Valencia purses her lips, then blows out a burst of frustrated air. "I've heard of Azrael. None of what I've heard is good."

"Haven't had the pleasure. For all they know, I'm at full speed, so it's a nuclear option. The longer this plays out, the more I figure it's a matter of time before our paths cross."

"And you really think Kenji is involved?" she asks.

"That's why I came here without calling, in case you decided to check with him. Up until recently, he was the only one who knew my real identity, and that I'm handicapped with this goddamn program."

"This *goddamn program* is saving your life, and mine, and countless others."

"Right, but my life would be a whole lot easier if I could just cut loose and let this play out the way—"

"Stop right there," she says, standing up and sticking a finger in my chest. "I get where you're at, but you're trying to give yourself permission to erase an entire year of progress."

"Would it be so bad to clear the deck this one time so I can live in peace? It's only a year. I can get back to counting days..."

"What's the point of stopping, then? Just kill someone whenever you have a problem. Next guy who cuts you in line at the bank, snap his neck."

"That's not what I mean."

"All we have is all we have," she says slowly, making sure to enunciate each word. "No more of that, okay? It's not good for you to hear, and it's not good for me to hear, either." She puts her hands on her hips and arches her back to stretch it. "What do we do now?"

"Check with Booker and Stuart. See if they know anything."

"Booker lives on Staten Island," she says. "Stuart lives in Astoria."

"I'd rather we handle this analog. No calls, no email, no texts, no trail. Do you know where Booker lives, exactly?"

"Yeah, we're in a bowling league together."

"You two are in a bowling league?"

She laughs a little. "He sucks. Don't say anything. He'll get upset."

"Okay, how about this," I tell her. "Can you go find him? I'll see if I can find Stuart. I'd like to see if he has anything useful to share, but when the time comes, I'd rather go at this with you and Book."

"Yeah," she says. "I can do that."

"Again, I'm sorry," I tell her. "For Espinosa. For coming to you with this. I don't feel great about it."

"That's why we're here, dumbass. You can feel bad, and you

should. Now you sit with those feelings and take the next right action. Meanwhile, I forgive you, because the person you were then isn't the person you are today. Welcome to recovery."

I fight with my face, to keep it straight. I don't do a great job, so to buy myself some cover I throw my arms around her, squeeze her tight. She lets me do it, and then she pats me on the shoulder and says, "Stop being a pussy."

We pull away from each other, temperatures having returned to normal. I nod toward the photos on the bulletin board. "You know I can't let that go. Looks like you're working again."

She huffs and walks over to it, regarding the different headshots. "You know my deal, Mark. I talk about it every week. I want to be a mom. I met with a sperm bank, got some potential profiles."

"Thought those were supposed to be anonymous."

She smiles. "Yeah. Not for people like us, though. There are things I'm looking for, things they might not disclose on the forms, and I need to be sure."

"Such as?"

She turns to me fully and her face softens. It is the most vulnerable I've ever seen her. "I want someone who doesn't have any kind of history of violence."

Oh.

That thing she saw in me, the last time I was here. Why she stopped me.

That maybe our genes were combustible.

"You think we're born this way?" I ask.

She offers a half-defeated smirk. "I'm not taking the risk."

I want to argue and say, no, we were molded into this, but the way my body buzzes when it's pumped full of adrenaline, the way my blood so easily converts to steam, I don't know if that's true.

It makes me wonder what hope there is for me, then. For any of us. It gives me something else to be terrified of. The thought that whatever's inside me can be passed down.

"C'mon," she says, moving toward the door. "Let's get to work."

Before she can open it I say, "Hey."

She doesn't turn. Her voice is barely a whisper. "Yeah."

"I'm not exactly an expert on the subject, 'cause I never really had one, but for what it's worth, I think you'd make a good mom."

Her hand drops to her side, and it seems like she wants to say something. Like she's preparing herself to let something fly. Whether it's a *thank you* or a *fuck you*, I can't tell. All I know is that I believe it. Then she reaches up and turns the knob and leaves the room without saying a word.

The R train rumbles toward Astoria. Astrid sits across from me. I plug away on my phone, the service going in and out between stops. I don't have much to go on for finding Stuart. I know his name. I know he's a serial killer. Based on some stuff he's said, I turned up a few unsolved murders around the city in the last two years I think could be him.

It feels very uncomfortable going to his home, but I need to check in. In part because maybe he overheard something that

I missed. Maybe he's in danger, too, and despite how I feel about him, I want him to succeed. Every meeting he goes to is a life saved. It makes me think of a Krav Maga instructor I worked with a long time ago. We were doing an active-shooter drill. Every second you stopped a shooter from firing, he said, you saved a life. And according to the Talmud, for every life you saved, you saved a universe.

He would walk around the mat, barefoot, point his hand in the air like it was a gun, and yell, *BANG! A universe.*

BANG! A universe.

BANG! A universe.

I need to remind myself of that sometimes.

Especially in moments like this.

Because Smiley is here, too. He's sauntering up and down the car with his empty Hennessy bottle, swinging it without care or fear of striking someone.

The train pulls out of 23rd Street and he sways out of time with the jostling of the car, talking to people who don't want to talk to him. His dark hair is greasy and unkempt. He looks more lit than usual.

And he zeroes in on Astrid.

He steps in front of her and she stirs a little, but I can't see how she reacts because he's between us.

Just a few stops to go. Astrid is a big girl. She can handle herself.

We can ignore him.

Four seconds in, hold for four, out for four, and . . .

Nope.

I get up and push between them. He has to move a little to

make room for me, and he looks more shocked than angry. Then he smiles when he recognizes me. "You back for more?"

Ignore.

Just stand here. That's it. That's all I have to do.

A gentle and peaceful deterrent.

"I was talking to her," he says.

Astrid looks up at me like, *What are you doing?*

Ignore. Ignore.

"You deaf?"

"Mark, c'mon . . ." Astrid says.

Ignore. Ignore. Ignore.

Four seconds in . . .

He shoves me. I've set my feet so I don't move, but it interrupts my breathing.

Just like I wanted him to.

To give me an excuse.

He says, "Sit down or I'm going to see red, motherfucker."

My hand lashes out before my brain can react. I grab him by the roots of his hair and yank his head back, exposing his throat. I want to sink my teeth into it. I want to tear a chunk of it out and spit it back into his face.

"You know how you can tell someone can't fight?" the Pale Horse asks. "When they say they see red. Like you're going to lose control and turn into some kind of animal. That's not how it works. The really dangerous people are the ones who can stay calm and collected under the most intense pressure imaginable."

I yank harder, causing him to arch his back.

"Mark!" Astrid says.

"Don't come at me with that tough-guy bullshit," the Pale Horse says. "You never know who you're picking a fight with."

I turn him around and smash his face into the subway door. He goes down, blubbering. I pick up his arm and set myself, ready to break it. I know how to do it so it'll never heal right. So he'll always have a little reminder, when it's humid or when he moves it the wrong way, that little ache will keep him away from thinking he's a man—

Astrid yanks me off him.

"Stop," she says.

He's crying, curled into a fetal position. I realize all I'm doing is stepping on an ant. I look up and expect, I don't know, something other than what I see, which is everyone squished to either side of the car, absolutely terrified.

At the most savage part of me.

I wish I could say I regret it, but I don't.

This is the perfect moment to call Kenji. And I can't.

"We need to go," Astrid says.

A few straphangers have their phones out and they're filming. Right. This'll end up on social media. Of course. Everyone looking for me will suddenly know exactly where I am.

When the doors open at 28th Street, Astrid pulls me off and we go aboveground, looking for a cab, as I clench my fists so hard they hurt.

This seems to be the place. The fries are good. Thin cut, crunchy on the outside, pillowy on the inside, perfectly seasoned. At our last group meeting, Stuart said something about scoping out a bartender near his place where the fries are really good. It wasn't a lot to go on, but I found four different food blogs praising the fries at Rusty's Tavern.

It's an old-man bar on the corner of 31st and Steinway. Lots of wood and old-school stools, and a mix of older clientele who just want to drown in a drink, along with wide-eyed gentrifiers who started flooding this neighborhood when they got priced out of Brooklyn.

It was a little busy when we came in, so after I went to the bathroom and washed the blood off my hands, Astrid and I found seats at the bar and ordered two pints and some fries. She doesn't touch her beer. I get halfway through mine—not enough to get tipsy, but enough to blunt the edge.

Astrid isn't speaking to me. I think she's spooked. She should be. I feel like this thing I've been grasping onto for the past year is slipping through my fingers.

And my suspicion was true. Twitter is blowing up—the video of me beating on Smiley is being shared around, and it's being politicized on both sides. The right thinks it's time to take our city back with violence, the left is condemning me for attacking someone like that, calling on the mayor for more funding for mental health services.

Here I am, stuck in the middle with my feelings of regret, and hard evidence for the Agency that I'm back in New York.

The bartender comes over to check on us. She's young and pretty—dark hair freshly blown out and hanging in shiny waves, piercing blue eyes, and the kind of smile that attracts zealous overtipping. "Need anything?"

"Yeah, actually," I tell her. "Got a question for you."

Her shoulders tense. I don't think she's explicitly creeped out by me, but when a strange man tells a pretty bartender he has a question for her, it's perfectly reasonable to put up some defenses.

"Got a friend, comes in here sometimes I think," I tell her. "He's either really noticeable or not noticeable at all. His name is Stuart . . ."

Her eyes twitch a little in response.

"So you do know him?"

She nods slowly. "He's your friend?"

"I shouldn't say 'friend,'" I tell her. "He's a guy I know. I need to find him. I'm Mark, by the way—"

"That guy weirds me out."

"Me too. If you don't mind me asking, has he ever done anything inappropriate?"

"No, he's perfectly polite. There's just something about him. It's like he's wearing a mask." She picks up a glass and wipes it down, then looks at me with some reservation. Probably because my face looks like raw meat. Finally she says, "He's always respectful and he tips well and he keeps to himself. He's the perfect patron, outside of the fact that he makes my skin crawl."

"I need to find him. Anything you can tell me—"

"He lives around the corner. There's a bunch of brick houses on the left-hand side, all in a row. I can't remember which one he lives in. They all look the same to me. But I saw him coming out of there once."

I peel a hundred out of my wallet and slap it on the bar for the fries and the beer. She slides it off, looking at me expectantly.

"Keep the change," I tell her.

As I'm dismounting the stool, she slips the bill in her pocket. "If you're looking for him, be careful, okay?"

Can't help but laugh at that. "Sure. I'll do my best."

Outside the bar the sun is dipping below the building tops and random flakes of snow are swirling through the yellow glow of the streetlights. Astrid is still giving me the silent treatment. I hitch up my collar and stick my hands in my pockets as we make our way toward the corner, passing stores and homes done up with twinkling colored lights.

"You gonna talk to me?" I ask.

"That was messed up, Mark. He was just a kid."

"Kid needed to learn a lesson."

"That didn't teach him a thing. Clearly he needs some kind of help he's not getting. He's not in the game, Mark. And you could have killed him."

Yeah. I could have.

And it would have felt good.

I put that thought out of my head as we turn the corner. The bartender was right. There are six two-story brick homes, all connected to each other. They look exactly the same. I've got a good eye for details and if I saw Stuart come out of one yesterday I wouldn't remember which one it was today. Out of the six, there are only lights on in two of them, so I pick the closest one and knock on the door. The mailbox on the railing is overflowing. I pluck out an envelope.

Stuart Bates.

He's a serial killer and his last name is Bates?

C'mon now.

"This is it," I tell Astrid.

Part of me feels lucky to have found him on the first try, but the abundance of mail and the lights on inside make me wonder how long that luck is going to hold out. The block is mostly empty. No cameras in sight. I keep a cheap lockpick set in my wallet—it's not going to get me through a secure door, but this isn't that. It takes about ten seconds to pop the pins and the dead bolt isn't engaged. I give one more look to make sure the street is clear, checking the windows across the street for any *Rear Window* types, then we slip inside.

"Jesus," Astrid says. "That stench . . ."

As soon as it hits me, I know whatever we find isn't going to be pleasant. The rot is so thick I can taste it at the back of my tongue: spoiled meat left in the sun. I'm used to the smell of fresh carnage—the way blood and viscera hang in the air, the way a body will shit itself moments after death—but I'm usually long gone before they ever get this far along.

There's blood in the entryway. I bend down to get a closer look. It's a thin film, dry and tacky. Been a day or two, at least. Maybe more. Right off the entryway is the living room, which is where I find Stuart, lying on his back, his head caved in.

Astrid puts her hand over her mouth and dashes outside.

The living room doesn't have any real personality. Gray couch, big TV, a coffee table with some remotes on it. No art on the walls, no rug on the floor. No books. Stuart is wearing jeans and a sweatshirt, and fat cockroaches chew on the shattered remains of his head.

This is not a professional estimate, but I'd say a somewhat educated guess: his head looks like it was stomped on by a boot. There's something about the uneven flatness of it that makes me think of a heel. Nestled in that mess is a hazy, milky eyeball gazing at the ceiling.

My stomach swirls with a mix of complicated emotions. The first thing that comes up is relief. Maybe the world is better off with him gone. But that makes me wonder if I'm really just imagining myself in his place.

After that, there's sadness. He really was trying.

Finally, there's a toxic mix of fear and confusion. How the hell did Stuart get involved in this? Why would someone come after *him*?

The *why* doesn't really matter, I guess.

It's more important that I get back and make sure Booker and Valencia are okay.

Lulu wordlessly fills our coffees, then goes back to the register. The man in the brown suit is sitting across the diner, like always, and there's no one else here.

"Nice cat," Booker says, nodding to the carrier on the table.

"He's a fluffy boy," Valencia says.

"So," Booker says. "I always figured you were serious. Didn't know you were this serious." He nods toward my beaten and bruised face. "But it seems that kid banged you up pretty good."

"You saw the video?" I ask.

"Nah," Booker says, then points toward Valencia. "She told me. I don't go on the Via Maris anymore. That shit is triggering."

Then he casts a concerned look at Astrid.

"How'd that shoulder heal up?" she asks him.

He rotates his arm in the socket. "Right as rain. Thanks again for that."

She smiles as she tips a mug to her lips. "It's what I do."

"Now, Stuart," Booker says. "Good riddance. Never trusted the guy."

"He was trying," Valencia says, her voice hushed.

"He was weird," Booker says.

"He was one of us," Valencia says.

It's Astrid's turn for a confused little look, but she doesn't dig.

"Let's focus," I tell them. "Someone tried to kill me, then killed Stuart. Kenji is in the wind. That changes the metrics here. Neither of you have noticed anything?"

"Nothing," Booker says.

"Nobody," Valencia says.

I spin my coffee mug. Two sips in and I don't want it anymore.

"What about Azrael. Booker? Do you know anything about him?"

Booker shrugs. "Whispers and rumors. Nothing solid." Then he snaps his fingers. "This Russian guy took your notebook, right?"

Booker, Valencia, and I all freeze at that. Silence strangles the table and after a moment Astrid catches on and says, "I think I need to use the bathroom."

She slides out of the booth and disappears to the other side of the diner.

Booker shakes his head. "Dragged that poor woman into this..."

"Couldn't be avoided. But yeah, my entire amends list. It's ciphered, but someone with half a brain and a full afternoon could probably crack it."

"What's in there that could be valuable?" Valencia asks.

"It's ten years of political assassinations and whatever side gigs I picked up on the Via Maris. The intelligence alone is probably worth a fortune."

Booker points at me. "That right there tells you something. You're about to start the ninth step, right? So you're supposed to go over it with Kenji. Decide who to make amends to. Who gets a direct amends and who gets a living amends. He wouldn't need to steal it if you were about to read the whole damn thing to him."

"I've been stalling," I say. "I think he knows that. Maybe he couldn't wait." I take a swig of coffee. "Or maybe we're all criminals at the end of the day and we can't change."

Valencia elbows me in the ribs. "Stop that."

"Let's just go to Kenji's," Booker says. "The three of us, together. See what the story is. You know where he lives?"

Yes, I do.

"No, I don't."

Because I'm not ready to find out that it could be true.

"How about this," Booker says. "You said the guy who attacked you at Dymphna's was Russian, right? Why not go ask the Russians?" He smirks. "I know someone, operates out of a club in Brighton Beach. I'm not gonna lie, they ain't gonna roll out a carpet for us. And whatever goes down, I need you to let it play out. But I think the three of us show up looking mean, we can get away with asking a few questions."

"I like everything except the 'three of us' part. This is my fight. I'm not putting either of you at risk for a slip."

I toss a hundred on the table, and the two of them look at me like I just spit in their faces.

"The fuck is this?" Booker asks.

"Both of you should get out of town," I tell them. "Take Astrid and the cat with you. This might get messy. We still don't know if someone is coming after you. I'll check into the drafts folder once I have a better handle on all this."

"Get right off with that cowboy shit," Valencia says. "If you're in it, we're in it."

Booker reaches over and finishes my coffee. "Let's go," he says.

"I don't feel good about this," I tell them.

"Get used to it," Valencia says. "Don't make me quote the Big Book at you."

"I just . . ."

Valencia rolls her eyes. "'The feeling of having shared in a common peril is one element in the powerful cement which binds us.'"

Booker nods toward her. "What she said. We ain't related, but that don't mean we're not blood. Pale Horse or not, you're not stopping us from following you. I'll be perfectly honest, you don't look that tough to me. You know who looks tough?"

"I swear to god, if you say you thought I would look like

Jason Statham, I'm going to slap the shit out of you right here in Lulu's."

He puts his hands up.

Astrid appears at the table. I think she can tell from the looks on our faces that she's not going to like what happens next. So when I take her outside and hand her the cat carrier and a few hundred bucks and tell her that the next thing I do I have to do alone and she should go back to the first hotel we stayed in, she sticks a finger in my face.

"You have completely inverted my life," she says, "and you are still keeping shit from me. I am tired of it. Soon as you get back, we're sorting out how to get the money you owe me, and then I'm gone."

She stalks off, looking for a subway.

It's for her own protection, I tell myself.

And I remind myself that letting people into my life has never gone well.

10

> Anger may in time change to gladness; vexation may be succeeded by content. But a kingdom that has once been destroyed can never come again into being; nor can the dead ever be brought back to life.
> —Sun Tzu, *The Art of War*

Jericho, New York
One Year Ago

Sara places the large green plastic bowl of popcorn on the coffee table, then slides onto the couch next to me, nestling into my side as I spread a pink fuzzy blanket over our legs. I reach for the bowl and balance it on my lap.

"Can't believe you've never seen this," I tell her.

"I'm sorry," she says, a little hurt trickling into her voice. "I know it's a classic. Just never got around to it."

"That's not a criticism."

She kisses the side of my neck, her lips warm on my skin. "I guess it's only fair, considering all the baking shows I subject you to."

"First off, I love the baking shows. Second off, I'm just excited to share this with you. It's my favorite movie of all time. And the only Christmas tradition I ever really had."

"One of your foster moms showed it to you, right?"

"When I was a kid."

It's a lie. But at this point I've told Sara so many lies, it may as well count as the truth, because anything from before I met her doesn't matter.

I hit the PLAY button, and the church bell rings as the Liberty Films logo appears, and then the title card: *Frank Capra's It's a Wonderful Life*, flooding me with a feeling of contentment, that I made it another year.

And we sit there in our flannel pajamas, the dim room lit by the television screen, the twinkling lights of the Christmas tree behind us—I can barely believe I'm here, or that I deserve this. The moisturized, manicured palm of domesticity.

The real truth, the first time I really saw this, was one Christmas Eve in the barracks, stationed in Kurdistan with a bunch of loudmouth meatheads. Something about the movie transported us away from that razor's edge between duty and terror. By the end of it, my face and my throat ached, because that wasn't a place you could safely cry. Ever since, I've watched this movie every Christmas Eve, by myself with a bottle of bourbon, and I would let the alcohol drown the complicated emotions it stirred.

But watching it with Sara, something about it plays different. As Jimmy Stewart's George Bailey stands on a snowy bridge, ready to throw himself off, I don't have that same feeling in my bones—of understanding where George was coming from.

Because when you spend as much time around guns as I do, sometimes you wonder what it would be like, to wrap your lips around the barrel. You appreciate the precision of death.

Right now I just want to reach out and offer him my hand, and I'm that much more thankful when the angel Clarence shows up to stop him.

The way someone can just reach out their hand to you like that.

It's been ten months now, of dinners and hiking and movie nights curled under a blanket with popcorn. The truth about who I am getting stuck in my throat. I've tried. One night I showed her *The Professional*, thinking I would tell her: that's kind of like me. That's what I do. But the way she cringed at the violence of it kept me quiet.

As the movie unspools and we finish off the popcorn, Sara pulls herself closer to me, and occasionally I glance down at her to make sure she's still awake, to see the smile on her face, and I can't tell which I enjoy watching more.

And when it ends, she looks up at me and smiles and says, "That was beautiful. Thank you for sharing it with me." She kisses me, long and soft, then pulls back and says, "There's still time to run, you know. You're sure about this?"

"Meeting your mom and your bro?" I ask. "Sure."

"It's a big step. I told you my brother can be tough on my boyfriends."

"Yeah, but I'm charming."

She smiles. "Mark . . ."

Her eyes go soft and she's treading water in a pool of something she wants to tell me. I recognize that look because I spend a lot of time there myself. The water tickling her nose, the threat of that true thing she wants to say, wondering whether it'll turn into a life preserver or the stone that drags her down.

And then she proves how much braver she is than I am.

"I love you," she says.

Every single other thing in the world drops away and nothing exists but the two of us on that couch. My breathing technique is useless, the air gone from my chest.

She kisses me again, then nuzzles my neck, and I can't tell if she's being intimate or trying to hide from the glare of the aftermath. "It's okay if you're not ready," she says. "Or if you're not there. Truly, I mean that. But I am, and it's how I feel, and I wanted you to know."

We kiss, again, and linger in that space. Her finding that relief, of having said the hard thing, and me wrestling down my shame, at not being able to return the favor.

Not now. Not in this moment.

Because I love her. I do.

And if I tell her that, then I owe her the truth about me.

She pulls away and smiles. "You're going to stay up for a bit?"

"You know me," I tell her.

Sara stands and pecks me on the forehead. "Oh, and hey, on your way up . . . don't slip, okay?"

My hand goes to the spot on my head that opened up when I killed Amato. "Never going to let me live that down, are you?"

"We never even got into the ice-skating rink, so, no, I will not," she says, then retreats to the kitchen. I click through the TV, hoping to find a documentary that'll bore me enough that I want to sleep.

Her words ringing in my ears.

It didn't use to be like this. It used to be that I slept like a baby pumped full of Ambien. That night I met Sara, after we had sex, I was up until sunrise, alternating between watching her sleeping form and staring at the ceiling, searching for words that could even skirt the edge of what I was feeling.

Still can't find the right words, still can't sleep.

On her way from the kitchen to the staircase she stops at the tree. We already stacked the presents we got for each other underneath.

I've never bought anyone presents before.

No one's ever gotten presents for me.

She adds one more to the pile, placing it down softly so maybe I won't notice, but of course I do, because I'm trained to notice things, but I give her the respect of pretending I don't.

"Don't stay up too late," Sara says as she climbs the stairs. "Early morning."

"That's what coffee is for."

Once she's cleared the staircase and I hear her footsteps padding around the bedroom, I go to the kitchen and pour myself a few fingers of rye, then restart *It's a Wonderful Life*. Because I want that little hint of my old life, but also, I want to understand what it is about the movie that suddenly feels different.

And as the whiskey does its work, I think I get it.

It's George's journey with Clarence. Touring George's life to discover how the world would look without him. His brother drowned as a child, the town in shambles, the people in his life sad and broken.

If I were gone, how would the world look?

A lot of people would be dead.

But a lot of people would be alive, too.

There were the six members of the Islamic Jihad Movement, planning a dirty bomb for Times Square during the summer tourist season. The fourteen members of the People's Liberation Front in Ethiopia behind an ethnic cleansing campaign. Twelve members of the Paraguayan Congress, a shadow wing of the country's communist Patria Libre party, which was responsible for hundreds of kidnappings, bombings, and other armed operations.

The math on those was clear.

Then there was Michael Albertson, the British journalist who uncovered direct evidence of Russian tampering in U.S. elections. A matter of national security, I was told. And Carol Gyzander, the environmental activist planning a debilitating attack on the Kuparuk River oil field in Alaska. People could die, I was told, plus all the chaos it would cause to the U.S. market.

Sometimes the math is fuzzy.

And even if I was saving lives, they were theoretical.

The only number that matters is the hard number of the people I've killed.

Some nights when I can't sleep, I sit and contemplate the paper crane that Kenji gave me. It sits on a bookshelf in my apartment, and I have yet to open it, for fear of how that might change the equation. And some nights, it's because I can't shake the scream of Antonio Amato's daughter, finding her dad dead in a bathroom in Bryant Park.

I take a sip of rye and savor the sting that trickles down the back of my throat.

My phone buzzes on the coffee table. I pick it up and find a text from Ravi:

Got a job for you. Tried to wait until after Christmas but it's an ASAP op. Flight leaves from JFK in three hours. I'm waiting in the Terminal B Chili's. Text me when you're close and I'll order you a drink.

I stare at it for a moment. I've been renting a storage locker close by for exactly this kind of situation, so I wouldn't have to go all the way home to get my gear. But I glance at the staircase, and the tree, and that wrapped first edition of *The Bell Jar* by Sylvia Plath that I am dying to watch Sara open, and there's not even a decision to be made.

Me: Sorry, bud. Got plans for the holiday.

There's a long pause. I imagine Ravi's expression of confusion and indignation. My heart slams against the inside of my chest.

Ravi: You don't get days off.

Me: Then I want to talk to my union rep.

Ravi: This is serious.

Me: Call in Azrael.

Ravi: Azrael is on something else. And the Director asked for you.

Me: I'm not available.

Ravi: No one sees these chats but me, Mark. So I'm speaking to you as a friend when I say: this is not a smart move. There will be consequences.

Me: I'm sorry, Ravi. I wouldn't be doing this if it wasn't

important. After everything I've done, I think I earned a night off. Merry Christmas.

And I turn off my phone.

Breathe in for four, hold for four, out for four, empty lungs for four.

A laugh erupts in my chest. That was easier than I thought it would be. I just said the thing. And sure, there'll be some fallout, but that's for tomorrow.

Anyway, what if I just quit?

I have enough money to retire. I could get a job, something normal people do, just to keep myself busy. No more math.

I don't even know what an exit strategy from the Agency would look like. If it's even possible. Then there's the question of the enemies I've made, none of whom know my identity, but if it ever got out, the danger I could put Sara in the path of . . .

Then I remember: I'm the Pale Horse. It'll be fine.

This right here, this is what I want.

When I get in bed, Sara will wake up a little and stretch over to let me kiss her, like she always does, and I'm going to tell her I love her, and I'm going to fall asleep in her arms, and tomorrow after her family leaves I'm going to tell her the truth about me.

Simple as that.

I can do this.

The rocks glass is empty. Probably one more will put me to sleep by the time this movie is over. I hit the PAUSE button and stand, my joints popping, and look at the present Sara placed on the pile. Pick it up and give it a shake. It's small. Something rattles inside but I can't tell what.

I'm about to put it back when I hear the subtle scrape of a careful footstep at the back of the house. Not wanting to create any noise, I slide the package into my pocket.

Everything drops away and I go into work mode, moving through the kitchen, grabbing a chef's knife out of the wooden block on the counter.

My phone is encrypted. Can't be tracked. I always watch for tails on my way over. There's no real way to tie me to being here.

Right?

Probably just a neighbor, coming home late or stepping outside for a smoke.

Unless the Agency thinks I went rogue. Did Ravi have someone watching me and now he's sending them in? In the sea of people I've killed, did someone figure out who I am and came looking for revenge?

Maybe not the first mistake this person has made, but definitely their last.

I move toward the sunroom at the back of the house, where there's a door that opens onto the yard. There's a figure jostling with the lock. I duck into the kitchen, standing on the other side of the open doorway.

If this were my own apartment, I would cut their throat and deal with the mess. But I don't want blood on the floor to spoil our Christmas plans. I need to subdue him, quietly, and figure out what the hell is going on.

My hand hurts. It takes a moment to realize it's because of how hard I'm gripping the knife. My vocation requires standing on the precipice of life and death, and usually I feel a vibration of excitement, something approaching serenity, like this is what I'm here to do.

For the first time, I'm angry.

Whoever this is, they want to come in here and take this all away from me.

The door creaks open and the figure steps into the house. From the reflection of a mirror near the front door, I can see more of him: bald head, thick neck, wide shoulders. Maybe this won't be quiet. I run through the Rolodex of hitters in my head, try to match someone to the shape. Can't come up with anyone.

I press myself flat against the wall and let him step past me into the living room. He's carrying a bag, which he drops when I come around him and wrap my arm around his throat, putting him in a blood choke. Cut off his oxygen. He tenses against me and with the other hand I bring up the knife.

"Make a sound and I will . . ."

He's strong, and I'm a little drunk and I let my anger cloud my judgment, so I respond a second too slow when he leans forward and tosses me over his back. I smash into a china cabinet, glass and shattered wood pelting my head and shoulders. The knife goes flying somewhere into the room.

Okay, so tonight may be the night I come clean to Sara, but that's not important right now. What's important is getting back on top. The guy comes at me and I sweep his leg. His front foot kicks out and he manages to stay up, his legs spread at an awkward angle. He throws out his arms to steady himself, so I slam my fist into his crotch, and his face scrunches as he tumbles to the floor. I scramble on top of him and crack my fist into his face so hard his head bounces off the hardwood.

"Do you even know who I am?" I ask. "And you come here like this?"

"Where is—"

I throw my fist and his nose shatters.

Again, and his breaking teeth gouge my knuckles.

I grab him by the collar and pull him close. That god-energy screams through every cell of my body, the most savage part of me fully in control.

Someone wants to take this away from me and I will not let them.

"The smart thing to do would be to keep you alive and question you," I tell him. "But I'm going to find out who sent you either way. And I want them to understand the depth of the mistake they made. What happens if someone ever even *looks* at that woman upstairs."

And I wrap my arm around his neck, bear down hard, and yank, separating his skull from his spinal cord.

Just as his body goes slack and I feel the life leave him and the god-energy crackles at my fingertips and I revel in the ecstasy of the adrenaline coursing through my veins, the lights flick on.

"Lucas!"

Sara is standing at the top of the staircase, holding her bathrobe cinched to her waist. Eyes wide, mouth open, staring at the body on the floor.

I'm thinking up an explanation when I realize she just said her brother's name.

With the lights on, with the haze of violence cleared from the air, I can see that the bag the man was carrying was full of presents, the carefully wrapped packages spilled across the floor. Sara dashes down the stairs as I check Lucas's pulse, as if regretting that he's dead might change the fact that he is.

Sara stands above us, and I suddenly feel smaller than I've ever felt. Words jumble and clog in my mouth. I have to remind myself to breathe. I stand, slowly, my hands up.

"Please, Sara . . ."

Her face twists through a messy jumble of emotion: disbelief, anger, fear. She doesn't know what to settle on. And I'm so desperate to fix it, so desperate to make this right, that I say the worst possible thing in this moment.

The cruelest thing imaginable.

"Sara, I lov—"

She puts up a hand to cut me off, her face red, and she screams, "Don't you *fucking* dare."

And she dashes up the stairs as my head swims and I struggle to keep down the whiskey in my stomach. I stand on unsteady feet and hear her voice. "Please, I need you to send the police . . . yes, he's still here . . . yes, that's my address. Please, hurry."

I want to plead my case. It was an accident. I mean, it wasn't an accident, it's what I was trained to do, but I didn't *mean* to. I want to open my chest and show Sara the ruins of my heart.

Sirens whine in the distance.

So I struggle into my boots and my coat, grab my wallet and my keys, and I'm out the back door, the cold Christmas Eve air searing my face.

And miles later, I stop in the shadow of a grocery store that's closed for the night to catch my breath, and remember that small box she placed under the tree, still in my pocket. I take it out and tear it open.

When I discover the positive pregnancy test inside, I fall to my knees and yell into the cold asphalt until my lungs feel scraped raw and there's nothing left for my body to give.

"Mark!"

Ibrahim is leaning over the counter at the front of the bodega, the maroon kufi on his head artfully askew, looking at me like I'm not wearing pants. I check to make sure that I am. Still in my flannel pajamas. Paired with a leather jacket and heavy-duty boots, it would look out of place anywhere else, but I'm in the West Village, so it flies.

"You good, bro?" he asks.

"Yeah, man, sorry."

"You been drinking?"

I run the fingers of my left hand through the webbing of my right hand, my knuckles cut up and aching from where I broke Lucas's teeth. "A little, yeah."

"Get some Gatorade and take a few Advil before bed," he says.

I turn my attention back to the freezer case, and the colorful pints of ice cream. All the delicious stuff I never get to eat. Cookies and cream. Brownie batter. Cannoli. There's a cannoli ice cream now? I'm out of the loop. Given my digestive circumstances, this isn't an area where I need to be well-versed.

I check my phone. Four missed calls. Two from Sara. Two from a number I don't recognize. The police will be looking for me. Doesn't matter. Sara didn't like to sleep in beds other than her own, and I told her my apartment had a roach problem, so we always stayed at her place. The cops have my first name, a fake last name, and the most dangerous organization in the world covering my tracks.

They won't find me because I'm not a person.

It wasn't them I was running from, anyway. It was the reality of who and what I am.

A monster, driven by blood and money and adrenaline.

I was fooling myself that I was worthy of her. I wasn't made for human things. And realizing that, what is there left to do?

George Bailey, I suddenly understand, lacked commitment.

I won't make the same mistake.

I open the freezer case and take out a pint of cannoli ice cream. Then cookie dough, and a cherry vanilla. I end up with six pints in total. I'll chase them with my SIG Sauer P365. Then the only person who has to worry about the mess is whoever finds the body. I'll do it in the bathtub. It'll be easier to clean. That seems like the kind thing to do.

It's almost funny, how easy it sounds.

But maybe that's because oblivion has been a constant companion.

A Pale Horse, and his name that sat on him was Death . . .

As long as I'm doing this, I may as well go full tilt, so I head for the shelves in the middle of the store, hunting for mac and cheese, the kind that comes with gooey cheese lava in the shiny pack. I remember having that when I was a kid. The one foster mom I actually liked, who went and got herself a boyfriend who wanted a "real" kid so she eventually sent me back, she would make it for me. I must have been seven or eight because the lactose intolerance developed when I was nine.

This is what I want. My last meal.

I'm going to eat all of this and enjoy these final moments of my stupid, cursed life.

It takes me a little searching to find—this isn't an item I generally go for—but then that perfect orange and yellow box leaps out at me, and when I grab it off the shelf, a little ball of fur peeks out from behind the gap and says, "Meow."

I jump back, dropping all the food I'm clutching in my arms.

"Hey, you found him," Ibrahim says from somewhere up front.

The cat is just past the stage of kitten but still not full-grown. A dull orange, his fur matted, he stands at the edge of the shelf and meows at me like an excited toddler. I give him a scratch behind his little ear and he flops forward off the shelf to the ground, then scrambles to his feet and rubs against my legs.

All that dangerous air built up inside me releases as I laugh. "You little dumbass," I tell him. I lean down and he leaps up, clinging to my chest, digging his nails into my leather jacket. I press him into the crook of my neck and have to stop myself from squeezing him too hard, like I can absorb the affection into my skin. I bring him to the front. "Does he have a name?"

"Some of the kids from NYU call him P. Kitty. Like the rapper?"

I stroke the back of the cat's head and he nuzzles closer to me. "Stupid name for a cat."

Ibrahim laughs. "I think it's an awesome name for a cat. You want him? I can't take care of him."

"You literally sell cat food. Every good bodega has a cat."

He nods toward the cook station. "You know Manny, on the morning shift? He's allergic. I can't lose him."

"Yeah, Manny makes the best sandwiches."

"The guy is in demand. Someone else will snatch him up if I'm not careful."

I scratch P. Kitty's neck. He exposes his throat, giving me better access. "No one else wants him?"

"One of the kids wanted to take him, but they're kids. I don't trust them. You live in the neighborhood. You're not going to ditch him soon as you go home for the summer." He smiles. "And the little guy seems to like you."

Animals have a sense, right?

If he feels safe with me, maybe I'm not a monster.

Easy enough to say, harder to believe. I did just brutally kill a completely innocent man in front of his sister—the woman I love, who is carrying my child—on Christmas Eve. Right in front of the tree.

The only thing I know for sure in this moment is: I can't kill myself now.

What would happen to the cat?

11

You hit bottom when you stop digging.
—*the Big Book*

Brighton Beach
Now

We make our way down the boardwalk, the shuttered attractions of Coney Island disappearing into the night sky behind us. The unencumbered wind hurtling off the water bites and claws at our skin.

We could have walked down Surf Avenue, gotten a little shelter from the weather, but I think Booker and Valencia feel the same way I do: the cold air is clarifying, and we're all processing the weight of what could happen.

Our destination appears in the distance: Ekaterina, a Russian restaurant and nightclub that spills onto the boardwalk. This part of the neighborhood is referred to as Little Odessa, for the Russian and Ukrainian immigrants who settled here in the 1970s. Even though the Russian Orthodox Church follows the Julian calendar, putting their celebration of Christmas on January 7, the place is decked out for the holiday.

People are crowded onto the worn wooden planks, smoking and chatting, many of them wearing novelty necklaces strung with flashing Christmas bulbs. In the sea of slacks and mink coats and sparkling jewelry, we are drastically underdressed.

As we approach the door, Booker pulls the wooden rosary out from inside his shirt and presses the cross to his lips, then breaks off and goes to the maître d', a man as short as he is wide, wearing a heavy coat and a black ushanka. A few cries go up from the people waiting in line. Booker and the maître d' lean into each other and whisper, first in a way that is not friendly, and then they warm up, before getting even more unfriendly. I still do not like putting the two of them in this position.

Especially because we're here to see Zmeya.

I've never met her. I don't tend to deal much with the Russians, though I killed more than a few. They're a different level of crazy. But you can't be in this line of work and not know who Zmeya is. She owns this neighborhood and, the whispers say, has a direct line to the Kremlin. In Russian folklore, the zmeya is a many-headed dragon, so I'm suspecting this isn't going to be a super-chill conversation.

Booker and the maître d' clearly come to some kind of understanding and he waves the three of us in. We walk through the outdoor patio, where people are huddled under space heaters, and then into the restaurant, where klezmer music slams into us. The place is all gilded and lined with heavy velvet drapes, that ostentatious Russian design sense that seems like a direct rebuke of the brutalism of communism.

There's barely room for the servers to navigate the sea of crowded tables, and across the room is a large stage full of showgirls in sparkling silver dresses and elaborate headpieces just finishing some sort of performance.

The three of us invite a lot of stares. At first, I think the restaurant is almost exclusively white, so a Black man and a Hispanic woman stand out. Then I realize the stares are directed at me. One man stands up, whom I don't recognize. Then another, and this one I do: Alexsei Zaitsev, a KGB directorate chief.

It's not every day the Pale Horse walks in, I guess.

My chances of getting out of here alive seem to be trending downward.

We're led to a door, behind which is a staircase. At the bottom is a storage room, mostly restaurant supplies. The man reaches underneath one of the heavy wooden shelves, flips something, and pulls it aside. The shelf swings out to a large room—an ornate lounge with a bar on one end and tables loosely filling the space. At one, there's a spirited poker game going.

As we walk through the space, the poker game stops and people stand from the tables, dragging them away, creating room in the middle of the floor.

Booker told us to hang back and trust him, so I'm giving him the leeway on that, but I drop into a loose fighting stance when out of the shadows steps a man who looks like a cross between a Rottweiler and a brick wall. He's massive, with a shaved head covered in faded, blurry, grayscale tattoos—the kind you pick up in a prison.

Between this Russian and my Russian, what the hell are they feeding these guys that makes them so big?

He smiles and cracks his sausage fingers, then shrugs out of a black blazer and throws it in the corner. He's wearing a tank top underneath, showing off fighter-jet arms. Booker is squared up: his right foot drawn back, his left heel planted forward, his hands at his waist.

The goon laughs as he moves toward Booker and throws a massive haymaker, which, if properly landed, would take Booker's head clean off. But he telegraphs it too far in advance, allowing Booker to slip underneath and slam a sharp, nasty hook into the brute's side.

The Russian winces but doesn't budge, then puts his weight into an elbow, snapping it down on top of Booker's head. Booker goes down hard, sprawling on the floor.

People are cheering now, trading dollar bills and rubles. There's a woman at the back, draped in shadow, so that I can barely make her out. All I can see is the burning ember of her cigarette and a slight sparkle in her eye.

The Russian lifts a massive boot into the air and is about to bring it down on Booker, who rolls out of the way and springs to his feet. He steps back, creating a little more distance, letting the Russian come at him, and his foot snaps out into a well-aimed and efficient teep kick, with just enough force to stop the giant's momentum.

As he stumbles, Booker follows it with a hard low roundhouse, wrapping his shin around the back of the Russian's knee. The Russian lands so hard on that knee I think I hear it crunch, even over the yelling. Then Booker follows with another hook, getting his entire body behind it. The tooth-shaking blow lands and the Russian jerks his head but still doesn't go down.

Booker manages to hook his arm around the Russian's throat as he throws his body over the man's back, yanking him to the floor and putting him in a choke hold, moving into a high-elbow guillotine on the ground. It's a smart move, good for smaller grapplers fighting bigger opponents. The Russian's head is tucked close to Booker's torso, and Booker curls his body tight against the man, trapping one arm and robbing him of leverage. The Russian swings wildly but can't land a solid blow.

From here, Booker just has to hold tight until the Russian tires himself out.

The yelling from the crowd intensifies, which causes Booker to tighten his grip. The Russian's face is red and he can't break free. He smacks Booker hard on the back a few times, and Booker lets go. The two of them get off each other, the Russian's chest heaving like he's breathing through a straw. They shake hands and the Russian retreats to the back of the room and disappears. Booker comes over to me, his face coated in sweat. He nods to me.

"She'll see you now," he says.

I pat him on the shoulder before heading over to the table in the back. The men sitting there get up and move away, leaving me and the woman by ourselves.

She's ancient, her skin like parchment, gray hair cut in a bob. She's wearing a black pashmina over a red dress, with minimal makeup and a heavy jewel-encrusted sapphire ring on the hand she's smoking with, which she uses to gesture to the seat across from her. She looks like she'd blow away on a stiff breeze, but even then, her eyes would be left behind in the wake. She has shark eyes.

"A celebrity in our midst," she says.

Tables squeal as they're moved back into place. The poker game resumes.

I nod over my shoulder. "What was that about?"

She stamps out her cigarette in a marble ashtray. "Dmitri and your friend had some unfinished business."

"Dmitri needs to work on his ground game."

She offers the briefest flash of a smile and points that ring finger at me again. "I have been telling him this, but he does not listen." She gives the table a little slap. "Please sit."

I take the seat across from her. "I'm looking for someone."

She savors a long sip of wine. "Aren't we all?"

"He's tall. Six and a half feet at least. Hair shaved into a Mohawk. On his arm"—I hold up my own forearm—"he has a tattoo. A dot, surrounded by four more. I'm told it's supposed to mean he was in prison."

"Yes," she says. "He was."

"You know him?"

She smiles at me, disappointed and upset.

Like, *How dare you?*

"What'll it cost?" I ask.

She waves a hand, showing off the room. "You are free to make me an offer. Though there is not much in this world I do not already have."

"I give a pretty mean foot rub," I tell her.

"Do you know who I am?" she responds, playful.

"Ulyana Semenova," I tell her, and when I say that, her façade drops for a second, delivered in the form of a fluttering eyebrow; most people probably don't know her real name. "You were an intelligence officer. A headhunter. You sought out and trained agents, won some American agents over to the Soviet cause. Story goes, you were a major player in Operation Horizon, back in the 1960s. Exposed more than a hundred foreign agents in the USSR and had them expelled from the country. Big victory for Khrushchev, bigger victory for the KGB. You were good at what you did. I suspect you did that until one day you decided you wanted to be rich. And now you're here. The Zmeya."

She picks up a box of Russian-brand cigarettes, plucks one out, and places it between her lips but doesn't light it. "And how do you know this?"

"You know who I am," the Pale Horse says. "It pays to be a student of geopolitics."

My experience thus far has been that every time I lean into my real voice, it strikes fear into the heart of whoever hears it.

She just smiles, plucks the cigarette from her lips, and gestures with it like a laser pointer. "In my restaurant, too. What an honor. There are a few people here tonight who would like very much to end your life. They would not do so unless I granted them the permission. Lucky for you, I am in a good mood. But you should be careful on the walk home."

Well. Looks like I overplayed my hand.

"So, this man," she says. "I will tell you who he is. Because now I have decided what it is I want from you." She pauses for effect. "A favor. To be decided upon at my leisure."

My heart drops into my lower intestine. She sees it happen and just smiles wider. There's a water glass on the table that looks untouched. I pick it up and drink, hoping it will loosen my throat. "What kind of favor?"

"I cannot tell you," she says. "I may ask you to kill someone. It is what you do. But I may become curious to know if what you say is true, and ask you to rub my tired feet one night. It will depend on my needs."

She puts the cigarette back in her mouth and lights it.

"I have money," I tell her.

"I have more," she says.

"What else would you consider?"

"Please," she says. "What is one more life to the Pale Horse?"

"It could put me in conflict with my employers," I tell her.

She shrugs. "Nothing in life is free."

"Fine," I tell her. "You get one favor. But I get veto power."

She takes a thoughtful drag.

"One time."

I think that's the best I'm going to do.

"Deal," I tell her.

She snaps her fingers, and a man appears with a chef's knife, a wineglass, and an open bottle of wine, which he places down on the table between us. She drags the knife softly against her papery skin, creating a shallow cut about an inch long on the meaty part of her forearm, and lets a few drops of blood fall into the glass. She wipes the knife with a clean napkin and hands it to me, handle first. I do the same. She then pours a small portion of wine into the glass and drinks before passing it to me.

This right here is why I don't like to deal with the Russians. Lunatics.

I take a sip, potentially ruining everything I've worked for.

"Viktor Kozlov," she says. "He is known as the Beast. It is a slightly long story of which I'm not sure all the details are pertinent, but he did spend time in prison. Orenburg Oblast, near the border of Kazakhstan."

"The Black Dolphin."

She smiles. "That's the one. Among the most brutal in all of Russia, and we are not known for our hospitality. He had made some enemies, but when those enemies were deposed and his friends came into power, he was recognized for the asset he was."

"Kozlov," I tell her. "I know most of the major players. Never heard of him."

"He has been in prison for a long time." She takes a long drag of her cigarette. "Given enough time he could be our *you*. Frankly I am surprised you have come to see me. Many assumed you were dead. An occupational hazard in this life. But your Agency has found itself on the losing end of a few operations. The loss of their golden child"—she nods toward me—"left a vacuum."

"What do you mean, losing end?" I ask.

"A bungled coup. A failed assassination. One of your assets was detained in Afghanistan and . . . broke under pressure. I am not sure by whom, but apparently many of your Agency's secrets were spilled, like blood across a table. Russia is watching this with a close eye, and is waiting to strike."

This, I did not know.

If the Agency is on the ropes, of all times to get me back in the game, this was it. Maybe Ravi knows more about this mess than he let on.

"Moscow always talks big," I tell her. "But you know how it works in an oligarchy. The second one of these knuckleheads thinks they're going to lose a couple of kopecks, they get cold feet and remind the Kremlin where the money comes from."

"Once, I might agree," she says. "Once."

"How do I find Kozlov?"

She shrugs again. "Wait for him to find you. I have met him, only once. He frightened me a little. I do not scare easy. You"—she waves a hand at me—"you have a kinder soul than I would have thought. Under different circumstances I would invite you to stay for dinner. I suspect we would have many stories to tell each other." She takes a final, hard drag on her cigarette and stamps it out. "Maybe if you live through this, you come back and see me. Well, you have to, I suppose . . ."

"I don't put out on the first date, just so expectations are clear."

That, at least, earns a genuine smile.

I stand from the table and nod to her. "Thank you for your time."

"I will be in touch," she says.

"For what it's worth, I wasn't kidding about the foot rubs."

But at this point, she's done with me. She waves her hand, and the men who were previously sitting with her come back.

They launch into a hushed conversation in Russian. Someone else takes away the wineglass and the knife but leaves the bottle, which she pours into a clean glass.

I return to the bar, where Booker and Valencia are both working on seltzers. Valencia is staring into the mirror behind the bar, but Booker is slowly shaking his head, and I am struck by a sudden, searing sense of shame.

We're barely out of earshot of the restaurant when Booker pushes me hard on the shoulder, nearly knocking me to the ground. "Why'd you take the drink, Mark?"

"I had no choice."

"You could have gotten up and walked away. That's a choice, too."

"You're the one who brought me here. I needed to know who was after me."

"And now that you know," he asks, "what does it change? What have you gained?"

"I know his name, which means I can find out more about him. I know things spiraled at the Agency after I left, so this puts them back on my list of suspects."

"And now you owe a favor to Zmeya. You know what that means, right?"

I step to Booker and get my nose an inch from his. That dark thing inside me, bubbling up. The scream of it reaching up my throat. "What does it mean? She'll ask for something and I'll say yes or I'll say no. And if I say no, who's going to do something about it?"

Booker sees where I'm at, and rather than match it, he takes a deep breath and lowers his voice. "This is a blood-in, blood-out kind of thing, Mark. Yours, or someone else's. We all know who you are and what you're capable of. But that isn't really an option for you anymore, is it?"

"Maybe it should be."

Booker and Valencia freeze at that.

"I'm exhausted by this shit," I tell them. "What have I gained? A whole bunch of people want to kill me and I can't do a goddamn thing to stop them because now I'm playing by a different set of rules. All I have to do is take the mittens off and I can know peace. Maybe that's worth it."

Valencia puts her hand on my shoulder. "'Adversity truly introduces us to ourselves—'"

I shrug her hand off. "Don't quote the Big Book at me. There's nothing in that book that'll help with this. I don't need recovery right now. I don't know what I need. I need . . ."

I need my sponsor. I need Kenji.

"I need to take a walk."

I don't look back at them. I don't want to see their faces. I stalk off down the boardwalk and they're smarter than to follow. The lights around me fade and I disappear into the depth of the black thing inside me. Maybe, if I'm lucky, I can wrestle it back into submission.

Or else I'll just let it loose and have it solve all my problems.

The front door of the apartment building offers little resistance. Nor does the front door of Kenji's apartment.

I stand in the doorway for a few moments, allowing the quiet to settle into the corners, and then flick on the light. The apartment doesn't look much different than the last time I was here. Bare to the point of barren; the floor is covered with tatami mats—made it feel more like home, Kenji said. There's a low chabudai table in the main living space, with two zabuton meditation pillows on either side of it. No television. No couch.

The kitchen is scrubbed to a microscopic level of clean. Trash is emptied, as is the recycling under the sink. There are some nonperishable items in the fridge. Nothing fresh. The bathroom is bone-dry; the shower hasn't been used in days.

Toothbrush and toothpaste are gone.

The bedroom isn't much more than a cheap mattress on the floor, a pillow and blanket folded neatly on top. The dresser is nearly empty, and there's no luggage in the closet. Given the hasty arrangement of the clothes, it looks like some stuff was quickly pulled out, the rest left behind.

Knowing what I know about him and about me, I poke around until I find a seam in the back wall of the closet and push it aside, revealing a hidden alcove. Inside is his katana, wrapped in a blanket.

I take it out and unsheathe it, hold it up to the light. Still sharp enough to carve an atom in half. A lot of us have a signature weapon, like my SIG Sauer P365, and it's recommended we dispose of it when we enter the program. I'm not surprised he still has this, though. He once told me it was made by a famous sword maker, whose practice can be traced back at least ten generations. The man utilizes tamahagane steel, which is incredibly rare and difficult to work with but results in a stronger blade.

This thing is priceless.

The rest of his stuff seems to be gone, but would he really leave without this?

I roam through the apartment, hoping to find something useful: signs of a struggle, something to tell me what happened to this man I loved, who I thought loved me.

There's a small end table by the door. The last place I haven't checked. I open it up and find a book-shaped gift, wrapped in sparkling white Christmas paper adorned with candy canes. Written with black felt marker in Kenji's delicate script is: *Mark*.

Underneath the gift is the one-year chip he was saving for me. I stick it in my pocket. It's almost mine anyway.

The gift I consider tossing into a corner, but I can't help myself. I tear open the packaging.

It's a handsome leather-bound copy of *Crime and Punishment*.

Despite myself, as hard as I try not to, I laugh.

Astrid is in bed, tucked under the covers, reading a book. She's scrubbed and showered, her hair still wet, face makeup-free. There are Chinese take-out containers on the little coffee table by the couch in the corner. P. Kitty comes wandering out from where he was napping in the corner. I place the signal jammer on the bedside table and sit on the edge of the bed and he hops on my lap and nuzzles me. I scratch behind his ear and he purrs into my hand.

"Nice of you to finally come back." She tosses the book to the side. "You're still in one piece, at least."

"Around two years ago . . ." I tell her, and I let that linger in the air for a moment. She seems to understand the gravity of it because the tension disappears from her posture. "I met this woman. She just saw clear to the center of me and I felt seen for the first time in my life, even if she didn't know the truth about me. Actually thought about quitting. Getting a normie job."

My feet are hot from walking, which is what I've been doing most of the night, so I lean down and take off my shoes.

"Last Christmas, her brother came into the house in the middle of the night. Probably supposed to be a surprise. But my brain goes to DEFCON 1, right? That's what I'm trained to do. I killed him. And she was pregnant . . ."

Four seconds in, hold for four, out for four, empty lungs for four.

I pick a spot on the wall, a little water stain on the wallpaper, and make it my entire universe. Something to keep me steady as the words flow out.

"Soon as I saw that positive test, knowing I was having a kid, I had this vision of decorating their ceiling with those little glow-in-the-dark stars. One of the bedrooms I spent some nights in as a kid, it had stars like that. They made me feel safe, because it reminded me there was a whole universe out there. That the world wasn't so small. That one day I might escape . . ."

Astrid starts to say something, then thinks better of it, and for that I am thankful.

"My son was born on August nineteenth," I tell her. "His name is Bennett. I have no delusions that his mom will let me into their lives."

There's a bottle of water on the nightstand. I pick it up and down half of it, then turn the bottle over in my hand.

"So then I did quit. Got into a twelve-step program for reformed killers. Kenji was my sponsor. First time I ever had a best friend, and he might have sold me out, or maybe he didn't. At this point I can't tell. Either way I need him and he's not here. The man who attacked me was a Russian named Viktor Kozlov. The Beast. I made a deal with the devil to find out. Probably jeopardized my recovery in doing so."

I put the water bottle back down and put my head in my hands.

"I want to kill someone. Anyone. Literally, anyone. I mean, not you. But I want to feel someone's life end in my hands. When I did that, I felt powerful, and now I feel powerless, and power is better. There's nothing in life that compares to death. In recovery we talk a lot about whether killing is a compulsion, and part of me never wanted to believe it. *I'm not addicted*, I kept thinking. But I was. It's how I was trained to communicate with the world around me. It's the only thing I know. It was how I proved I was a man . . ."

I consider looking at Astrid, but I'm not ready yet.

"I'm tired. And this is hard. If I find Kenji, and he did betray me, I may end up killing him. The only way to stop Kozlov is to kill him. A Russian power broker is going to call in a favor soon and probably make me kill someone. All roads lead to this. I've been running from who I am. You told me to tell you the truth. There it is."

I finally turn to Astrid.

The expression on her face is blank.

Then she reaches her hand to me.

I take it, feel the warmth of it, her skin, and then I pull her toward me, and I kiss her, knowing that this might be the exact wrong thing to be doing, but I need to feel something, to feel accepted by someone in the searing light of my sins, and to my relief, she kisses me back.

I wake to the sun in my eyes and an empty bed.

I think maybe Astrid is in the bathroom, but the door is open and the light is off. The room is empty. Her clothes and bag are gone. I get up from the bed and feel a tug on my stomach. There's a fresh bandage on the knife wound. I look for the signal jammer on the bedside table, and it's gone.

There is a lot happening, but for a moment only one thing matters: I'm alone. Astrid is gone. I sat here and cracked open my chest and spilled out my soul and she left. I sit in the silence as it closes in, reminding me what the truth has cost me.

No, not silence. There's an echo reverberating in my chest. I cock my ear and listen.

It's the most savage part of me and it's saying: *I told you so.*

I slide down to the floor, my back against the bed. P. Kitty jumps into my lap and I tell him, "It's gonna be okay."

Except I'm not saying that to him, I'm saying it to me.

And it's not sinking in.

The shaking starts in my chest until it travels through my body, and then I'm clutching P. Kitty, sobbing into his fur, holding him for dear life, because without him, I have nothing. And to his credit, he just stays close and purrs into my skin.

Ms. Nguyen doesn't answer her door. She's probably out grocery shopping, or doing tai chi with the other ladies down in the park. I consider leaving P. Kitty in his carrier outside her door, but I don't want to abandon him like that. What if she's gone for longer?

I head up to my apartment. As soon as I walked in the front door of the building I smelled the smoke, and it intensifies as I climb the final set of stairs to my loft, which takes up the whole top floor.

The door is busted open and crisscrossed with police tape. I step into the remains of my living room. Everything is black scorch and white ash. I put P. Kitty down at the entrance, and despite the destruction he knows he's home. He scratches the caged door on the front of his carrier and yowls, but I don't want to let him out. Too easy to lose him, or for him to get hurt.

"It'll be fine, buddy," I tell him. "Ms. Nguyen is going to give you a better life. More snacks, for sure."

The bookshelf is in ruins. I look for the paper crane Kenji gave me, but it's gone. After retrieving the password inside I did my best to fold it back up, though it didn't look as neat and precise as when he gave it to me. Now I can't even find the ash, like it never existed.

There are still a few pieces of clothing intact at the back of the closet, but they reek of smoke. I get down on the floor and feel around between the floorboards until I find the finger latch, and pull up. The safe underneath is still intact. I key in the combination and open it. There's a duffel bag crammed into the corner of the closet. I drag it over and load wrapped stacks of hundred-dollar bills. Each stack is ten thousand dollars, so I count off fifty of them. Not too heavy, and enough to get me started.

I'll earn it back once I get into the groove of working again. Maybe I'll take the rest down to Ms. Nguyen. Give her a crash course on how to spend it without attracting the attention of the IRS.

Once I've got my money situated, I keep digging, to the bottom of the safe. To the thing I told Kenji I got rid of, and didn't.

But hey, he kept his katana.

My SIG Sauer P365.

A beautiful piece of death-dealing machinery. Striker-fired subcompact, tritium X-RAY3 day/night sights, and a ten-round magazine. Stainless-steel frame with a polymer grip module. I dig a little deeper and find a box of 147-grain hollow-point bullets.

It's not flashy, but it's reliable.

It's also ended a lot of lives.

Just holding it makes me feel like I can take on the whole world.

This is always the way things were headed. I'm not a man. I'm a tactical drone with a heartbeat and a dairy allergy. It used to be that weapon was aimed and fired by someone else, and I allowed it to happen. The only difference now is I'm going to aim it for myself. Find my peace, and then maybe a farm, and woe be unto anyone who dares try to take that away from me.

I am the Pale Horse.

It was silly to pretend otherwise.

I dig around in my pockets until I find both the one-year and six-month chips, and I toss them into the safe. Then I dig out the urban carry holster stashed with the gun and get it set up on my hip.

There's not much else to do at this point. I go to the bathroom to take a piss. Wonder where Astrid is. Why she disappeared like that. Maybe the gravity of all this sank in. Taking the tracker felt like she was making a point, but I don't know what.

Whatever. It's not like I was falling for her. Not like opening up to her was a last desperate attempt to save myself through truth and vulnerability.

P. Kitty meows at me.

"I'm fine," I tell him.

There's a commotion from outside: horns honking, someone yelling, so I move to the window and peek my head out. There are four black SUVs blocking the street, and a bunch of cars lined up behind them. I don't need anything to confirm that this must be for me, but when Ravi pops out of the lead car, I duck back inside before he can look up.

I grab P. Kitty's carrier and sling the duffel bag over my shoulder and make for the building's air shaft, which is between this building and the one behind us.

The Agency troops will eventually get around to checking the shaft and they'll find the handholds I installed, as well as the door at the bottom, which I can slip through to get into the building behind mine. Then they'll find the unmapped door to a utility tunnel, inside which I carved out enough room to let me slip into the sewer system.

If that door were on a map, they'd have someone stationed down there, but lucky for me, New York City is a maze of shit built on top of shit. Spend enough time looking around and you can find a decent escape route. I'll be long gone by the time they find it.

I lower myself out the window, holding tight to P. Kitty's carrier. He doesn't make a sound. Probably too scared. Thank god. Last thing I need is for someone to look out a window and see me. But given the proximity of the windows between the buildings and the lack of privacy, most people have curtains or blinds.

I make it down about ten feet when I hear ". . . caught him on a camera around the corner, not ten minutes ago."

It's coming from Ms. Nguyen's apartment. I stop and brace myself, just to make sure she's going to be okay. Ravi wouldn't hurt her, probably, but I want to be sure of that.

"I was out running an errand," she says. "I don't know if he even came here. I haven't seen him since the fire."

"Damn it, Fran, I pay you a lot of money, and you have one job. Keep an eye on him. And you couldn't even do that . . ."

"First off, don't speak to me like that," she says. "Second, I retired. I was done. I agreed to do this because it was low impact. No chance of getting hurt. I worked too hard to risk my life like this."

What?

"We're going to search the area," Ravi says. "If you see him, you know the drill. Call me ASAP."

A few moments of silence, and then Ms. Nguyen asks, "What kind of mood is he going to be in?"

"Probably not a very good one. But he has no reason to suspect you, right?"

"Right."

"He'll come to us. We have his friend. If he's going to be pissed at anyone, he's going to be pissed at me. When he hears what I have to say, he'll understand."

Wait.

The Agency has Kenji?

Does that mean he didn't sell me out?

I've lingered too long. But there's no sound above me. Are they not in the apartment? I wait another second, my free hand hovering by the pistol, which suddenly feels hot and alien on my belt. After a moment, I risk it and climb back up. There's no sound, no nothing. I clamber back in, then dash over to the window and watch the SUVs pull away from the curb.

If the Agency has Kenji, then he didn't turn on me.

They're using him to draw me out.

And since I got rid of my old phone, and the secured messaging app I used to communicate with Ravi, he had no way to get in contact with me.

Breathe in for four, hold for four, out for four, empty lungs for four.

What do I know?

Zmeya told me the Agency had gotten slapped around a bit and was currently on the ropes. So it behooves them to get me back to work. But Ravi knew where I was this whole time; he was paying Ms. Nguyen to keep an eye on me. Which, putting aside the discomfort of knowing that my life isn't exactly what I thought it was, it raises the question: Why didn't he come to me sooner?

This all started with Kozlov, who stabbed me, planted me with a tracker, and took my notebook.

He stabbed me, but left me alive.

Oh.

Enough of the picture snaps into place that I can at least see the outline of what's happening.

This is a power grab.

Some foreign player is looking to depose the Agency.

The notebook serves two purposes: it gives that player a ton of intel about Agency operations, but it also sends me into panic mode, turning me against them—and if you want to hurt an organization like the Agency, your best bet is to turn their biggest asset into an enemy.

The Agency must have some kind of inkling about this. And even if they don't know about the program, they knew where I was—they must know I'm close to Kenji. So they scooped him up, maybe to protect him, maybe for insurance, maybe to help find me.

I go back to the safe, open it, dig out the six-month chip, press it to my lips, and place it in my pocket. The one-year chip stays. It doesn't feel right to carry something I haven't earned yet. I stash it with the gun, remove a few stacks of bills from the duffel bag, and shove them in my coat.

Only one thing matters: Kenji is alive and the Agency has him.

So I'm going to get him.

Lulu throws me a little eyebrow when I step through the door of the diner. The place is mostly empty. The old man in the brown suit is doing his crossword at the back, and there's an MTA worker sitting at the counter, nursing a cup of coffee. I walk to the register and tell her, "I'd like the hungry man's breakfast, please. No sausage, extra bacon."

Lulu stares at me for a moment, like she didn't understand what I said, then without moving her eyes from me, raises her voice and says, "Rodney, we need to close up for the day."

The MTA worker looks over and shrugs, throws some money on the counter, and leaves. The man in the brown suit remains. Once the door closes behind us, Lulu crosses over and locks it and flips the CLOSED sign, then leads me back to the kitchen. I put P. Kitty's carrier behind the counter and follow. The kitchen is cramped and immaculate, the stainless-steel surfaces gleaming, like you can't tell the last time it was used. She takes me to a door in the back, which opens onto a narrow staircase. We head down into a basement that smells like standing water, where there's another door, and she fishes a heavy key chain out of her apron, then opens it up.

Inside is a room roughly the size of the diner, the walls adorned with lighted panels that softly flicker to life. Each one is loaded with weapons, from pistols to assault rifles.

"What do you need?" she asks.

"Nonlethals."

"What's the gig?"

"Agency headquarters."

A laugh grows deep in her belly and reverberates through the room. "And you want nonlethals for that?"

I shrug at her, and she shrugs back.

"Okay, then," she says.

Like, *It's your funeral.*

Maybe it is.

She crosses to the far wall, pulling a rolling table alongside her. She takes a pair of what look like brass knuckles off the wall, but they're heavy black plastic with metal tips.

"Just got these in," she says. "Stun knuckles. Like a Taser."

"Nothing with electricity. Can't risk sending someone into cardiac arrest."

"Jesus, you're not making this easy. Okay."

She plucks a pistol off the wall. It's slightly bigger than a normal gun. The body is black but the slide is orange, and there are two fat barrels on the front.

"Air pistol, loads with pellets that disperse a cloud of pepper spray. The clips hold five pellets each." She holds it up and points to the bottom barrel. "You drop the CO canister in here. First trigger pull breaks it. When you reload a clip, you have to put in a fresh canister. It's slow and they sometimes jam if you fire too fast."

"I'll take two, and as many clips as you have."

"Then you'll want this." She places a gas mask on the table, with a wide, clear faceplate. "Won't obstruct your vision. Hypoallergenic coating on the inside to prevent fogging."

She rummages around in a drawer and comes out with a foam handle about seven inches long. She hands it to me. I test the weight—light as a freshly fallen feather—then snap it out to full length.

"Steel friction baton, twenty-one inches," she says. "I tend to dislike the grips on most batons, but this one holds up pretty well."

I slam the point on the counter to close it and put it on the table.

"Great," I tell her. "Next?"

She lines up thin cylindrical grenades on the counter. Six in all.

"Flash-bang," she says. "Nonfragmenting, nonbursting aluminum body. Anti-rolling so it'll stay close to where you toss it. Three bursts of sound and light." She places a slim piece of plastic next to them. "And you can set any of them to remote detonate."

"I could use a vest."

She opens a large drawer and pulls out a black vest and holds it up to me. "Looks about your size. Rated level four, with full side protection, and it has a cooling mesh liner."

I test the weight, then feel the front, find it free of the

telltale level-four bulk. "How do they claim that without rifle plates?" Before she can answer, I find a tag on the side with a Hebrew symbol. "Ah. Gotta love Israeli craftsmanship."

"It's still in development, but I got a preview," she says. "A thirty-ought-six round is going to crack a rib, but it shouldn't break through." She sticks an excited finger in the air. "One last thing. This is a fun little bit of business."

She places a small black box with a wrist strap on the table. I pick it up and put it on.

"It emits a laser that'll overwhelm the optical nerve," she says. "There's a button that fixes on the palm so you can wear it without interfering with trigger pulls."

I aim the device at the far wall, hit the button on my palm with my middle finger, and a thick dot of flashing green light appears.

"Nice. You got any kill switches?"

She nods, digs around in another drawer, and comes out with a USB stick, which she places next to the rest.

"And I could use some cutlery," I tell her.

Not that I'm planning to open any throats, but a knife can be useful in so many other ways. She opens another drawer and comes out with an eight-inch blade snugged tight within a sheath. "Clip point, flat grind. It's not very resistant to corrosion and sometimes gets stuck coming out of the holder, but you can use it as a pry bar without worrying about snapping off the tip."

I pull it out—the sheath does offer a little resistance, but it's not bad—and check the edge of the blade. Looks plenty sharp, and the rubber handle is nice and grippy.

"What do I owe you?" I ask.

"Let's call it thirty grand," she says. "Your credit is usually good with me, but considering what you're about to do, I'd like you to pay me now."

"Business is business," I tell her, and dig the money out of my coat.

As I stack the bills on the table she asks, "You sure about this?"

"Not really, no," I tell her.

"What you and the others are doing, the whole group thing—it's good. You know that, right?"

"How do you know about that?"

She smirks as she places a duffel bag on the counter so I can load up the gear. "You and Kenji don't keep your voices nearly as low as you think." She looks around the room as I pack up. "You're a good customer. You're probably going to get killed, but it'd be nice if maybe you didn't."

"Thanks, Lu," I tell her. "And you're tougher than a mouthful of thumbtacks. One last question: How do you feel about cats?"

She nods. "If you don't come back, I'll make sure he finds a good home."

"You're a doll." I throw my gear over my shoulder and leave Lulu to get the room straightened up. On the way out of the diner I stop at the register. One last thing: I grab a black felt marker off the pad next to the register.

Never leave home without one.

I put the carrier on the counter and open the door. P. Kitty was napping—I guess he just got used to the travel. I don't risk holding him too tight, because then he'll just squirm away from me and get lost in here somewhere. But I hold him up and look him in his eyes—or, eye, considering one seems to be pointed at the wall.

"I'm sorry for all the times I called you dumb," I tell him. "You saved my life. You are a good cat, and I love you, and I hope to see you again, okay? Either way, thank you."

"Meow," he seems to say in response, as I load him back in the carrier.

I hang up the phone. Booker accepted my apology, and my thanks. He promised to find Valencia and complete the favor I asked of him. I was worried it might be asking too much at this point, but it wasn't.

Because the feeling of having shared in a common peril is one element in the powerful cement which binds us, and it's on me for forgetting that.

Satisfied that's covered, I lean over the edge of the roof. Cold wind blows through my hair and my stomach dips. The Agency building rooftop is about twenty stories down. I check the harness around my waist one more time to make sure it's secure.

Funny the way life comes full circle.

My career with them started, and will officially end, with jumping off a roof.

I move to the other edge, to where I can clearly see the

trash can on the sidewalk. There are still too many people around it, so I wait. I don't have much of a plan, other than to stroll into the Director's office, introduce myself, show him how easy it is to get to him, and demand they hand Kenji over.

Maybe not the most elegant plan, but I've certainly rolled out with less.

I've been inside before, but only on the lower floors. It used to be the tallest building on the block, but then developers got obsessed with these super-tall residential skyscrapers, and the security inside them sucks as much as you'd imagine. A bored ex-cop at a desk and a camera system I can walk straight through without attracting any undue attention.

Surely the Agency caught me on the city's CCTV, and they know I'm nearby. They probably assume I'm coming in the front door. Which I hope they continue to believe. I'm going to help them believe it, if the space around the trash can would just clear a little.

As soon as I land on the roof they'll register my presence—there are some electronics scattered about that look pretty innocuous but I'm sure can count the pebbles on the surface of the roof. Need to take them out quick. There's an emergency access panel near the stairwell door that looks promising.

The space around the trash can finally clears, so I take the remote out of my pocket and hit the button. A flash-bang goes off with a thump I can barely hear and a burst of light, then two more in succession. With the way the trash is compacted around it, it immediately catches fire. Bystanders duck for cover or pull out their phones to record it. I wonder if any of them actually call 911 or if they're just posting it to Instagram.

As soon as I see flames, I jump off the edge of the building, rappelling my way down, and when I land on the roof, I sprint for the emergency panel. It's locked, so I slip the knife inside and lean into it, prying the panel off. There's a USB port and a small computer screen with a keyboard, so I stick in the kill switch and run the prompt to start it. The security here is a little more robust than in most places I would use this, but still, it'll buy me some time, and . . .

"Hey, Mark."

I turn to find Ravi standing twenty-five feet away, his hands behind his back, like he's waiting his turn to order coffee. He's wearing a white dress shirt, navy slacks, and an expensive pair of Italian loafers. There's a tactical vest under the shirt and a handgun strapped to his belt.

"Hey there, bud," I tell him. "You seem awful lonely up here. Where's the goon squad?"

"I wanted to talk," he says. "You and me. I figured you'd come in through the roof. I know you. I didn't share that with anyone else."

"How kind of you."

Before he can blink I've got one of the air pistols cleared from the holster and trained on the spot directly between his eyes.

He squints and tilts his head. "That a toy?"

"Pepper spray pellets. It won't kill you, but it won't feel nice, either."

He nods slowly and takes a step, keeping the same distance, walking a circle around me. "At this point, I have to figure, you know that I know. Dymphna's. The paper cranes. The last year. Sara and Lucas. Everything."

"And you were just waiting to, what? Pressure me back into the game?"

"No, Mark, I've been trying to protect you. The Agency has been looking for you since you went into the cold, but do you really think they'd let you walk on killing a civilian? If the Director knew, you'd have been dead within a day."

"What happened, then?"

He pats his chest. "I did. I made it go away."

"Do you want a medal?"

"A little thanks would be nice."

"Why'd you do it?"

"Because regardless of what you might think, I like you, Mark. It was easy enough from the crime scene details to tell it was an accident. I could just imagine how it tore you up. Finding you with the paper cranes confirmed that. I thought you deserved a little peace."

"And now you want me back. You even assigned me a chaperone."

Ravi sighs and puts his hands on his hips. "First off, Ms. Nguyen was one of our best agents. She was there to *protect* you. Second, there's some shit going on that would take about six hours and a slideshow to explain. Instability in Eastern Europe. Regime shuffling in the Middle East. High-level targets we've been watching for years taken out. There's been chatter about some kind of concentrated effort here, but we can't see the full picture yet. The only thing I can surmise is that Kozlov was hired to take you out, so the board would be clear."

"See, Ravi, here's my problem," I tell him. "I know that you're lying."

"How's that?"

"You're breathing. When we had lunch in Singapore, you said you didn't know who he was."

"C'mon, Mark," he says, raising his voice, getting agitated. "I had to play a little dumb. I still had no idea why you showed up. And I'm juggling that with the fact that the Director wants you in his office. Azrael is waiting downstairs, by the way . . ."

"Good. I could use the workout. Where's Kenji?"

"He's downstairs. He's safe."

"He better be."

"I figured whoever was coming after you would chase him down next to draw you out. We extracted him. He knows the whole story. You'd know that if you checked your messages. I've been trying to get in contact with you to set up a meet."

"I've been busy."

He nods, continuing to walk around me, maintaining that distance. It's not lost on me that the distance is twenty-five feet. I take a few steps toward him, closing the gap. He notices but doesn't react.

"Come downstairs with me," Ravi says. "Peacefully. The Director is out for blood. I can talk him down. I'm willing to stake my reputation on it. He's going to want you back. And that's something we're going to need. When you realize what's happening, you'll drop all this recovery bullshit and help us put things right."

"It's not bullshit."

"We need you, Mark. We need the Pale Horse. A lot of people are going to die without you."

"A lot of people will die no matter what."

"You can make sure it's the *right* ones."

"That's not true, and it never was."

Ravi puts his hands together in mock prayer. "Please, Mark. I'm your friend."

"A friend wouldn't be telling me to throw out everything I worked for over the past year."

"A friend is someone who sees you," Ravi says. "And I see you. I get why you struggle. I do, too. If you didn't, you'd be a complete sociopath. But in the end, the world needs bad men to keep other bad men from the door."

"Did you just quote *True Detective* at me?"

He pauses, a little embarrassed. "Shit, you saw that?"

"Remember what you told me in Singapore? When I asked why you picked me for this?"

Ravi starts to say something, then stops.

"That it was my temperament," I tell him. "That I wasn't some militia nut. That I had high scores and a strong will. It was all bullshit. You picked me because I was a scared, lonely kid, desperate to be told he was good at something. Am I right?"

His lip flutters into the makings of a smile, which is all the answer I need. Then he sighs, his body going slack for just a second.

It's a distraction. I know it is. By the time he's reaching for the gun on his holster, I've got a pellet sailing his way. It lands on his chest with a crack. I expect there to be some kind of hissing sound, or to see a cloud of dust. I wonder if these things are defective, but then he starts hacking and grabbing at his face.

He falls to his knees, choking.

"See you around, Ravi," I tell him.

At the bottom of the stairs is a door, which leads to the elevator bank serving the top floor of the building. Beyond that is a dim office area that looks mostly empty. The Director's office is, presumably, past that.

Standing between me and my goal are twelve men and women in tactical gear—black body armor and heavy goggles, all strapped with FN P90s, a compact submachine gun designed for tight spaces that spits out fifty rounds in a blink.

At least I have some air pistols.

As they raise their weapons in my direction, I duck back into the stairwell and a voice rings out, "We *will* shoot to kill."

"I'm sure at this point you know who you're dealing with," I yell around the corner. "You want to go home healthy, now's the time."

In response, the lights snap off.

Which is exactly what I was expecting.

My vision goes completely black, and I'm sure the strike team is turning on their night vision goggles. I pull a flashbang off my belt and throw it through the doorway, not really worried about aiming.

"Grenade!" someone yells.

The first bang hits, followed by a flash. I've got my eyes

closed and my hand over my face, but even still some of the light seeps through. With their night vision goggles amplifying the light, it probably looks like staring into the face of the sun from ten feet away. It must not feel nice; I can tell that from the screams.

When the third and final bang-flash combo goes off, I swing around the doorway with the air pistols raised. The members of the strike team are yelling and struggling to get their goggles off. I squeeze off the nine shots I have left, not so much worrying about hitting the men and women in the hallway. I just need to crack open as many of the pellets as possible.

I duck back into the stairwell and pull down the gas mask and hear coughing.

"Lights, lights," someone yells, choking through snot and phlegm. "Hit the lights!"

The first thing they see when the lights come on, if they can even see yet, is me moving down the hallway, the baton raised, placing the weapon onto knees and elbows and helmets. At this point it's like a ballet. I see every angle, how to move from one swing into the next, hitting the targets that are going to inflict the most damage you can get without killing someone. A few of them squeeze off shots, their guns thundering in the tight space, slamming into the walls and sending up puffs of drywall, but they can't get a bead on me.

My old friend adrenaline does its job, screwing with time. I'm moving so fast it feels like forever. And by the time I reach the end of the hallway I'm the only person standing. I'm feeling pretty good about it until another guy in tac gear comes around the corner and unloads two slugs into my chest.

Suddenly I'm airborne and I land hard on my back. I tuck my chin so I don't smash my head against the floor, then slap at the searing pain on my chest to make sure the bullets didn't go through. Worked fine, and that's why I go to Lulu.

The shooter moves in, holding the gun out, and I blast him in the face with the optical distractor. He shields his eyes, which gives me enough time to roll out of the line of fire, get to my feet, and throw a sharp hook into his side, where his vest doesn't cover. Then I snap the blunt end of the baton against his forehead.

The numbers on all the elevators are increasing, so I pull the fire alarm. The emergency lights flash, a high-pitched whine ringing out through the space, and the numbers stop growing. This is too easy. I take a moment to reload the air pistols, then turn the corner into the office area. After turning a few more corners I find a double set of wide oak doors. I'm moving toward them when a figure steps out from an alcove.

The Neck.

His face is bruised, but probably not nearly as much as his ego. He's furious, and he points a thick finger at me and says, "Time for some payback, motherfu—"

I grab the finger and twist it toward the ceiling and he throws his head back and yelps. I use the leverage to bring him to his knees and then use my knee to shut him up.

Back to the doors. I head for them, when something hits my back and sends me flying. I throw myself forward with the momentum and combat roll to my feet, turning to find Ravi. His eyes are red, his face raw. He's in a loose fighting stance.

"I was trying to protect you, you dumb son of a bitch," he says. "Now we're past that."

I whip up an air pistol and send a shot Ravi's way, but he ducks forward hard, bending almost to the floor, and the shot goes wide. Before I even get it retrained on him he smashes into me.

My mistake; he was only twelve feet away.

We plunge to the floor and he grabs me by the throat, setting his grip, and headbutts me hard. My vision goes fuzzy and he brings up an elbow to smash me in the head, but I manage to get a knee between us and then lift him up, sending him flying over me. We scramble to our feet, resetting ourselves.

"Didn't know you could rumble," I say.

"Don't send people to do work you aren't willing to do yourself."

He snaps a kick at me, and I grab his foot, yanking him back hard, taking him off balance, and then slam my fist onto his knee. Not enough to break it, but enough that he'll need to ice it tomorrow. I'm expecting him to go down but instead he leans into me, gets some leverage, and brings the other foot up. He goes briefly airborne before slamming his free foot into the side of my head, and I crash into an empty cubicle, landing in an awkward pile.

He disappears from my field of vision and comes back with a roller chair lifted over his head. I bring the baton down hard on his foot. It staggers him, and I roll onto my hands and horse-kick him in the stomach. He falls, dropping the chair on me, which hurts, but it hurts him more.

Before I can get back to my feet he tackles me, and then we're grappling on the floor. It stops being a clean fight. The two of us struggling for purchase, trying to find a place to slip in and score a shot. The blows land, but I'm too amped up to feel them. Finally I manage to roll on top of him and throw my fist into his jaw a few times.

He drops back, his eyes swirling in their sockets. I climb to my feet and he says, "Whatever happens next is on you, Mark."

In response, I take the other air pistol from my belt, reload it, and put a pellet into his chest, sending him into another coughing, spasming fit.

Then I reach for the double oak doors.

They open onto a handsome but sparse office that demonstrates money without bragging about it. It's longer than it is wide, with a desk at the end, perched beneath floor-to-ceiling windows overlooking Midtown. There are two chairs in front of the desk, and one behind it, facing away.

I hold up the pistol, wondering what kind of man the Director is. I never met him. I had dreams that one day I would. He'd call me into his office to tell me how good I was at my job. A dumb fantasy, I now realize. Doesn't matter. I don't need his approval. The people at the top are all the same: terrified when faced with the consequences of their own actions.

Otherwise they wouldn't need people like me.

The chair rolls around and I'm greeted by the last person I expected to see.

"Astrid?" I ask.

Her face looks different. Cast-iron eyes, and that smile. Not like any smile I've seen on her. Knowing and mischievous.

She's been waiting very patiently for this moment. She's wearing a black shirt, black pants, and a harness, strapped with enough weaponry to storm the Bastille.

"Azrael," she says.

Huh.

"Thought Azrael was a man," I tell her.

"That's sexist." She pulls a gun from her lap and points it at me. She's more than the minimum safe distance. "And sort of the point."

"Is that an FN Five-seven?" I ask.

She tilts the gun. "High-velocity rounds. From this distance it stands a decent shot of cutting through a level-three vest."

I pat my chest. "Level four."

"Really? It doesn't look like it has plating."

"Israeli."

"Ah, that makes sense. Guess I'll just go for the head."

"Kinda wish you wouldn't. As you can imagine, I have questions."

Like, a lot. It does verify a few things: why she can fight, why she stuck with me through all this. But those realizations just raise more questions. The one thing I can say for sure is that seeing her, oddly, brings me some level of comfort.

"I bet," she says. "But first we're getting out of here. Turn around, hands behind your back. Any sudden movement and you get to find out how good a shot I am."

With most people, I'd get to work, calculating the odds, figuring out how to turn the tables. Astrid—Azrael—is a pro. I'm not inclined to push my luck with a pro. Better to listen until an opportunity presents itself rather than try to manufacture one.

And right now, at least, it'd be nice to get some answers.

She takes my hands and zip-ties them tightly behind me. Then she shoves me forward.

"March." As she pushes me through the oak doors, there's a hiss of static and she speaks into her walkie-talkie. "I'm bringing him out. Clear a path to the parking garage. Director's orders."

Ravi is dragging himself to his feet. "I didn't hear that order."

"You wouldn't have."

There's a sharp crack from behind me and Ravi's head jerks back. His body folds to the floor like a rag doll.

A few seconds ago I could have watched him get skinned alive while munching popcorn. But my anger is clouded over by the memories of us traveling the world, eating well, sharing laughs after a job. He was still an important part of my life for a long time, and a deep well of sadness swirls through the anger.

"Jesus, Astrid," I say.

"He bet on you and he lost. That's just one in a series of screwups. Like I said, Director's orders."

When we reach the elevator bank, the only evidence of the mayhem from earlier is the battered furniture and the bullet holes in the walls. Astrid presses the DOWN button and a door opens.

"Right corner," she says. "Face the wall."

I lean against it as the elevator begins its descent. "So," I ask, "how in the hell did I end up at your apartment before Singapore? Was all that by some kind of design?"

"It was good timing. I moonlight as a black-market trauma surgeon. I was a medic in the Special Forces. That was before I was recruited by Ravi. Patching people up, it's something to earn a little extra money, and to keep my ear to the ground. Like I kept saying, you boys love to brag."

"And Ravi didn't know you were with me?"

"Just kept telling him I was right behind you, and he bought it. I've been trying to get my hands on Kozlov. Soon as you mentioned him to your friend on that phone call, I knew it was him. I didn't have his name at that point, but I knew exactly who you meant."

"What did Kozlov do to you?"

"He killed someone important to me. He left that scar on my back. Did you ever wonder about why I stuck with you? Anyone with sense would have run. When I found out you were the Pale Horse, I thought I could use you to draw him out. Maybe soften him up. I didn't know you were the one who went soft."

"I didn't go soft."

"Okay, Gandhi."

The elevator doors open onto a cavernous parking garage. It's half empty, spots occupied mostly by black, anonymous-looking sedans and SUVs. Astrid steps out first and tells me to follow. I consider hitting the CLOSE DOOR button, but it probably won't shut on her in time.

"The white van, over there in the corner," she says.

There's only one, so I head toward it. "You know, Gandhi said if he had to choose between cowardice and violence, he'd choose violence."

"Then he's tougher than you."

"I'm not a coward," I tell her.

"Coulda fooled me."

"You know how hard it is to spend your whole life doing what I did, to be good at it like I was, and to decide to stop? I didn't make that choice once. I have to make it every single day."

"Look where it got you."

"It worked until it didn't. Why did you take the signal jammer?"

"Once I realized you were useless to me I figured I would draw Kozlov out. But he hasn't turned up. Then I got the call from Ravi. Figured our paths would cross eventually."

"Why did you sleep with me?"

She hesitates. "Girl's got needs."

I can't see her face, but from the way she paused, I can tell that's not the whole truth.

"Where's Kenji?"

"He was gone two minutes after you disabled the security," she says. "Saw an opportunity and took it, I guess. Heard it on the radio right before you came in. At this point I don't need him. I just needed you."

I stop at the back of the van. She waves the gun so I'll back off a bit, and she opens the door. The inside is completely stripped, and there's a metal cage between the back and the front.

"You understand killing Kozlov won't bring that other person back, right?" I ask.

"Get in the van," she says.

"You know what anger like that is?"

"What?"

"Drinking poison, hoping the other person dies."

"Get in the van."

I climb in and lower myself to the floor as she slams the door. She walks around and hops onto the driver's seat, stashes the gun on the passenger seat, taps on her phone a little, and drives. We wend our way through the garage and onto the street. It's hard for me to sit comfortably, so I settle for lying on my back.

After a couple of blocks she says, "I don't get it."

"What?"

"The not-killing thing. I know what we do isn't going to win us a seat in heaven. But how far do you take it? Say you could go back in time, right? Wouldn't you kill Hitler?"

"Why does it have to be about killing him? If you could go back in time, why not go back further, to when he was a kid, and show him the love and understanding he never got? Dissuade him of all the messed-up notions he had? You haven't saved seventy million people. You saved seventy million and one."

"But he's Hitler. Doesn't he deserve to die?"

She doesn't sound like she's taunting me now, not exactly. She sounds genuinely curious.

"You could make that argument. But this is a thought experiment."

We drive in silence for a little. Then she says, "You know what pisses me off the most, though?"

Before I can ask what, something smashes into the side of the van and my stomach lurches as we go airborne. I ricochet off the hard surfaces, trying to protect my head, which is impossible with my hands behind my back, and when we finally come to a rest, I think upside down, my vision is fuzzy and my brain feels like a half-deflated and well-used soccer ball.

"Astrid?" I ask.

No answer.

The back door opens behind me. I can't see who it is, but I can venture a guess. Before I can say something smart, a canister lands next to me, spitting out white vapor. I'm too winded to hold my breath, and it smells sweet, and then . . .

12

Grace means that all of your mistakes now serve a purpose instead of serving shame.
—Brené Brown

Lower East Side
One Year Ago

"I'm glad to see you again," Kenji says.

He's standing with his hands tucked inside his long black jacket, and he offers me a little bow. I offer one in return. He's a bit older now, his hair a little more gray, but he looks different than that last time I saw him, on that snowy rooftop.

He doesn't seem as burdened.

He also snuck up on me, which is a hard thing to do. I guess some skills never go away.

"Long way from Prague," I tell him.

"Would you walk with me, Mark?"

He doesn't wait for an answer, sensing I will. We weave though the dense crowd on Delancey Street. It's a Tuesday. Three whole days since I tried to end my own life and then found P. Kitty, and I'm taking that as a win. The thought of finishing the job snuck up a few times since then and lucky for me the cat would always do something dumb—go in the bathroom and cry at the tub or fall off the bookcase.

It was just enough to get me to open the paper crane, inside of which was the password for the forum on the Via Maris: *anxious phoenix.*

We walk for a bit until Kenji stops in front of a dilapidated church. The doors are painted red, worn and beaten by age. The stone façade is crumbling. Had we not stopped here, I might have walked past and not even registered it.

"Do you know the story of St. Dymphna?" Kenji asks.

"I know there's a bar in Alphabet City named after him. That's the best I got."

Kenji nods. "*Her.* St. Dymphna was a princess, born in Ireland in the seventh century. When she was fourteen she swore a vow to Christ. Shortly after, her mother died. Her father was a petty king. He took the death very hard and searched far and wide, looking for a woman to marry who matched his wife's beauty. He eventually settled on his own daughter."

"Gross," I tell him.

He doesn't laugh. "She fled to Belgium, where she opened a hospital for the poor and sick. A year later her father found her, and when she rejected his advances, he cut off her head."

"That's some real family dysfunction there."

Kenji turns and gives me a hard little stare.

"Sorry," I tell him. "Please."

"A church was built in her honor in Geel, the town in Belgium where she died," he says. "People came from all over Europe, seeking help for psychiatric conditions. Thus began a tradition that still persists today, where the people of Geel take in those who are sick and suffering. They call them boarders, not patients. They are welcomed as part of people's families. It is not meant to be treatment or therapy. It is purely a thread of kindness that has stretched for hundreds of years.

"This church is named after her. This is where we meet. Every Tuesday night. We picked this location because the pastor is a friend, and I knew we could be safe here. I do not believe in coincidence, but the name of it felt a bit like providence."

We stand there in the silence, surveying the building.

"There are rules," Kenji says without looking at me. "We are modeled on Alcoholics Anonymous, but the meetings are small, so they can be less structured. We do not reveal the names we worked under, and we do the best we can to obscure our political affiliations. That is for everyone's safety. No one must know you are the Pale Horse but me."

"Thank you."

"Normally there is a vetting process," Kenji says. "And that takes time. But from what I see, I believe you are ready to join us tonight."

"And what do you see?"

He turns to me, looking me up and down, and zeroes in on my eyes. His gaze is so searching I feel compelled to hide from it, but I know that's not the thing to do. The thing to do is stand here and let him see me.

"Sadness, that you carry like an anchor," he says. "But more than that, a desire to put the anchor down rather than follow it into the deep."

"Sounds about right."

He leads me to the side of the church, down a short flight

of stone stairs, and through a door, then a darkened hallway, and around a corner. The church basement is sparse, but large enough to fit a few dozen people for a mixer or a fund-raiser. There's a folding table holding a coffeepot and an open box of donuts. The walls are robin's-egg blue and the floor is a black-and-white-checkered pattern.

In the center of the room are four chairs facing each other, just close enough that the people sitting in them could lean forward and stretch and hold hands. Two of those seats are occupied: a Hispanic woman and a Black man, both of them immediately recognizable by the smell of gunpowder in their blood.

"This the guy?" the Black man asks. "Doesn't look very tough. You sure he's one of us?"

I get a little closer, let his eyes meet mine, and he nods.

"Yeah, guess he is." He offers me his hand and we shake. "Booker."

The Hispanic woman offers me her hand. "Valencia."

I return the shake. "Like the orange."

"No," she says, pulling her hand away, her face going dark. "Never like the orange."

Booker puts his hands up. "This is a safe space for everything but that."

I put my hands up in mock surrender and look around. Kenji gestures to the folding table. I pour myself a cup of coffee, just to have something to do with my hands.

"Now," Kenji says as I sit, placing down a small silver lipstick-sized device. "This will disable any listening or recording devices and obscure our voices. A measure of security, given the things we discuss. And at the start of every meeting, we review the steps:

"One, we admit we are powerless—that our lives have become unmanageable.

"Two, we come to believe that a power greater than ourselves can restore us to sanity.

"Three, we make a decision to turn our will and our lives over to the care of a higher power, as we understand it.

"Four, we make a searching and fearless moral inventory of ourselves.

"Five, we admit to our higher power, to ourselves, and to another human being the exact nature of our wrongs.

"Six, we are ready to have our higher power remove all these defects of character.

"Seven, we humbly ask it to remove those shortcomings.

"Eight, we make a list of all persons we have harmed, and become willing to make amends to them all.

"Nine, we make direct amends to such people, wherever possible, except when to do so would injure them or others.

"Ten, we continue to take a personal inventory, and when we are wrong, promptly admit it.

"Eleven, we seek through prayer and meditation to improve our conscious contact with our higher power, as we understand it, praying only for knowledge of its will for us and the power to carry that out.

"Twelve, having had a spiritual awakening as the result of the steps, we try to carry this message to others like us, and to practice these principles in all our affairs."

Kenji pauses, giving the words a moment to sink in. Then

he says, "No one among us has been able to maintain anything like perfect adherence to these principles. We are not saints . . ."

"Damn straight," Booker mutters.

"The point is that we are willing to grow along spiritual lines," Kenji says. "Now, Mark, as this is your first meeting, you're welcome to share. Would you like to tell us what brought you here?"

My head spins a little. I'm not used to talking about my job. Or my feelings. Or anything at all, really. And here are three people waiting for me to open my wrist and spill blood all over the floor. I press my hands together, crack my knuckles, hoping words manage to spring forth, but not really knowing what to say.

Booker raises his hand, a pair of wooden rosary beads wrapped around his palm and dangling down his wrist. "I can share. To get us started."

His voice sounds different. Softer now, and warmer. I nod at him.

"My name is Booker and I haven't killed anyone in two years," he says. "So for the past week I've been doing this guided meditation to get to sleep at night. I thought it was working pretty good. And then last night I woke up in the middle of the night, and he was back, like he never left. The boy . . ."

His voice drifts and his eyes grow dark, then sad.

"It was a night mission, and we had bad intel. Everyone in the house was supposed to be fighters on the other side. When the bullets stopped flying and we tried to clear the place, I found him. He had gotten out of bed, made it halfway across his bedroom. I don't know if it was my shots that cut him down. Probably not; this was on the second floor and I was on the first. But I was there, you know? I was part of it. And so last night, I woke up in the middle of the night, which happens, you know, going in and out of sleep."

He drops his eyes to his hands, which he folds in his lap.

"The boy was standing at the foot of my bed. He's a regular, so I see him pretty often. But I guess, four nights is the longest I've gone without seeing one, you know? And so I thought maybe I'm out of this. Maybe this meditation thing is working. I got so mad. Like, man, I thought this worked. It made me mad at the world. At the people I used to work for." He regards the rosary wrapped around his hand. "You spend your whole life learning 'thou shalt not kill,' and then you get in the service and it's 'thou shalt not kill, unless we tell you, then it's fine.' How doesn't that mess you up?

"Anyway. I wanted to say I was sorry. But it's always the same. When I see them, something happens. I can't speak. One of the PTSD docs told me it was a night terror. That it was a dream and I just believe it's real. I think he's full of shit. Things are always weird in dreams, right? Nothing ever looks right. But every detail, from the color of my sheets to the curtain over the window to the two bullet holes in the kid's chest—spot on. And then how do you account for the ones I see during the day? I feel silly even saying any of this..."

He pauses. I speak before I even realize I'm going to do it. "Have you tried melatonin?"

He frowns. "Gave me nightmares. Vivid ones."

"Crosstalk," Valencia says.

"Crosstalk?" I ask.

Kenji nods. "In meetings we're supposed to let people complete their shares without offering advice or judgment."

"Except we end up doing that anyway," Booker says with a smirk.

"We never said we were perfect," Kenji says.

Everyone looks at me again.

"It's the god stuff that's throwing me," I say, a little spark of anger flaring in my chest. "That higher-power thing. I'm supposed to believe in god after the things I've done?"

Kenji shakes his head. "It doesn't have to be god. It just has to be something greater than you. It can be god, or the Buddha. Nature, or consciousness. This is especially important for people like us. We acted like gods. Sometimes we need to be reminded that there are powers beyond us, because one of our greatest weaknesses was the way we were seduced by our own power. There's a saying in AA: *Let go and let god.* I believe it to be a good motto. It reminds us to recognize that decisions over life and death are not for us to make."

It's not the answer I came in here looking for, but it feels like it's approaching one.

"If you'd prefer not to share . . ." Kenji says.

"A few nights ago . . ." I say, then I stop. "Actually, I'm sorry. Hi, my name is Mark and it's been, uh, three days since I killed someone. So, I met this woman. And I fell for her, hard. I never told her what I did for a living. I did what I'm used to, you know? Made up a lie. We dated for nearly a year, and man, every time I looked at her, it was like seeing a sunrise for the first time. She gave me this feeling of peace, I guess, that I never really had. I was ready to hang it all up for her. But then, Christmas Eve. Her brother came into the house in the middle of the night. He was there to surprise her, to drop off presents. But I was awake. And of course, I figure this is someone here for me . . ."

I rub the cuts on my knuckles hard enough to bring the pain back.

"I was angry, that someone wanted to take that peace from me, so I killed him. Didn't even think. Just did it. Killed her brother. Turns out, she was pregnant, too. And I never wanted to be a dad. It's not something I ever really thought about. But when I found out, I realized I had this chance to create a better version of myself, and I ruined it. Then I went home and thought about eating my SIG. Then I met a cat. Then I got in touch with Kenji. Now I'm here."

Everyone nods slowly, creating a space for these feelings to reverberate through the room.

"I just keep thinking about that first night I met her. It was February, and there were these trees around Bryant Park, and they looked like hands. Like skeletal hands reaching up to the moon, which was glowing in the sky. And removed from the context I guess it seems like a bit of a spooky image. But I keep thinking about how those limbs were reaching for something beyond their grasp. And that's what being with her felt like. Like there was something greater I could be reaching for. Something beyond myself, but I guess, also within myself? I don't know. Like, the more you reach the more you realize there's something worth reaching for . . ."

The words I've been struggling to find finally come to me.

"Before I met her, my life felt very small. And afterward, it felt a lot bigger. I know that I've made mistakes, and I don't want to *be* those mistakes. I want to be something else. I don't know what that something else is. I just know that I want it."

Valencia leans forward and squeezes my hand.

"You don't need to know why you're here," she says. "You just need to be here."

"I just . . ."

There's more I want to say, but the sob that's been building in my chest explodes outward, and then I'm hunched over, crying like a baby, and these three people, they put their hands on me. Hands they've used to kill, but tonight, just feeling the weight and the warmth of them, they knit together the things inside me that are broken.

13

> If you had not committed great sins, God would not have sent a punishment like me upon you.
> —Genghis Khan

Somewhere . . .
Now

A burning sensation starts in my nostril and moves through my body, the warm blanket I've been wrapped in suddenly ripped off. I'm ejected into the cold air, my skin ringing like an old bell. Then a sound: something hard and plastic hitting the floor. There's so much to take in at once, my brain can't keep up.

Instead it doles things out in phases.

My hands are bound behind me. Metal cuts into my skin.

There's a song playing softly in the distance. Something familiar.

Smells like a pine forest, but we're inside.

Deep breath.

The song that's playing is "Ave Maria." I'm sitting at the base of an enormous Christmas tree. The kind you know is expensive because it's real and doesn't have any kitschy ornaments. It reaches toward the top of the cathedral ceiling, and the white stars pulsing in the center are the only source of light in the room. Beyond the tree are floor-to-ceiling windows overlooking the city. I catch a corner of Central Park in the panorama. I think we're looking north. The sun has set but it's a clear night and we're so high up I think I can see the curvature of the earth.

Sitting across from me, bound to a chair, her face bloodied, is Astrid. She looks like she's waking up from a nap. Probably coming out of whatever put me under.

She has a little red bow on her head.

I think I do, too—something's tugging at my hair.

Seated to the right of us is Kozlov.

He's not bound. Just lounging on a chair turned backward, his arms draped over the top rail, smiling like we're all friends.

"Dobriy vecher," he says.

"I wouldn't call the evening *good*, all things considered," I say. "I was wondering when I'd run into you."

"Before this gets started, I would just like to say"—he puts his hand to his chest—"I am a big fan. I know it would be silly to say 'no hard feelings' after what happened"—he leans back, waving his hand around his gut—"you know, with me stabbing you? But I hope in time we can get past it."

My nostril still burns. "What did you dose us with?"

"Just now?" He nods toward a small, plastic nasal injector on the floor. "Naloxone. To counteract halothane with a small amount of fentanyl."

"Didn't they use that in 2002? The hostage situation at that theater in Moscow?"

He smiles and looks at Astrid. "See? This is why he is the best."

Astrid lunges forward, but she's tied too tightly to the chair. Kozlov looks at me with a sheepish little grin. "She is not a fan of me, it seems."

"I'm going to wear your skin to FaceTime your mother," Astrid says.

Kozlov smiles. "That is a good one. But my mother is dead. Anyway, the boss has no use for you."

"And who's the boss?" I ask.

Kozlov looks at something over my shoulder. "He is here, now."

"Ave Maria" has been playing—the Bocelli version, I think—but almost as if on cue, footsteps approach, and a soft, awkward voice joins in:

Ora, ora pro nobis peccatoribus
Nunc et in hora mortis

The translation is not lost on me: "Pray, pray for us sinners, now and at the hour of our death."

The footsteps stop directly behind me.

"You brought me some presents. Thank you, Viktor."

That voice.

No . . .

A clammy wave passes over my skin as it erupts into goose bumps.

A pair of hands take mine and undo the cuffs. They clatter

to the floor, and those same hands untie the ropes holding my legs.

I stand and turn, yanking the bow off my head, to find Stuart.

He's barefoot, wearing an oversize maroon sweater and a pair of khakis. His entire demeanor is different. Gone is the scared-animal energy he had at the meetings. He seems to have grown a few inches since the last time I saw him, which I thought was: stomped to death on the floor of his apartment.

"Merry Christmas, Mark," he says. Then he looks at Kozlov. "The bows are a little theatrical, but I'll give you the points for effort. Why don't you give us a moment? Don't go far."

Kozlov crosses to the other side of the room. Stuart turns the chair around, scoots it back a few feet, and sits, draping one leg over the other. He points to my empty chair and says, "Please, sit. We haven't been introduced. Not properly, at least. You probably know me better as Hannibal Khan."

"You son of a—" Astrid starts.

Stuart turns to her and says, "Speak again, I will carve your tongue from your mouth and feed it to you."

Astrid complies, more frustrated than intimidated.

I sit on the chair to keep my knees from buckling, my body moving on autopilot.

Stuart snaps his fingers. "You have questions." The confidence in his voice is deeply unsettling.

"Many," I tell him.

Though I know the biggest mistake I made thus far was dismissing him. And the corpse. That was the only piece of this that didn't fit. Why Stuart? And I forgot one of the most basic rules of this job: don't ruin the target's face, or else you could kill someone else and pass them as genuine.

He points a finger at me and smiles. "I see the wheels turning. I needed something to throw you off, just in case you came looking. Which was impressive that you found the apartment, you didn't have much to go on. It was a homeless guy, panhandled around the corner. Same body type. I let him take a shower and borrow some clothes and once I was done driving my boot into his skull, it was an easy enough mistake to make." He puts his hands out, in mock-worship. "Even for the great Pale Horse."

"How'd you know?"

He shrugs. "I pieced it together." Then he smiles and gestures toward the windows. "Isn't this place the tits? Fourteen hundred feet above the park. Three floors. Seven bedrooms, four bathrooms. Seventeen thousand square feet total with the highest residential terrace in the world. Which surprised me, because you'd figure they'd have something like that in Dubai, right? But then again, who wants to be closer to the sun in the desert? I just moved in, but I got the tree set up. 'Tis the season. Now, if I told you how much this place cost, you wouldn't believe me."

He looks at me with the energy of a child showing off a drawing of a puppy that looks like a melted puddle of mud with legs. When I don't bite, he pouts his lips and frowns.

"Two hundred fifty million. Paid in cash. Not bad, right?"

I look for something to use as a weapon. Stuart doesn't look to be carrying anything. Kozlov might have a weapon, I can't really tell from here. I've got jack shit. An empty room and a woman who is more acquaintance than ally, tied to a chair.

"So, let's start from the top," Stuart says, "I started the Via Maris as a way to sell drugs. *Lots* of money in drugs. But it developed into a Craigslist for life and death. Which was great. More money for me. I mean, the processing fees alone." He leans back in his chair, gesturing with his hands as he speaks. "But the bigger it got, the more I started to think, there's a chance to make a real difference here. Looking at all the chatter on the boards, seeing who was getting taken out where, I realized I could predict which way the political winds were blowing. I began to recognize the ebb and flow of the world's power structures. And I saw an opportunity."

"What kind of opportunity?"

"You think governments kill bad people, Mark? They do not." He shakes his head. "They kill *troublesome* people. The Agency isn't trying to make the world a better place. They have an agenda. What if we could restructure the way that worked? What if instead of oil executives using the hammer of the gods—using people like *you*—to destabilize the Middle East to shift the market, what if we went after those same executives, who were using their power and influence to destroy the planet? Instead of killing a political leader because they dared to question the efficacy of capitalism, we could leave them *in power* and take out their enemies, so they could *empower* their own followers to fight the system. We could level the playing field. Make things *right*."

"And what's right, to you?" I ask.

"Anything we want."

"You keep saying *we*."

He sticks a finger in the air and says, "We'll get to that." Then he stands and strolls over to the window, clasping his hands behind his back and gazing out over the city, like it's something to be conquered. "In order to do this, I need to break the Agency. Create a vacuum, which I would then fill." He turns and offers me a rattlesnake smile. "I've been doing what I could, setting them against the Russians, letting both sides tire each other out. Make my job a little easier. But I needed a more targeted strike. I had to find an Agency employee to cause them some inner turmoil." He claps his hands. "So I got in the Paper Cranes forum. Figured I could not-so-gently persuade them to get back in the game. The whole serial killer thing was a bit. I could never pass for an assassin. You'd sniff me out. But a serial killer? Serial killers have gotten in before. And all of you would think I was grotesque, so none of you would look at me directly. It would provide me with just enough cover to hide in plain sight. Granted, I had to kill a few people, to establish a pattern and plausibility, get past the vetting process with Kenji, but it was worth it. Because I got luckier than I could have imagined." He raises an open palm toward me. "You."

"Not gonna lie, bud, doesn't feel that way to me."

"I bet. Anyway." He jerks his head to the imposing figure across the room. "I hired Kozlov to cause you some grief. I figured it'd smoke you out, and in turn, the Agency. I orchestrated that whole thing with throwing the suspicion on Kenji, too. You should have been watching over Gaius's shoulder while he was working. He called me up on a chat immediately." Insult creeps into his voice. "There's no god mode. There's no tracing anything back. I told him to tell you the thing with the username. I just needed to break you out of this bullshit recovery thing, get you back on the horse, as it were, and wait for you to dismantle the Agency. Because even if you didn't suspect them, you'd realize they wouldn't let you live, and then it was you or them." He shakes his head. "I thought you'd raze that place to the ground. I really thought I would have broken you by now. That part of the plan didn't work out. Still, I can work with this."

I readjust myself in the chair a little, wonder if I could tackle him, but no, Kozlov is still waiting in the wings. Best to keep him talking. "To do what, exactly?"

He turns to me and sighs, thrilled to finally be explaining this. I bet he's rehearsed this in front of a mirror. "We're going to use all the data I've collected through the Via Maris to start our own Agency. All in one centralized, online, easy-to-access location. Now, every leader needs a team. You'll be my chief of operations. Kozlov, our man in the field. That's a pretty good starting point, right?"

Oh.

"You think I'm going to come work for you," I tell him.

"With me, Mark. *With* me. You're the best." He bows a little, the gesture meant to be respectful, but given the circumstances I can't interpret it as anything more than obscene. "I want you to teach me how to do what you do. I want you to steer the ship through choppy waters. You don't even have to kill anyone for now." He waves a dismissive hand. "You can stick with . . . whatever this phase is."

"It's not a phase."

"Mark," he says, his face twisting like he's in pain. "Mark, please." He takes a deep breath and screams, "If you really wanted to make amends you would turn yourself in." He settles himself, and his voice drops back to normal. "Been dying to say that, ever since the first meeting I attended. Seriously, this whole recovery thing, it's weird. You know that, right?"

"Standing in front of a judge isn't going to fix the problem. The problem is me."

He rolls his eyes. "I'm tired of unpacking feelings. Look, I ordered Chinese, figured we could all sit and eat and talk logistics, but it seems like you're still coming around to the idea. Fine. In the meantime, we need to straighten up a bit." He raises his voice. "Viktor? She's all yours."

Kozlov smiles, cracks his knuckles, and advances on us.

I stand in front of Astrid.

"Gonna have to go through me," I tell them.

"I don't need you to save me," Astrid whispers.

"At this very second, I think you do," I tell her.

"She would have gutted you if she had to, Mark," Stuart says, drawing closer to me.

"She didn't," I tell him. "Your man did."

Stuart nods. "Fine fine fine."

And he snaps his foot out so fast I don't even see it coming. It lands on the side of my head and sends me spinning to the floor. He circles me and pulls the sweater over his head as I struggle to get my bearings. He's shirtless underneath, and while he's not big, he's carved out of granite. He turns his arms out a little, posing a bit, then rubs his triceps.

"Not bad, right?" he asks. "I have more money than you can imagine. And time. With all that money and time I've trained my mind and body. More fighting styles than I can list. Targeted weight training. Hell, I constructed a mock Hell Week to complete, which I did, in record time. You were a SEAL, you remember what that was like."

I get to my feet and he throws another kick at my head, so fast I can't get out of the way.

"The thing is, I'm not like you," Stuart says. "I'm not lying to myself."

Kozlov wraps his hands around Astrid's throat, and I forget about Stuart for a second and launch myself, slamming into the both of them, knocking them to the ground. I'm about to help Astrid out of the chair, when Stuart grabs me from behind and sends me sailing. I hit the window and bounce off. Mercifully, it doesn't break, but it's hard enough that stars bloom in my vision.

I clamber into something like a fighting stance as the knife wound on my side screams at me. I can feel warmth spreading across my skin. Must have ripped the stitches again.

Stuart spreads his hands out, palms up. "C'mon, Mark. You were born for this life. All I had to do was apply a little bit of pressure and what happened? Okay, you didn't kill anyone. Congratulations. You did everything *but*. You fell right back onto the power of your name. You used fear as a weapon. You want to have it both ways. Be the Pale Horse *and* Mark. You're one or the other, my man, and I think you know which one it is."

Of all the blows I've taken in the last few days—and some of them have been pretty serious—that's the one that lands hardest. That's the one that makes me forget my box breathing and the serenity prayer and just about every other thing I've achieved.

Because he's right.

I didn't just fall back into my old patterns.

I did a shit job of convincing myself I wasn't enjoying it.

But I was.

I loved every second of tapping into that god-energy again.

My existential funk dissipates when I realize Kozlov is advancing on Astrid, but she's managed to wriggle free of the chair. She throws a hard kick into Kozlov's shin, which causes him to throw his head back and howl. She stumbles out of the room, heading deeper into the extravagant apartment. Kozlov goes after her. I turn my full attention to Stuart and wait for him to come at me, but he doesn't. He stands and waits.

Smart.

Making me come to him.

I don't indulge. I circle a little, trying to get the pathways of my brain firing again, get my muscles warm.

Pet the bunny closest to the bench.

"Why'd you take the notebook?" I ask.

"Oh, that," he says. "I mean, if I'm going to dismantle the Agency, I need more data on them. But I also needed a little more data on you. Pressure points, you know? I didn't really think you would accept my job offer right off the bat."

"I mean, not ever, probably, you psycho."

He winces a little, the word leaving a mark on his skin. "Like I said, pressure points." He takes a phone out of his pocket and waves it at me. "I've got two men stationed outside that house in Jericho. They're watching Sara and Bennett right now. All I have to do is say the word and there won't be anything left of them but wet smears."

"And if I take your job you'll let them live?"

He pauses, not expecting my laid-back reaction.

But the bluster comes charging right back.

"I know this isn't the best incentive, but hey"—he shrugs—"if it works, it works."

"I guess there's only one thing for me to do," I tell him.

Stuart smiles. "And what's that?"

"Tell you to take your job offer, turn it sideways, and shove it up your ass."

He frowns. "You think I'm kidding." There's a crashing sound from deeper in the apartment, which draws his attention for a moment. Then he turns back to me and says, "Well, okay." He dials a number and sets it to speakerphone. When the call picks up, he says, "You can move on the woman and the boy. Keep the phone on so we can listen to what happens."

A voice comes back: "Stuart? Is that you?"

Booker.

Stuart's face drops.

There we go. My turn to give him a little bow. "I did kind of figure whoever took the notebook was looking for something I did," I tell him. "But I knew it could expose Sara, so just to be safe, I sent some friends to keep an eye on them."

"Hey, Stuart," Booker says. "Always knew you were an asshole."

Stuart growls in the base of his throat and tosses the phone across the room.

"That must suck, huh?" I ask. "I'll admit, I missed a few pieces, but everything else I pretty much figured out on my own. The only mistake I made was thinking I was up against a real player. Russia. China maybe. Not some kid with delusions of grandeur."

Stuart tries to respond, but the words come out in a choke as his face twists in anger.

There's the nerve I wanted to hit. I keep digging.

"You know what I think, Stu?" I ask. "I think you're full of shit. You make me this nonsense pitch about changing the world. In your expensive apartment, which you can't wait to show off. Then when I said no, you showed me the muscles you bought. You're not trying to change anything. You're just like every other one of these assholes. You want to be rich. You want to feel powerful. You got a little money and bought your way into the game. But you're a tourist. I think you just want to *be* me. You want the kind of power I had. And you never will, so the next best thing is to buy me, like you buy everything else."

Stuart's face morphs from anger to rage to pure fury, and he charges at me.

Which is exactly what I wanted.

Get him to see red.

Red means stupid.

He comes at me with a roundhouse. It lands hard, but I've

got my block up and take it on my forearm. I throw a cross and he slips, and then I go to sweep his leg and he hops around it. He actually is pretty good at this, but again, he bought this training on a mat, in a gym. He didn't earn it on the asphalt, where the person on the other side of the fight is trying to kill you.

It makes a difference.

He comes at me with a teep and I sidestep, grab him under the ankle, and lift, which acts as a lever, sending him to the ground. I could kill him six different ways from this position. But I don't. I let him get to his feet and come at me again, slipping and blocking, letting him tire himself out. Then I dance back a little, creating some distance, and when he charges, I duck out of the way and use his weight to smash him headfirst into one of those pretty, expensive windows. He falls into a heap and scrambles to his feet. Then he's flailing at me, screaming like an animal. I do my best to block him, waiting for my opening and, when I find it, send my fist so deep into his stomach I leave knuckle prints on his liver.

He doubles over and before he even hits the ground, I'm sprinting through the doorway, looking for Astrid and Kozlov.

Never let an opponent get behind you. But I can't abandon Astrid. I follow the sound of their struggle, through a series of hallways and an empty library, and find them in the dim lighting of a massive white marble kitchen. Astrid is lying on the island in the center of the room, and Kozlov is straddling her, his hands around her throat.

"Still pissed at you, by the way," I tell him, and use my momentum to take a running jump with my knee out and slam into him. As I land on Astrid he goes flying across the room and slams into a cabinet. It stuns him for a moment, and Astrid leans forward, hacking the air back into her lungs.

Given our last meeting, I'm not giving Kozlov the chance to breathe. I hop off the island and go at him fast, driving my knee into his head so hard it cracks the cabinet behind it. His eyes roll around in his head for a second and I'm about to throw another, when he strikes me on the side of the knee and my body crumples to the ground.

I'm going to feel that tomorrow, but for now, the adrenaline is working.

He gets on top of me, but as he does I manage to place my foot on his sternum. I buck my hips and push up hard, throwing him into the air behind me. He hits the refrigerator, denting the stainless steel. By the time I get to my feet he's already waiting on his.

There's a trickle of blood dripping down from his hairline, which he wipes with the back of his hand, smearing it across his forehead.

"Don't hold back," he says. "Please."

From there, it's a dance. The two of us throwing blocks and blows in a mad, buzzing flurry. It reinforces the thing I learned the first time we met: we're pretty evenly matched, and now it's about who finds the first opening.

Which is me.

He drops his guard just enough that I'm able to open-palm smack him on the ear, hard.

Hard enough to pop his eardrum.

He screams and staggers, falling to his knees, but before I

can take advantage of the opening, something slams into me, pushing me onto and over the kitchen island.

"He's mine," Astrid says.

I attempt to clamber to my feet but my knee buckles. "Are you kidding me?"

She brings her foot up high, ready to bring it down on his face, but he throws a hard fist into her crotch and she bends over in pain. There's a crashing sound from somewhere deeper in the apartment. I turn to look for Stuart but don't see him.

Then there's a sharp crack, and Astrid staggers back.

Kozlov has a small handgun cradled to his chest.

I hope she's wearing a vest, but she presses her hand to her side and comes back with a fistful of blood. Kozlov is training the pistol for a better shot when I yell, "No!"

So he turns to me, sending a bullet into the meat of my left shoulder.

At first, it feels like a punch. Adrenaline still working its magic. But whatever he hit, it mattered, because suddenly I can't move the arm. The pain is howling at the door, and I go down to one knee. Kozlov gets up and comes toward me.

Astrid is writhing on the ground, but he's lost interest in her. He's stalking toward me now. Whatever went down between them was personal, but not personal enough to distract from the opportunity to put down the Pale Horse.

"Ultimately," he says, "I didn't think it would work out. It was always going to be you or me. But I appreciate the opportunity."

He aims the gun at my face.

This is it, I guess.

When you enter this life, you don't expect to leave it clean. When I got into the program, I thought maybe there was a chance. And there's still a part of my brain saying: *You can do this. You can fight back. You can survive.*

Just give over to that thing you've been denying about yourself.

Be who you're supposed to be.

Except I don't want to be that.

And I don't have to be.

"It is a privilege to take your life," Kozlov says.

He tenses, ready to fire.

And the point of a long blade erupts from his chest.

He drops the gun and his eyes roll back. He's dead before he slumps to the floor.

Kenji is standing in Kozlov's place, his face bloodied. Every ounce of his concentration is directed at keeping his body vertical, and I know without him having to say anything that Kozlov isn't the first person he's killed today to get here.

My heart shatters on the tile floor, the fragile glass shards of it cascading around us.

When he sees me, he just gives me that bemused smile, like someone told a moderately funny joke. He opens his mouth to say something, but there's another explosion. He puts his hands to his chest and falls to his knees, then collapses into my arms.

Blood blooms hot and sticky on my legs.

Too much blood.

Kenji coughs and sputters, his eyes rolling around in his head before they lock on mine. He reaches out, and I take his hand. He squeezes it, hard, and says, "It's . . . okay . . ."

His grip loosens.

And then he's gone.

Another hand appears on my shoulder. "You see? In the end, Kenji understood."

Stuart.

His voice is soft and warm, like he's comforting a scared child.

"This is all there is," Stuart says. "That thin line between life and death. Only people like us can navigate it. So, c'mon. I get this wasn't the smoothest way to go about things. But let's put all that aside. Let's work."

That black, noxious thing in me bubbles to the surface.

And I am tired again.

A different kind of tired.

I am so tired of fighting that thing inside me to a standstill every night just for it to rear its head every morning. I'm tired of the effort it takes to be different, when being the same is just . . .

Math.

"You're free now," Stuart says.

I grip the hand on my shoulder and throw my whole body forward, flipping Stuart onto his back, and scramble on top of him.

"You wanted me, here I am," the Pale Horse says.

And I hit him in the face so hard I break a finger.

Then I do it again.

And again.

There's a voice in the back of my head trying to tell me something.

I ignore it.

Adrenaline coursing through my veins like liquid gold. That thing I denied myself. Pretending I didn't need it. Slowing time and allowing me to savor every swing of my good arm, hammering him until my fist is wet and shattered. Until all that rage bubbles out and spills onto the floor and the most savage part of me fills every square foot of this stupid giant apartment.

Until I breathe smoke and taste metal and the building shakes because I am a god.

The voice persists, and I can just barely make it out, but it's not strong enough. This feels good. So good. It's not going to bring Kenji back, but it sure is going to make me feel better.

It dawns on me that it's probably past midnight.

The one-year anniversary of killing Lucas.

This is a hell of a way to celebrate.

And just as I'm about to deliver another shot to his jaw, with the express goal of splitting it clean in half, he wriggles and I slam what's left of my fist into the soft part of his throat.

It crumbles.

Because the trachea has the tensile strength as a soda can. You have to be careful how you hit it. Just right, the person can't breathe. Can't breathe, can't fight. Do it too hard, they're unable to take in air and they choke to death.

He's choking to death.

He reaches for the crushed remains of his face, gasping, gargling blood, spitting it up, going flush. The sight of it snaps me out of my rage just long enough for the voice to slip through.

Sara.

Don't slip.

The trick to not falling.

So simple that it's almost ridiculous, and I didn't hear it when I needed to, but I hear it now. Loud and clear.

Don't slip.

Simple as that.

I climb off Stuart to find Astrid crawling toward me, a trail of blood streaked on the floor behind her, a kitchen knife grasped in her hand.

"We have to help him," I tell her.

"Let him die," she says.

I don't see a phone handy. No way we can get an ambulance here in time to save him. I need to save him. I need to keep my fist from closing around the paper crane I've been cradling in my heart. I came too far. Maybe Stuart deserves to die. No, he does, he really really does. But it's not for me to decide.

I'm not death.

We can do a tracheotomy. I pull the felt marker out of my pocket, yank the ends out with my teeth. "Astrid, please." I offer it to her. "I don't know how to do this."

She falls onto her back, staring at the ceiling, breathing hard. "No."

"If he dies . . ."

She spits. "If he dies, what?"

"I don't know, I don't know," I tell her, searching for the words. The right thing to say. Some perfect thing that will convey this impossible feeling inside me. It's just there, at the edge of my fingertips, and I need her to see it. I need her to see me...

"The world will be a better place without him," she says.

"And if he dies, I'll be worse. Look at what this life gave us. This isn't living, Astrid."

She laughs, long and deep, her eyes closed. "You think we can change? It's kind of adorable."

"We *can*," I tell her. "We can, okay?" And I find it. That perfect thing to say: "Yesterday matters. Today matters more."

She turns over and stares at me. I think that did it. I think she sees it, that pulsing light at the center of me, dimmed for my entire life and finally free. That feeling that the world used to be so small, and now it's bigger.

She rolls her eyes and pushes her body into a crawl. She gets over Stuart and holds out her hand. I give her the marker. She looks at it for a moment, studying it, like she's never seen one before.

Then she tosses it aside and plunges the knife through Stuart's eye.

He stops choking.

His body goes slack.

Astrid falls back onto the floor. "You're right. Today matters more."

I slump on the floor next to her, close my eyes. Adrenaline abandons me and the pain comes roaring through the door, rattling the foundations. I allow it to sink its teeth into me. It covers up all the other things I'm feeling in this terrible, crushing moment.

14

We're all just walking each other home.
—Ram Dass

Jericho, New York
One Year Later

Breathe. Four seconds in, hold for four, out for four, empty lungs for four.

I peer through the scope, into the front window of the house. The living room is empty. My phone vibrates in my pocket. I shouldn't check it. I don't want to be here longer than I have to be. Someone could spot me.

But most of the driveways on the block are empty. People gone for work, or traveling for the holidays, or scrambling to buy Christmas gifts at the last second. I risk it. It's a text from Booker.

BOOKER: You done yet?
ME: Almost.
BOOKER: We're running out of time.
ME: I got three hours.
BOOKER: Google says they close at 4.

Me: I called. Holiday hours. They're open to 6.

Booker: That's not what Google said.

Me: Google doesn't know everything. I called to make sure.

Booker: Don't fuck me on this, Mark.

Me: Calm down, tough guy. I got it covered.

Booker: Ask for Maritza.

Me: This better be worth it. It's out of the way. I like that place on Bleecker.

Booker: Remember the last time you went hard in the paint for someone? Your judgment remains suspect.

Me: You're never going to let me live that down.

Booker: Real talk, man, I've been thinking I'm nuts for a long time. Seeing ghosts everywhere. It was actually pretty affirming that my gut was right on that. Means my radar still kind of works.

Booker: But no, I will absolutely not let you live it down.

Back to the scope. I shift it to my right arm, giving my left a chance to rest. Kozlov's bullet missed the tangle of bone and major blood vessels in my shoulder, but it tore out a chunk of my deltoid muscle. Six months of rehab bought me a little strength and range of motion, but it's never going to be at full capacity.

Could have been worse.

I spend a lot of time thinking about what Kenji did, sacrificing his recovery, and then his life. In the movie version, I'd chalk it up to some cutesy hitman code like "You live by the blade, you die by the blade." The honest truth of it is, I think Kenji loved me as much as I loved him.

My service commitment: organizing and leading the weekly

meetings, keeping an eye on the Paper Cranes forum, taking on sponsees of my own—that's the best way to honor his memory.

I'm still waiting for that last part. I think I'm ready. Another thing he was right about. Being a sponsor isn't about saving someone else. It's about reinforcing your own recovery and saving yourself in the process.

One life, plus another.

Even though we haven't had any new recruits, I've been practicing the paper cranes, which contain the password for the new forum on the Amber Road, the site that took the place of the Via Maris. It feels good to keep that part of the tradition alive.

I always wondered about the origin of the cranes and never asked. I feel silly now, for not asking. It was one of those things I figured we would get to eventually, and then *eventually* turned into *too late*.

The story I've decided to tell myself is that Kenji wanted to use his hands, the hands that inflicted so much pain and death, to create something delicate and beautiful.

Finally, there's movement against the lens of the scope.

Sara walks into the living room, Bennett toddling after her, and it takes me a moment to realize I stopped breathing. He's got the same color hair as me. He goes to a kitchen playset and slams plastic toys together, pretending to cook. Sara sits on the couch, clearly exhausted, but content. The Christmas tree twinkles in the background.

This is the first time I've seen Bennett and it's all I can do to keep the scope steady.

My son.

The next time Sara goes outside, on the porch she'll find a box wrapped in sparkling red paper with a big green bow on top, placed out of view from the sidewalk so no one walks off with it. Inside is half a million dollars and a typed note, explaining how to spend it to avoid the attention of the IRS.

In the bag at my feet is another note—this one handwritten, explaining who I am, what happened, everything. Along with that: a gift-wrapped present for Bennett. A package of glow-in-the-dark stars for his bedroom ceiling.

The whole ride over I nearly managed to convince myself there existed a reality in which knocking on her door would be appropriate. By the time I rounded the corner of her street, I realized how selfish it would be.

She might guess the money is from me, though honestly I hope she doesn't.

And if she does, I hope she keeps it.

This isn't about clearing a debt.

I like to imagine at some point I'll make an in-person amends, but for now I have to settle for a living amends. Which means sticking to the program, doing my best to make the world a better place, and keeping an eye out to ensure nothing from my past ever blows back on them.

If Bennett can be happy and know what it means to be loved—that can be enough.

That can be more than enough.

I stash the scope in my bag and turn onto the sidewalk, head for the train station that will bring me to the Lower East

Side and that little cupcake shop that offers the promise of a peaceful Christmas Eve with friends.

As I walk, I feel lighter. I'm not sure why. I don't think it's the money. Maybe it's the freedom of knowing I could catch a bullet in the back of my head at any second, and the lights would just go out, *Sopranos*-style, which means nothing matters, but at the same time, everything does.

As I step through the door of the cupcake shop, a young Hispanic woman with curly brown hair and a shiny nose ring looks up from the counter.

"Maritza?" I ask.

"You must be Mark," she says, sliding a white cardboard box across the counter. "Booker called. Said you were coming."

I check my pocket to make sure I've got my Lactaid. "Yeah, he was hyped. Sorry if he got a little intense?"

Maritza makes a confused face. "Intense? Booker comes in all the time. He's like, the sweetest."

I stifle a laugh as I pull out my wallet. "Fairytale of New York" by the Pogues starts in on the café's speakers. I point toward the ceiling. "Best Christmas song there is."

"Agreed," she says before placing a small cup of coffee next to the box.

"I didn't order that," I tell her.

She points with her chin at something behind me, toward the seating area on the other side of the shop. "She did."

I turn to find Astrid sitting in the corner, bundled up in a heavy black bubble jacket, a paper cup of coffee on the table in front of her. I don't know what's more unsettling—that she's here waiting for me, or that I didn't notice her when I walked in. She gives me a little wave, and I wave back, which seems like a ridiculous greeting considering the crushing gravity between us.

I stuff a hundred into the tip jar, wish Maritza a Merry Christmas, take my coffee and cupcakes, and approach Astrid like I'm navigating a minefield. I stop in front of her table and she raises her cup of coffee to her lips, takes a long drink, and puts it back down, all without taking her eyes from mine.

"Hey," she says.

"How'd you find me?"

"Would you join me?" When I don't, she takes another sip of coffee. "I'm no Pale Horse, but I'm pretty good at my job, too. I'm not here to cause trouble."

I pull out a chair and sit across from her, take the lid off my coffee to let it cool. "If you were planning to kill me, I never would have seen it coming. Maritza has seen your face, the shop has a camera, and there's a CCTV across the street. Too many variables."

"Just wanted to talk."

"Right," I say. "Talk."

A chasm of silence opens between us, and it's hard to tell from the vibration of it what kind of silence it is. There are too many emotions swirling inside my chest for me to have any hope of untangling them.

Astrid's eyes are sunken, her body concaved. She looks like she hasn't slept since the last time I saw her.

"You still in the city?" she asks.

"Got a little cabin up in the mountains. Off the grid. I come in for the meetings, but otherwise, there are way too many people around here who want to kill me. It's pretty nice, besides the mice."

"P. Kitty must be in heaven, then," she says.

"Oh, no, he has no predatory instinct whatsoever. The mice have the run of the place."

"Why don't you kill them?"

"I don't work for free."

She nods. "Speaking of, happy anniversary."

"Anniversary?"

"Last year, didn't you say you were at a year? You'd be at two years now."

"Ah, that." I laugh, and it starts small but then grows bigger, and her face twists in confusion. "Actually, I'm back to a year. After what happened, I started from scratch. Went back to counting days. Square one on the steps."

"Was it because of what I did?"

I shrug. "I needed to do it. I decided being in the program wasn't as simple as killing or not killing. The second shit went sideways, I went right back to how I used to be. Riding on my reputation, using fear to get what I wanted. It scratched the itch." I turn my cup of coffee on the heavy wooden tabletop, hoping the words I've been struggling to find for the past year will suddenly reveal themselves, written on the surface of it. "Turns out there was one last person I needed to kill."

"The Pale Horse," she says.

I bow my head in affirmation.

Astrid's eyes drift to the corner. She picks up her coffee but doesn't drink from it.

"What was the thing that pisses you off the most?" I ask.

"What?"

"When we were in the van. Before Kozlov rammed us. You said that."

She nods and places down her cup of coffee. "Sticking with you wasn't just about Kozlov. I wanted to understand you. To be honest, I resented you. You were the go-to guy. I was second string. And it pissed me off when you said you quit. Like you were wasting your potential." She pauses. "Like you weren't just physically better than me, you were suddenly morally better, too."

"I was good, Astrid," I tell her. "But so are you. Speaking of, how are things at the office?"

"Messy. That guy Stuart, he kicked over the apple cart and then stomped on all the apples. There was a lot to clean up. They've got a new golden child in, too. He's been getting most of the work, so I'm back to the B squad. People call him the Viper."

"If Ravi were around, he'd be called Leviathan or Nephilim or something."

For the first time since I sat, Astrid smiles. "The guy did love his biblical references, didn't he?"

"I wonder if he was religious." I take a long drag of the coffee. It's still a little too hot, but it feels good to do something to fill up the sharply awkward edges of the space. "Didn't know him well enough to say one way or the other, I suppose."

"You were right, by the way."

"How's that?"

"Drinking the poison." She cranes her neck to look around me, but Maritza is in the process of wiping down the counters, preparing to close—out of earshot. "For years, all I thought about was killing Kozlov. Then he was dead and I didn't feel any better."

"That's the way it tends to go."

"Are you mad at me?"

"For what?"

"For screwing up your recovery."

Again, the right words elude me, even though I've imagined this conversation, despite never expecting to have it. I drum my fingers on the table, waiting for something to come to me, and when nothing does, I settle on the truth. "Yeah, for a while after. I blamed you, and I thought you killing him was the same as me doing it. The more I sat with it, the more I realized I was mad at myself. It's up to me to clean my side of the street."

"Yesterday matters," she says. "Tomorrow matters more."

"Sixty percent of recovery is cute slogans."

"It took me a little while to hear, but I heard it."

"Sometimes they take a minute to land. Believe me, I know."

"I want out."

The word burst out of her, like a frothing river held back by a dam. Once they're free and floating in the air between us she holds her breath. She said the hard thing. A thing she's wanted to say for a while now. And I can feel pieces of her falling away in the white-hot aftermath.

"Hey." I look her in the eye, tossing a rope into that raging river. I know where to throw it because I've been there myself. "Do they teach box breathing in Special Forces?"

She shakes her head, hard and fast.

"They teach it in the SEALs. Calms your central nervous system. Breathe in for four seconds, hold it for four seconds, breathe out for four seconds, hold your lungs empty for four seconds." I put my hand on my chest. "With me, okay?"

She nods her head with the same fervor, and together we breathe in, hold, breathe out, then hold.

We do it once, twice, three times.

She closes her eyes and then looks back up at me, the waters now placid.

"Thank you," she says.

"You're welcome."

"I don't know if this whole program thing is for me."

"It might not be," I tell her. "But you could give it a shot."

"The whole 'god' part of the recovery process—"

"Don't worry, we cover that."

"Excuse me," Maritza calls from the other side of the store. "Sorry to rush you off, but we have to close."

"No, it's all good." I toss the mostly empty coffee in the trash can next to me. "It's Christmas Eve. We all have places to be."

Astrid and I gather our things and step outside. Maritza locks the door behind us. Snowflakes swirl in the air and perch on our shoulders. The street is empty, the city taking that deep, peaceful breath it takes once a year for Christmas, when everyone either leaves or heads indoors, seeking out a little bit of light in the dark.

"You got any plans tonight?" I ask.

"No," she says.

"I'm getting together with Booker and Valencia. And my old neighbor, Ms. Nguyen. She was in the game, too. She's great, even though she gets a little handsy when she's drinking."

"So it's like a recovery thing?"

"Sort of, but not really," I tell her. "It's part Christmas party, part baby shower for Valencia."

Astrid smiles. "She's pregnant?"

"Close to popping. You will not be surprised to hear it's not doing much for her demeanor. But she's going to be a good mom. She's so excited."

"I don't have anything to bring."

"Me and Booker got a bunch of cool stuff. We'll throw your name on the card."

She hesitates. "Are you sure that's a good idea?"

"No." I offer her my free hand. "But it could be."

She lets out a light laugh that feels warm and familiar—like it was back when we were on the run, when I thought there might be something between us. "We're not holding hands, Mark."

"Right," I tell her, sticking my hand in my pocket. "C'mon, though, worst thing that happens"—I hold up the box—"is you get some cupcakes."

"What kind?"

"Red velvet. Best in the city, according to Booker."

She surveys the empty street, and the sparkling lights and decorations, and the swirling snowflakes, and the enormity of what it means to decide you want to change.

Both the impossibility and the simplicity of it.

"Okay," she says. "Lead the way."

I turn in the direction of the subway, and for a few steps, she follows, until she falls in alongside me. The snow picks up, dusting the street, the stunted and barren trees lining the sidewalk and reaching up to the streetlights, and even if this is all a ruse, even if her ultimate plan is to kill me, it's hard not to appreciate this moment.

ACKNOWLEDGMENTS

Thanks to Todd Robinson, Jordan Harper, Shawn Cosby, Eryk Pruitt, Alex Segura, Mia Gentile, Chantelle Aimée Osman—for reading pages and offering input, or just letting me ramble and bounce ideas. I'd like to give a special thanks to Pruitt, his wife, Lana, and the rowdy crowd of regulars at Yonder Bar in North Carolina, where I stress-tested the first chapter at a live reading, and got the encouragement I needed to keep writing.

Thanks to my friends in recovery programs who shared their journeys and wisdom with me. I'd thank you by name, and for obvious reasons will not, but I admire your strength and appreciate you deeply.

If you're reading this and you think AA is something you might want to explore, visit www.aa.org.

ACKNOWLEDGMENTS

Thanks to my agent, Josh Getzler, his assistant, Jon Cobb, and the whole team at HG Literary, for busting their tails throughout the entire process of developing and selling this book.

Thanks to my editors, Mark Tavani and Daphne Durham, and the whole team at Putnam, especially Aranya Jain, for their tireless efforts in turning this from a Word document into the book you're holding in your hands. It ain't easy.

Thanks to Amblin Entertainment—Lauren Abrahams in particular—for seeing the potential of this book, and my film/TV agent, Lucy Stille, who once again proved why she's one of the best in the business.

Finally, thank you to my daughter, Abigail, for inspiring me to be a better writer, and a better person.